sarah dawson powell
writer of real-life fiction

the fragile line series

- beautiful.
- damaged.
- falling.
- pieces.
- changes.
- karma.
- invincible.
- breakable.
- dreams.
- nightmares.

Fall 2024:

Burn the Past- Book 11

Winter 2024:

Bury the Ashes- Book 12

stand alone// coming of age

The Truth About Gracie

In the Moonbeams

www.sarahdawsonpowell.com

In the Moonbeams

a novel

Sarah Dawson Powell

Content warning: swearing, substance abuse, unplanned/teenage pregnancy, child abuse, self-harm, mild violence, some sexual content, mention of sexual assault.

Copyright © 2023 by Sarah Dawson Powell

All rights reserved.

No part of this publication may be reproduced, distributed, or transmitted in any form or by any means, including photocopying, recording, or other electronic or mechanical methods, without the prior written permission of the publisher, except as permitted by U.S. copyright law. For permission requests, contact sarah@sarahdawsonpowell.com.

The story, all names, characters, and incidents portrayed in this production are fictitious. No identification with actual persons (living or deceased), places, buildings, and products is intended or should be inferred.

First edition 2023

For everyone who has ever thought they weren't good enough.
For everyone who has ever thought they needed someone else to make them whole.
For everyone who has ever felt unloved or abandoned.

You are enough.
You are whole.
You are loved.

Stay beautiful
@Sarah Dawson Powell

Six Months Earlier

Mike

Melissa looks at me from the other side of the bar while I mix her drink. She's been in here every night I've worked for the past two weeks. "You here by yourself again?" I ask.

She nods. "No one ever wants to go out on a weeknight."

"That's no fun," I say as I set the drink on a coaster in front of her.

The first time I saw Melissa in here, she was celebrating her thirtieth birthday with friends. Intoxicated and flirty, I didn't think anything of it. Until she started coming back in every time I worked, sitting at the bar quietly.

"You don't have a boyfriend or anything?" I ask.

She sighs. "No, it's just me and my cat."

I chuckle and wipe the bar near her where no one had sat all night, trying to look busy. "What's your cats name?"

"Pluto."

"That's unique."

She smiles. "What about you? You have a girlfriend or a cat or anything?"

Her casual way of asking if I have a girlfriend is cute. She's cute. "No cat. No girlfriend. Just kids."

"Kids plural?"

I nod. "Four."

Her eyes go wide. "Four? You're not old enough to have four kids."

I've heard this before. "Probably not, but I do."

"How old are they?"

"My girls are fourteen, fifteen, and seventeen. My son is sixteen."

Her jaw drops. "You have four teenagers?"

"Yep."

"How old are you?"

"How old do you think I am?"

"Well, I thought you were, like, twenty-eight or so, but now I'm not so sure. Definitely didn't think you were older than me."

Her compliment makes me feel good. "Thirty-five."

"No way."

I nod and step away to grab a beer for another customer. Then I busy myself with restocking the napkins, figuring that Melissa's interest in me is done. Usually when a woman finds out I have four kids that's basically the end of the conversation. I used to try to hide it, but then I'd end up hopeful for more and decide to drop the bomb, so to speak, just to be told over and over they weren't interested anymore. So now I lead with it. No point in getting my hopes up anymore. Maybe when I'm down to one or two kids at home I can find a divorced woman with her own kids or something.

"Hey, Mike," Melissa calls out. "Do you get to see your kids often?"

I shake my head. She's hoping I don't. But the truth is: "They live with me. Their mom has been gone for years."

"Oh," she says softly. "I'm so sorry."

I walk over to her. "Don't be sorry. It's not your fault she went to prison and never contacted us when she got out."

She studies my face, curious. "Tell me about your kids."

No one has wanted to know about my kids, other than their names maybe. Which is a story in itself. But that's not the story she wants. She doesn't want to know that Amy Jo and I named our children for all things above because the first night we met we laid under the night sky so she could name constellations for me.

"Skylar is the oldest. Goes by Sky. She's an old soul, always looking out for me and her siblings. In school she's pulls decent grades. Stays out of trouble, keeps the house clean, does laundry, and cooks." I smile. "Someday she will run her own family seamlessly."

Melissa rests her chin on her hand, seeming truly interested in what I'm saying.

"Orion is next. He's a lot like I was at his age. I just hope he can enjoy his teens and twenties more than I was able to." I give Melissa a small smile, wondering if she's done the math in her head to figure out how old I was when I started having kids. "He gets in a little trouble here and there, but nothing major. He plays basketball, but he also likes to party and likes girls a little too much. But he's got common sense. His priorities have shifted some over the summer," I say with a light laugh.

"Boys can be like that, I guess," she says. "I have two brothers. They both went though some wild years. Well, I'm not sure my youngest brother is quite out of his yet."

"Boys will be boys," I say with a smile, disbelieving she is still listening to me. "Sunny is number three. Sunshine is her real name, but no one calls her that. She's the one who never disappoints me. She's always had perfect grades, never even a B, and is her class president. Besides all her brains and drive, she is absolutely gorgeous." I hold up my hand. "Yeah, I know, I'm partial as her dad and all, but it's like she got the best parts of me and the best parts of her mom and became something more beautiful than either of us had ever dreamed of creating. She has more focus and motivation at fifteen than I've ever had in my entire life.

"She sounds amazing."

"She really is." I sigh when I see someone come in the door of the bar but am relieved when they go to the bathroom before sitting down. "Starla is the baby. She just turned fourteen. She's small for her age. When she was born, she was only four pounds, the others were all at least six pounds. Aside from being small, she's also really quiet and reserved. She doesn't have a lot of friends, but she does have a boyfriend that she started dating in sixth grade and they just never broke up. I probably worry about Star the most. It seems like she has things to say but for some reason she doesn't say them." I shrug.

"Sounds like you've done a good job raising them."

"I'm doing my best." I step away to wait on the customer who went in the bathroom. Overall, my kids are pretty amazing, and I think I have a pretty good relationship with each one. I can't wait to see what the future has in store for them.

I glance over my shoulder at Melissa while I grab the whiskey off the shelf. She's watching me, and I wonder if there's any future for me and her.

Part One

Skylar

Ten minutes is hardly enough time to spend with the one you love, but when you're in love with someone who shouldn't even be on your radar and your dad calls, beckoning your cooking and cleaning skills home, you can't rightly say, "Hey, no, Dad. See, I'm over here and…."

Nope.

I sigh and look at his gorgeous face. "What a spectacular end to the summer."

"You could come back later." His smile is gentle, knowing I won't. Not tonight.

"School in the morning. Gotta start senior year out right," I say with a teasing smile.

"I'll see you there."

I roll my eyes. "Yeah. I know." Another sigh escapes me, one that's sad and tired. Disappointed. "This sucks. Now we have to go back to the old way."

"It'll be over before you know."

It doesn't seem that way. Nine months of school, one-hundred-eighty more days of government required education before my ransom will be paid. I'll be eighteen in five weeks but that doesn't mean a thing in my situation.

I pull the Ford Taurus I share with my younger brother Orion around the corner and spy two cars in my drive. One is the Sante Fe belonging to Ray, my youngest sister Star's boyfriend. The other is the rusty old pickup Austin drives- Austin being the biggest pain there has ever been in my ass. In addition to that, he is like my brother's conjoined twin. When you see one, you see the other.

I park on the street, planning to kick out both of those losers per Dad's very specific orders.

When I walk in, the scene is exactly what I expect: The house is a disaster (it always is), Orion and Austin are stuffing their jaws at the kitchen table, my sister Sunny at the table with them (never eating, especially not in front of Austin), Ray's younger brothers are on our couch in their swim trunks (likely wet) watching a tired episode of SpongeBob Stupidpants, Ray and Star are incognito. Of course. Likely upstairs doing the deed.

Austin watches me walk into the kitchen, his eyes taking on that familiar I-just-saw-a-ghost look. I point at him and say, "Out."

He swallows whatever was in his mouth and widens his eyes. Orion, though, he says, "Mind your own, Sky. He didn't even say anything to you. Besides, who died and made you boss?"

I start emptying the dishwasher. "Dad. And while he may not be dead, he did call to say Melissa is coming over for dinner."

Orion and Sunny trade looks. "Seriously?" says Orion.

Our dad hasn't dated anyone seriously enough to bring home since I was in third grade, but he and Melissa have been dating for about six months. So this was kinda big. A change from whatever he usually does on the weekends when he doesn't come home after working a shift at the bar.

"Seriously." I start to rinse the dishes in the sink and load them into the dishwasher. "And he said no one here except us." I look at Sunny. "So go find Ray and tell him to get gone, too." I switch my eyes to Austin, who I'm sure has been staring at me the whole time. "Goodbye, freak."

Orion

Don't ask me. I don't know a thing.

                    Except this:
Austin keeps Sky on
a pedestal in the sky.

          Sunny would give her right eye to have Austin
                look at her like she is the sun in his life.

Sky is over the moon in love,
and not with Austin.

                    Sunny doesn't shine as
                    bright as she once did.

I wish I had three brothers
and not three sisters.

                My mother was never a mother,
                  just a baby popper-outer.

My dad needs
a good woman.

                          That is all.

Starla

Have you ever gotten stuck in mud? Like, when you're walking? Mud so thick your shoes come off and you're left in your socks? What do you do? Count your losses, move on? Or do you pry those shoes from the mud and try to salvage what there once was?

That's how I feel. Stuck.

I can't go forward, not like this at least. And, oh, *what I would give to go back*.

My shoulders are red from a day at the community pool with Ray and his little brothers. Sunburn, like shoes stuck in the mud, like a life stuck in neutral in a dead-end town, like a relationship that's suffocating you, are all things I cannot control.

Ray sits on the edge of my bed watching me stare at my reflection. *God, what does he see when he looks at me that makes him so consumed by me?* "Come here," he says quietly.

I face him, our eyes meet. I am in love with him. That mythical kind of love that other girls my age only dream about. Our whole life is planned out, from now until eternity, every step will be in accompaniment with Ray Douglas. Part of me is wild about the idea, part of me is scared to death.

I take a few steps toward him, and his hands come around my waist. He pulls me onto his lap, my legs straddling his, our faces close. His kiss is like a drug I cannot get enough of, his touch the balm to cure any hurt.

My swimsuit top comes off, finds its way to the floor, his mouth replaces where it had been. Soft hands are what he has, not being the type for work that causes calluses. Give my Ray the controller for a video game and he'll be happy as a lark, though I must say, he prefers our present activity to those found on a television screen.

Who wouldn't?

Me. That's who.

He knows we don't have much time. Sunny was home when we got here, and Orion and Austin came in right after us. Dad will be home in about thirty and I'll need to shower so he doesn't catch a whiff. Besides, we left Dylan and Lucas downstairs with a yellow sponge babysitter.

One thing, though, I will say, is when Ray is loving me in the way only he ever has, I don't feel suffocated or stuck. I feel powerful, controlling him, controlling what he so desperately wants.

Another thing I will say is that love, this type of love, can lead to unwanted things if you get what I mean.

And tomorrow I start high school.

Ray

Star shines in my life as bright as the brightest star.

There is nothing and no one who can capture my eye like her.

That first day I saw her,
when I was just a seventh-grade newbie in this Podunk town,

I smiled without meaning to.

Good thing she smiled back.

Sunshine

I creep quietly up the stairs and stop when I get to the top.

Listening.

No, not to my sister and her obsessive boyfriend in the bedroom we share. I listen for Austin's departure, hanging on to a thread of hopelessness that my name might grace his lips on his way out the door. Even if it's just *goodbye*, at least I'll know he acknowledges my existence.

"Count on a text later," says Orion. "I'm sure this chick will be bogus. She'll take a look at us and be, like, 'See ya' to my dad. I'll be looking for alternate activities, ya know?"

Austin chuckles. "Alright, man. Hit me up."

The door shut without him remembering to say goodbye. I bite my cheek, gnashing my teeth into the already rough skin, tasting the salty warmth of my blood.

There. That's better.

I rap quietly on my bedroom door. "Star?" I wait a moment for an answer. No way will I walk in. Did that once. Learned two things that day: 1) People look awkward when they're doing *that*; and 2) My younger sister lost her virginity before me.

According to my calculations, I'm the only virgin living under this roof.

"What?" Star snaps behind the closed door.

"Um, Sky's home and says Dad's bringing Melissa over for dinner." I pause for her reaction. "She says Ray and them boys gotta go and we need to get this house cleaned up." I pause again. "Star?"

"Okay!" she yells. "Give us a minute!"

OMG. *Are they doing it right now?* Like, while she was talking to me? Gross. Creepy. Gross. Ew. I'm gonna be sick.

Seriously. It seems like the thing to do.

I'm in the bathroom before the thought fully processes, kneeled before the porcelain throne, my fingers assuming their usual position in my throat. The watermelon I ate at 12:43 p.m. today tinges my view pink. I gag and gag, feeling myself empty of everything inside; heart, soul, and being, feeling and emotion, anything that might get caught up in a spider web. When the purge is nothing but transparent saliva, I lean back against the bathtub.

God, I feel better. Lighter. More alive.

The door opens suddenly startling me back into reality (Reality: I'm fat and half dead). Star stares down at me, her shiny blue eyes laying judgment on me like a steel cloak. Thankfully she took the time to half-dress in underwear and a t-shirt. Her eyes shift to the toilet. "Is that blood?"

"Watermelon." I stand and grab my toothbrush as I flush the toilet. Star pulls back the shower curtain and turns on the water while I scrub the disgustingness from my mouth.

"Dad's really bringing her here?" she asks as she strips. She's sunburned.

"I guess." I watch my naturally skinny, perfect-bodied sister as she tests the water temperature.

She scoffs. "Should be interesting." Getting in, she disappears from my envious view.

I want to be mean and tell her to make sure she washes away the stink Ray leaves on her body, but she could likely retort with a million things about me.

Things like how kids are starving in Haiti and would love to have the food I waste on a daily basis.

Austin

Orion and I go way back.
All the way back to when girls had cooties.
And the worst cooties came from his sisters.

Cooties are infectious.

They get in your brain and make it think weird things.
Then they manipulate your heart and make it beat funny when a girl comes into the room.

The most obvious symptoms of cooties are the complete lack of comprehensible speech when a girl is around, and the horrible side effects of obsessing over something unreachable.

Skylar

I'm proud of the fact that I taught myself to cook. Thanks to Pinterest, I can feed my dad and siblings all kinds of meals we never knew existed outside of restaurants we can't afford. For sixteen years we lived off frozen chicken nuggets and corndogs ala carte. Tonight, in celebration of the hope that Dad has found The One, we are having chicken enchiladas. It was a stroke of luck when the food pantry had canned chicken yesterday. I felt bad taking two cans, but I have a big family.

Hope this Melissa chick likes Mexican.

Actually, I don't care if she does.

I made them for *him*, and *he* loved them. And *he* is the reason I learned to cook. A good woman cooks for her man. It's never too soon to practice being a good wife, but in my case, my hope is we'll be saying our vows in less than a year.

Dad thinks I've just taken a fancy to cooking, and that's fine. No reason to alarm him or the officials before it's necessary.

Sunny is setting the table when the doorbell rings. It's like a fire alarm in that we all follow Dad to the door anxious to see the mystery woman worthy of meeting us. Before he opens it, he looks back at us, lined up like dominos behind him. His face clearly tells us not to ruin this for him. *For us*. We could all use a female role model in our life. Star needs guidance (and probably birth control), Sunny needs to feel love (and not from a worthless POS like Austin), and Orion needs to know there are good women in the world (that they're not all trash like Mom). Me, I'm knocking on the door to womanhood, soon to leave the nest. I don't need anything or anyone but *him*.

But my siblings? Yes, they need a mommy.

The potential mommy at the door is pretty, petite, and blonde. I expected someone who looked rough, like she'd seen her better days. No, not Melissa. She's well-dressed in a sundress that meets her knees, strappy sandals that I would wear. Her hair is shoulder length, and you could tell time had been taken to make it look just so. She looks like someone's mom. Someone whose mom cares about them.

I sigh. Dad'll be lucky if she sticks around until dinner has been digested. A woman like this doesn't date a single dad with four ornery teenagers, living in government subsidized housing, who works two jobs, one of which pays cash so we can keep our Section 8 and food stamps.

Introductions are made and she doesn't seem overwhelmed. She smiles easily, comfortably. We gather around the table to break bread and enchiladas.

"So," Star says. "Tell us about you, Melissa."

She smiles while she finishes the food in her mouth. "I want to hear about you kids."

Okay. They might be kids, but I *so* am not. *Strike one, Melissa.*

Orion snorts next to me. "No, you really don't."

She laughs. "Teenagers don't scare me."

Now Dad says, "Not yet anyways."

Melissa divulges. She works for the state office that oversees professional licenses, like for nurses and doctors (state jobs pay well in theory). She lives in the next town over, the town she grew up in, owns her home (Orion asked), it has three bedrooms (Orion asked that too), she has a cat (Pluto), she's thirty and met Dad on her birthday while she was out with her friends at the bar that pays Dad cash to dole out drinks to drunks.

She's thirty. My dad is thirty-five. And his eyes are lit up like candles during a power outage as he watches Melissa fill our ears. For his sake, I hope we (they) don't screw this up for him.

"Oh," she adds as a P.S., "and I have two brothers. My older brother Ben is a truck driver. He lives in Missouri. My younger brother, you probably know him." She nods and looks at each of us. "He teaches at the high school here. Algebra."

My stomach does a cartwheel.

"Jake Morris?" She says the name as an inquiry into our knowledge of her brother.

Before I can process that, Orion laughs so loudly I'm sure the neighbors heard him. Under the table, his leg hits mine with so much force I'm jarred slightly.

"Mr. Morris is your brother?" Orion hoots.

Melissa nods unassumingly. "I take it you know him?"

My leg whacks into his now. So his answer is appropriate. "I play basketball and he's the assistant coach. Oh, and I'll have him this year for algebra." He looks at me. "Sky had him last year. *Really* liked him."

It's okay, Orion, I'll kill you later.

Melissa looks at me. "He's a good teacher?"

I nod. "Yeah. Sure." *What else could I say?*

Orion is laughing again. I'm seriously gonna kill him. Everyone's gonna start wondering what's so damn funny.

Oh, wait. Too late.

"Orion," Dad says, a smile entertaining his lips, "what is so funny?"

He doesn't stop laughing when he says, looking at me, "So, like, if you guys get married, that will make *Jake*, like, our uncle?"

Melissa and Dad give each other a look. A look that says it all. It says it doesn't matter how ornery or bad or misguided we are. They are in love with each other and when they get married Jake *will* be our uncle. "Yes," they say regardless of the unspoken communication.

Later, in the solace of my room, after Melissa had gone, and Dad drilled us for our thoughts on her, I called *him*.

When *he* answered, this is what I said: "So my dad's new flame. Her name is Melissa. She claims you're her little brother."

Jake

Yes, this may pose a dilemma.
Sky is where I have hung my heart.

I don't care that she's seventeen or a
student where I teach numbers.

She doesn't care that I'm twenty-three
and fell in love with her from in
front of a classroom.

The dilemma lies in that Melissa
loves this man who happens to be Sky's dad.

Why didn't I make the connection before?
Melissa hopes for a ring,
much as Sky does.

But can I marry my (step)niece?

Starla

Today a new chapter of my life starts. High school. Freshman year. Oh, yippee.

Some people get nervous, but no, not me. I have three older sibs that have paved the way for me, plus Ray who won't lose me in the sea of hormones.

I roll over in bed. Sunny's already up, so I'm alone in the room. I lay flat on my back and pull my blanket to my chin. Lifting my shirt, I run my hands along my flat stomach. I note that my shoulders are still sore from sunburn. Sitting up, I suck in a deep breath and feel nausea consume me.

I'm gonna puke. Like, seriously.

I jump up, cover my mouth with my hand and fly to the bathroom, whip open the door. What I see doesn't surprise me. Sunny is huddled around the toilet upchucking exactly nothing. How do I know? Because she ate a total of four bites of enchiladas last night and threw them up promptly afterward.

It doesn't matter. I don't have time to wait for her. I gag into the sink, wrenching my guts until nothing except yellowy-greenish bile makes its appearance.

"Nice," Sky says behind me. "You're doing that shit now, too, Star?"

I don't look at her because my stomach is sending another round of bile to the sink.

"Hurry your pathetic selves up," she demands. "I need to get in the shower."

Yes, you know, because God forbid the Queen go without a shower for a day.

I hear her now across the hall. "Go check out the bulimia twins," she says to Orion.

He laughs. "Star might disappear if she pukes too many times."

I open my eyes and turn on the faucet to wash away the evidence. Sunny is looking at me with her angry eyes.

"What. Are. You. Doing?" she asks with clenched teeth.

I narrow my eyes. "It's not me you're competing with, so don't worry about it."

Sunny makes me so mad. She makes all of us mad, really. She's not fat, not at all. She's as tall as Sky, about five-foot-eight, while I'm a measly five-foot. None of us are overweight, or even what you would call stocky. I get teased about being underweight and get compared to ten-year-olds regularly. Sky and Sunny, well, they weigh about the same. Sunny's argument is that she has to purge to keep looking that way. As if one extra calorie might send her over a cliff into the sea of obesity.

It's whatever. I have my own problems. Like why the hell did I just puke first thing in the morn, and why does a candy cane sound so good in August, and why haven't I had a period since May?

Orion

The sun shines today.
Of course it does.
It's the last Friday in August, the first day of school.

And like the sun:
Sunny comes out of her cave and
smiles like she is without the burden
of bulimia.

Star twinkles bright,
downright shimmers
when Ray is around.

Sky is on top of the world knowing
she will get to see Jake every day
again.

Me, it's just another day in the shadows of them. Much
like my name, people forget I'm there, don't often look
for me.

But everyone sees the sky, the sun, and the stars.

Sunshine

I get out of the backseat of the nasty old Taurus and survey the parking lot. I spot Austin's truck. It kinda sticks out, being more rust colored than black and all. I straighten my posture and pull my cami down to cover my gut. I fall into step with Orion despite the look he shoots me. Sky is on his other side, her phone in hand as she texts. Star rides to school with Ray. He's a sophomore like me, but rumor is that he was held back in elementary school, so he turned sixteen in May. The first one in our class to get a license.

I stick close to Orion, knowing he'll lead me to Austin. As we walk, I exchange hello-how-are-yous with friends I pass. As sophomore class president, it's important that I keep up the image I've manufactured.

Friendly and sincere. Outgoing and capable.

When in fact I'm: Desperate and lonely. Jealous and pitiful. Insane and neurotic. Bulimic and suicidal.

Haley Johnston slithers up to us, her snake eyes on Orion. Haley and I were best friends before high school. Until she became a vamp, obsessed with boys. Obsessed with showing her boobs to them, and whatever else they want to peek at.

"Hi, Orion," she says in her sly, cunning little skankspeak.

He barely smiles at her. "Hi."

She looked at me. "Sunny, wow. You look great. Have you lost weight?"

I look down at my disgusting body. Why did I wear these shorts? You can see every fat dimple on my thighs. God, and this cami isn't covering anything. "Um, I don't think so," I say.

"Maybe it's your hair," Haley says. "Either way, you look *hot*."

"Thanks," I mutter, feeling my cheeks flush. Then Austin comes up behind Orion, lays a heavy hand on my brother's shoulder. My heart flutters in my chest and the blood that flushed my face twenty seconds earlier is quickly draining into my butt, making it look huge, I'm sure.

"What's up?" Austin says to no one in particular. His eyes travel over Haley, then shift to Sky. He nods at her.

Sky rolls her eyes and scoffs before walking away. He watches her go.

"Hi, Austin," Haley says.

"Hey," he says with an easy smile. He glances at Orion. "So you have algebra with Morris first hour?"

"Oh, yeah," Orion says. "I gotta tell you about this chick my dad brought home." They start to walk away. I so desperately want to follow, but I don't dare.

Morning moves through like a fog, waiting until lunch when I can see Austin (not that he sees me). While I stand over the salad bar, debating over iceberg and romaine, Haley finds me.

"So how was your summer?" she asks.

"Fine. How was yours?" I choose iceberg. Iceberg equals water. Water equals zero caloric intake.

"Good. We went to Wisconsin Dells for a week. It was *amazing*!" She squeals a little. "I met this *gorgeous* guy there. He's from Michigan. He was *so* hot!"

"That's cool. What's his name?"

She crinkles her brow. "Logan. No, wait. Landon?" She giggles. "Oh, well. It was only a week, and I haven't talked to him since." She waves her hand in the air as we sit at a table with the group of sophomores we'd been a part of forever. "Summer love, you know?"

As if I have a clue.

"What's your schedule look like?"

I hand it to her and proceed to cut my lettuce into tiny pieces. She's rattling off my classes, citing what we have together. I finish cutting and put one leaf, half-inch in diameter, in my mouth and note the time. 11:22 a.m. I face Haley. She's stopped talking.

"What?" I ask.

"Sunny, I miss you." She gives a vulnerable smile. "I want things to be how they used to be with us. What do you think?"

I shrug and snatch my schedule from her skankhands. "Sure."

She smiles and I feel mighty and powerful. Even if it's just Haley, someone wants me.

Not that that changes who I am or anything else. After three more pieces of lettuce, I excuse myself to the little girl's room (not that I am little by any means) and allow the lettuce to escape the confines of my beached whale body.

Austin

Her brush-offs have zero effect on my self-esteem.
I swear.
I'm not saying Sky loves me or even wants anything to do with me.
What I'm saying is that once upon a time, not all that long ago, she did want something to do
with me.
Sure, she might say it was all in fun, a time to learn and a time to grow, but I see it
differently.
Why else would she give me the priceless gift that she did?
One thing's for sure:
No matter where the universe takes her, she won't forget her first time.
My first time.
Our first time.
Together.

Skylar

I watch Sunny whiz past me on her way out of the cafeteria like she didn't even see me. From the head of the lunchroom, I see the crowds gathered around the tables, wondering where I really fit in. At the one long table in front of the window sits all the popular kids no matter the grade. I can see Sunny's backpack on an empty chair next to Haley Johnston. Was she really sitting there? Haley is a straight-up skank. The things I've heard about her, and not just from Orion, but I know he wouldn't lie, so I believe the rest of the stories too.

Orion is sitting off to the side near the salad bar with the rougher looking kids. Sometime last year, he and Austin transitioned from hanging with the jock-asses to hanging with the crew who liked to hit bongs instead of balls.

Star sits with Ray at one end of a table. No one else sits with them. Actually, I'm not even sure she has friends besides Ray.

My siblings aren't my concern. Jake Morris is who I want to sit with, but he is nowhere to be seen. Guess I should have asked him where he goes during lunch. Maybe it's somewhere I can go too. Hopefully somewhere we could be alone and not get caught.

Resigned to being just a student, I sit with my friends at the far end of the table nowhere near the window. I half-listen and half-participate in the juvenile conversations around me about who had hooked up with who, who was wearing what, and so-and-so who had gotten a new car.

Kylee is going on about Maci Pendleton and the rumors she had an STI when I see Sunny come back into the cafeteria. Her face is slightly flushed, which actually gives her the color she usually lacks. I follow her with my eyes as she snakes through the cafeteria, purposely passing the table where Orion and Austin sit.

Her eyes are locked on Austin, but he never even glances up. Orion does, though. After Sunny passes, he glances at Austin, then his eyes find mine.

Wordlessly we say: What does she see in him?

Well, that's what I said. Orion was probably saying something like: Why is she such a stalker?

I don't care anymore because Jake just walked into the cafeteria. He's scanning the room and I wonder if he's looking for me. I so badly want to stand up and shout, "Hey! Babe! I'm right here. C'mon, I saved you a seat."

But that would likely result in the loss of his job, and possibly a jail term.

So instead I stay seated, watching, waiting for him to find what he's looking for.

It's me. Our eyes lock and I say (wordlessly, of course): *I love you*. And he says (again, wordlessly): *I love you, too, Skylar Hollis. I love you more than anything*.

I am sure that's exactly what he's saying.

He leaves then, giving me notice that the only reason he appeared was to see me. And that is more than enough to make my day.

Jake

Yes, I know it's wrong, but let me tell you why it's so right.

Exactly five years and forty-three days passed on the calendar between my birth and hers.

I'm not that much older than her.

In the arsenal that we have prepared for defense there are the following facts:

1.) My dad is eight years older than my mom, having married when my mom was twenty.

2.) My brother's wife was eighteen when they got married. He was twenty-one.

3.) Sky's mom was seventeen when she was born. Her dad was eighteen.

And the latest fact:

4.) Sky's dad is five years and one-hundred-nineteen days older than my sister.

We did the math last night.

In addition, we love each other. Don't dwell on the wrongness but be happy for our love. It's not like I became a teacher to find a wife. But I became a teacher and found a wife. Her name just happened to be listed in my grade book.

Starla

After the mundane first day of high school, I guess I felt the need to mix things up. Ray, however, did not. We drove to his house after school, which had been routine once he got his license last year. He'd pick me up at the middle school and we'd come here where no one else was home.

I know what you're thinking, and you're wrong. That's not when we started doing it. That was a long time ago. Ray asked me out when I was in sixth grade, and he was in seventh grade. When he was nearing the end of eighth grade, I was thirteen and he had turned fifteen, and I started to fear losing him when he went to high school.

And I knew this much about s-e-x: Sky, my older, mother-like sister, had s-e-x with Austin. He became infatuated with her.

I wanted Ray to look at me the way Austin looked at Sky forever. I assumed s-e-x was the way to get that. But what I didn't realize was that Ray already loved me. I didn't need to do that to gain his devotion. But once he had a taste of s-e-x, he became infatuated with it.

Sometimes I felt like I was an intruder in his relationship with s-e-x, that he wanted that more than me, but he needed me for that.

Or did he? Because there were plenty of other girls who gave it away like sand in the desert. So, maybe it was me he wanted, not just s-e-x.

He sits up on the couch next to me, polite enough to hand me the clothes I'd shed on the floor. Once our bodies are concealed, he scoots closer. It's 3:45 p.m. We've been at his house for twenty minutes.

"Ray," I say quietly as I lay my head on his shoulder.

"Hmm?" he responds, taking the remote with one hand, my hand with his other.

"My period's late." I pause. "And this morning I threw up."

I'm not sure what I expect, but he sits unmoving while I watch the secondhand circle the clock three times.

Finally, he says, "My parents are gonna kill me."

Yeah, that's likely. But only, "If my brother doesn't kill you first."

He sighs loudly and lowers his head to his hands, the TV remote forgotten. "I knew you should've gotten on the Pill."

I nod. "Probably would've been a good idea."

"Jesus Christ, Star. You're fourteen!" He sits back and looks at me. "You started high school today." I nod. "How is this happening?"

"Like, biologically?"

"No, I know the sex ed stuff. I mean, like, why?"

I shrugged. "I haven't taken a test or anything yet. So let's not freak yet."

"How late are you?"

I look at the clock. 3:52 p.m. "I don't know. Like, three months."

He jumps up and yells, "Three months! And you're just now telling me?"

"Don't yell at me."

He sits beside me again. "I'm sorry," he whispers, drawing me into a hug. "I'm sorry, but why did you wait so long?"

I melt at his touch. "I don't know." I lift my chin and find his lips with mine, anxious to wash away his anger, anxious to make it all better. All the while knowing there weren't enough kisses or enough s-e-x in the world to fix this.

"Okay," he says with an authoritative sigh. "First, you need to take a test to see if you're really pregnant. Then we'll go from there. If you're not, which I'm really hoping is the situation, you are definitely getting on some birth control. If you are, well, I don't know." His eyes find mine. "What would we do?"

I shrug.

"You have to have thought about this already, Star. Do you want to have a baby?"

"I don't want an abortion, if that's what you're asking."

"It's not."

"And do you think I could carry a baby for nine months and then just let it go?"

His face softens, and I commit the confusion in his speckled blue eyes to memory, set it right there next to the way his pale blond hair curls on the ends, the gentle slope of his nose, the ruddy color of his cheeks. "I don't know." His lips curl into something like a smile. "I guess that's why we have parents. They'll tell us what to do no matter what we want."

Something about that settles easily with me. Yes, I am too young to be making a decision of this caliber. Then again, I suppose I was too young to be having s-e-x when I was thirteen. But there's something about being in love that makes you see things through rose-colored glasses. And from where I stood, s-e-x equaled love and devotion, not a baby.

Ray

Not in the plans.
Not in the plans at all whatsoever.
Absolutely no freaking way.
I love Star, but my life goals are laid out like a marble walkway.
They do not include a baby at sixteen.

Yes, I plan to be with Star forever and have three kids, but not until she is done with college.
That's in eight years.
This cannot be happening.
I can win this, though, without her hating me.

Our parents will see we are too young, they'll demand an abortion
(will they, really?)
or adoption
(could I part with a part of me
and a part of her after watching it grow
for so many months?).

Sunshine

Sometimes I wonder what happened to our mother. I mean, we know our dad's version of what happened. The abridged tale goes like this: Mom and Dad were losers. Dad was a small-time meth dealer, Mom a full-time junkie. Dad was in and out of jail. Men were in and out of our house when he was gone (hence the question of why Star looks like no one else). Mom found a new sugar daddy while our daddy was in lock up, when he got out and came calling for us kids, he found us in the care of the new man, mom who knows where. She returned eight days later and accused dad of kidnapping, police were called, we went back to Mom. It wasn't long after that when a neighbor called the police because Sky went to their house asking for food and her mommy. Mom was arrested (when she finally showed her face) and we've been with Dad ever since.

We all expected to hear from her when she was released, but that was about ten years ago.

I'm at the kitchen table with the laptop the school gave our family a few years ago because we couldn't afford one, when Orion comes through the front door. I sit up straight, hoping Austin follows, but the door just slams shut. I slouch down, partially crushed, partially relieved. Without Austin here, I feel less on edge.

"No Austin?" I ask.

He goes straight to the fridge. "Nah."

Odd, but I don't dwell. "Hey, O? You ever wonder where Mom is?"

"No. Why would I?"

I shrug. "I don't know."

"Do you?" He looks at me from across the room, waiting for my response.

"Yeah."

"Why? Do you think life would be better if she was around?"

"Not necessarily. It's just that I don't really remember her. And there's, like, no pictures." I sigh. "And the ones we have are of either you or Sky with her. None of me or Star."

Orion sits across from me with a plate of leftover enchiladas. "There's nothing to remember, really, Sun. She was a piece of shit. We're definitely better off without her."

"But that's Dad's side of it. There's two sides to every story, you know."

"Sure there is. But I remember some of it. And so does Sky."

"I know. It's just, that maybe…I don't know."

"You think that maybe you wouldn't be so messed up in the head if you had a mom?"

I stare at my brother, wondering how long I would have to choke him before he died.

"Sunny, I'm not trying to hurt your feelings. But you're a bigger mess than the rest of us. Having a mom isn't gonna fix that. It's not gonna make you like your body or make Austin or any other guy fall in love with you." He pauses, probably assessing the damage. "It's not gonna make Sky any less a control freak or Star any less obsessed with Ray."

"And you're just perfect, I suppose?"

"Having a mom isn't going to change me either. I have no interest in a relationship, getting married, or having kids. Probably because of her."

"Maybe not, but it would be one more person to slap you in the face when you're out of line. Like right now."

He scoffed, finished off his enchiladas. "Right. I'd knock her out if she ever touched me." He got up and went to the sink, dropped his plate in and grabbed a soda from the fridge. "Have you tried Facebook?"

"Facebook?"

"To look for mom?"

"Oh, God. No."

"Why don't you?" He comes back to the table and sits beside me.

I sign into Facebook. Then I search for her by her married name: Amy Jo Hollis.

"They're divorced," Orion says.

"I know, but maybe she still has our name."

And she does. Her profile is the first one that pops up.

There she is, our despicable mother, staring back at me and Orion, a smile the size of the universe on her lips. A young child sits on her lap.

"Click on it," he whispers.

I do. Her profile is public, and we spend the next hour learning things we would have been better off not knowing. Like: she lives about an hour away, she is apparently a waitress at TGIFriday's, she is in a relationship with a man named Johnny Pearl, and she had a baby about four years ago, named her Rainn. She is happy in her pictures. She looks clean and healthy.

"She looks like Sky," I say.

"She does," my brother agrees.

We hear a car door slam outside and look at each other. Quickly, I hit Home on Facebook and pretend to scroll through my newsfeed. Orion jumps up and opens the fridge.

It's Sky who comes through the door. We're both staring at her when she enters the kitchen. "Why do you guys look so guilty?"

"Guilty?" Orion retorts. "I don't think either of *us* are committing daily crimes."

Sky rolls her eyes. "I'm not committing any crimes. And shut up." She glances at me, back to Orion. "Where's the meat I told you to get out?"

"I forgot," he says easily. If it were me who forgot, I'd be facing her wrath for a week. Sky and Orion share some bond that I doubt I'll ever have with anyone.

Sky sighs and says, "Worthless." She opens the freezer, pulls out the meat in question and sticks it in the microwave to defrost. "I need the computer," she says to me. "Have to look up the recipe on Pinterest."

I glance at Orion, wondering if she'll be able to see that we looked up mom.

"What were you guys doing? Watching Internet porn?"

Orion laughs. "Yeah. With my sister. You're a sicko."

I log out of Facebook, close out the Internet completely, grab my backpack and go upstairs. I hear Sky say something about me trying to hide something by closing out the Internet, but I keep walking.

I almost wish I was watching porn. I'd feel less guilty.

In my room, I reach under my mattress and grab out the thing I keep hidden from everyone. See, everyone knows I puke everything I eat. Well, everyone but Dad. But no one knows about this.

I set it on the edge of my bedside table and take off my shorts, ignoring the fat bulging over my underwear. The cuts on my left leg are still scabbed over, but my right thigh is healed, ready for new ones.

Without allowing concentration, the razor is in my hand and the next thing I know *one two three four* the blood is dripping down my fat thigh. I want to cut the fat out of them.

Four slices hidden from sight just below my underwear.

Four slices in equal length going from left to right.

Four slices deep enough to draw blood.

Four slices are not enough to kill me.

How many would be?

Note the time: 4:36 p.m.

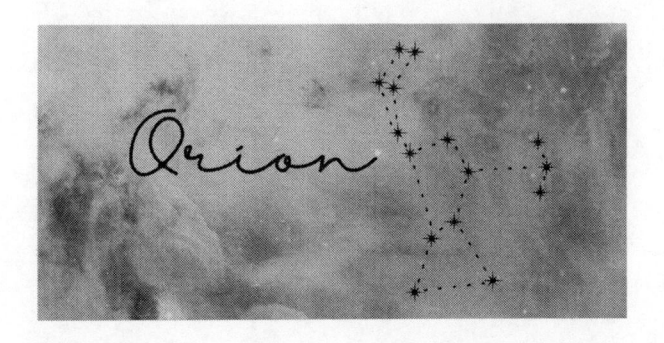

Orion

                    Mom.
            Don't care.
            Don't want to know.
                  But I do.

She's happy with her new kid, also named from all that's above.

                            Does she think of us?

                Does she search us on social media?

                      Like I do every chance I get?

Does she know what a mess she left behind when she went on that last bender?

          When she left behind her four babies

                              for some blow?

Skylar

I will be so glad when I am out of this house. These kids are so weird. Probably *were* looking at Internet porn. Freaks. But I guess Sunny has to learn somehow, though I know for fact she'd like to learn the same way I did- trial and error with Austin.

The thing about it is, I didn't really learn anything. Jake, though, has taught me so much more than a thing or two. And not even about the physical act of love, but how when tied to the heart, the term *making love* makes sense.

I'm not saying we were in love from that first fateful day, but we went into this endeavor eyes wide open, well aware of the consequences that could damn us both. Okay, well more him than me, but whatever. We're still not in the clear, but now we're devoted to this. We will be together, even if he does lose his job and goes to prison.

I will wait.

After school, I walked to his house and let myself in, letting Orion take the Taurus wherever stoner boy goes. He knows about me and Jake, and he is the only one. I had to tell someone, someone I could trust. I didn't find any of my friends worthy of that secret, so I told my brother. I wish I never said a word, but no use looking back now.

Jake arrived home, smiling at the sight of me. "I was hoping you'd be here when I saw Orion leaving school in your car." He put his arms around me and sealed our love with a kiss. "It was strange today. You know, seeing you and not being able to act…I don't know, normal?"

I giggled. "Normal? What's that?"

He chuckled. "Not this." He kissed me again, this time with more meaning, more passion. More desire and more want.

Jake gives me more than Austin ever could. He knows there is more to love than checking out a person's body and getting them into bed. He knows to say the right words, ones like *beautiful* and *forever*, instead of *hot* and *maybe someday*.

I lay cradled in his arms, feeling the nip of tears in my eyes. "I don't want to go," I whisper.

He squeezes me. "I don't want you to go either."

In the summer we had more time. Lazy, long days. Now that school has begun, our time will be vastly limited to an hour or so after school, except on nights when my dad's working at the bar. And the weekends. But, God, how I longed to leave this house with him. Go on an actual date.

Can't chance getting caught.

"One-hundred-seventy-nine days to go," I say.

"You know that only counts actual school days, right?"

I groan. "Don't depress me any more than I already am."

He laughs and sits up. "We should talk about this situation with your dad and Melissa."

I ignore him, reach out to touch his bare chest.

"I wish I would've realized who she was talking about. Mike. He has four kids. How many guys named Mike could there be raising four kids on his own?" He looks down at my hand.

"I say we go back to Plan A."

"What was Plan A?" He takes my hand in his, kisses each fingertip.

"I drop out on my birthday."

"No, no, no, Sky. You're finishing school."

"GED?"

"No."

Now as I slice the steak for stroganoff, hopeful that top round steak (since it was the cheapest) instead of flank steak (what even is the difference?) doesn't ruin the recipe, I go back to the option of dropping out. It would make everything easier. I would be eighteen and an adult. I wouldn't be a student at Monroe High School. We could get married, and I could live with him. No more being mommy to these *kids*. No more cooking for my dad. No more having to answer for all my unaccounted-for time.

Why didn't Jake see that?

I can still go to college with a GED. It wouldn't really change anything except we could be official about our relationship sooner rather than later.

"Hey," Dad says over my shoulder. "Smells good. What is it?"

I smile. "Beef Stroganoff."

He nods, though I know he's never heard of it. "Where's everyone?"

"Upstairs, I guess. O and Sunny were acting weird." I shrug. "Not sure what's up with them. Oh, and I'm actually not sure Star is even here. Should I text her?"

"Could you?"

I do. She texts back that she's on her way. When she comes inside, her face is red, and she storms upstairs. Dad and I hear her and Sunny yelling at each other, then Sunny storms downstairs.

"She's a psycho, I swear," she says.

I stifle a laugh. Star is actually pretty even tempered. Sunny is the psycho.

Dinner is a roundabout of everyone's first day of school. The salty scent of dinner lingers in the air. Then Dad says, "Melissa liked meeting you guys last night. She wants us to come to her parent's house for a Labor Day cookout." He wipes his mouth with a paper napkin.

Orion looks at me, then at Dad. "Will Mr. Morris be there?"

"Who?"

"Her brother."

"Oh, I don't know." He looks at each of us, settles on Star. "It's tomorrow. None of you have plans already, do you?"

Star narrows her eyes. "No, Dad. Ray's family is cooking out on Monday. Like they always do."

"Don't be so defensive, Starla." Dad looks at the rest of us. "How about the rest of you?"

Sunny and I have no plans, of course. It's Orion who says, "I wouldn't miss it for the world."

Mike

I've tried my best with these kids.
And I think I've done well considering the cards
stacked against me from the start.
I was young, so was Amy Jo.
                      I did drugs, so did Amy Jo.
I had no interest in being a father,
          Amy Jo had none in being a mother.
After Sky you'd think we'd figure out how not to
make more mistakes, but no.
    b a m ,   b a m ,   b a m ,   b a m
Kids were coming out of nowhere with no end in sight.
Fifteen months between Skylar and Orion,
twelve between Orion and Sunshine.
Between Sunshine and Starla,
if I do the math, I don't like it,
but thirteen months.
They're not that bad. They pull passing grades.
Stay out of trouble.
    Sure, maybe Star is a little too involved with Ray,
and perhaps Orion lights a blunt now and again,
                  but Sunny and Sky are golden.
I couldn't ask for better kids.

Starla

"I have to go to a cookout at this Melissa chicks house," I tell Ray over the phone after dinner.

"Get out of it, Star. We have to figure this out."

"I can't. I have to go."

"Play sick."

"Ray, c'mon. I won't be there all day. You can pick me up from there and we'll get the test then."

"How about I come get you now?"

I sigh and roll over in my bed, pull my tattered comforter around my shoulders. "I'm tired. Tomorrow."

He's quiet for a moment. "Star? I'm scared. Like, scared to death."

"Me too." But am I?

We hang up and I contemplate whether or not I am scared about being pregnant. I should be scared, but I'm really not. It's like it's someone else that this is happening too.

Hold up.

I'm not even sure yet, but on the other hand, I'm sure. I'm as sure as the stars shine at night that there is a piece of me and a piece of Ray growing inside of me.

Sunny is losing her dinner in the bathroom. She's gonna kill herself doing that, I swear. I hear a video game coming from Orion's room. Nothing from Sky's room. She's probably downstairs cleaning up. I get out of bed and debate what to do. I really don't want to deal with Sunny. I could sit in Orion's room and watch him kill zombies or whatever. Or I could go downstairs and sit with Sky and dad.

Life is all about decisions. Some I can make (like, what to wear), some I cannot (like, whether or not to have a baby at fourteen). And some decisions are never yours to make in the first place (like whether to be born).

If I were this baby inside of me, would I want to be born to parents who are much too young? What would my life be like having a mom too young to even make a decision? Would I rather be dead? Would I opt to never have a life in the first place? What if I ended up like Sunny, a little off in the head, destroying myself from the inside out? All because my mom couldn't decide if I should be born.

Maybe I should talk to Sky. She's the closest thing I have to a mom.

I find her sitting on the couch downstairs, sans Dad. "He had to work, and I'm leaving in a bit," she says matter-of-factly. Well, duh. It is Friday night. Where else would Dad be? And in that case, why is Orion still here? Surely there's some loser party for him to attend.

Then, as if on cue, the doorbell rings and Austin comes in before me or Sky can react. "Hey," he says to Sky.

I'm not even sure he sees me standing here.

Sky pulls her legs to her chest and stares at the TV. "He's upstairs."

Austin stands by the door. He wants to say more, I know he does. But he doesn't. He goes upstairs, leaving us alone.

I sit beside Sky. "I'm not even sure he saw me standing there."

"He did. If he didn't, he would still be there trying to come up with something brilliant to say."

That makes me smile. I've seen how uncomfortable Austin gets around her. It's entertainment, really. Almost as entertaining as when Sunny the circus side show loses her words around him.

Me and Ray never had that problem. "Me and Ray were never like that."

She rolls her eyes. "Well, no. You and Ray were just kids when you got together." She scoffs. "Hell, you're still kids."

I want to remind her that Ray is sixteen and she's only seventeen, so if Ray's a kid, then so is she. But I don't. Instead, I say, "Yeah, well, I think I'm pregnant."

The Netflix surfing stops but she doesn't look at me. "Are you kidding me?"

"Do you think I would kid about this?"

She finally looks at me. "You're not on the Pill?"

"No. Are you?"

"Yes."

"Does Dad know?"

"That I'm on the Pill? I don't know." She shakes her head. "Why do you think you're pregnant? Did you take a test?"

I shake my head. "No. But I'm late, and this morning, when you saw me puking, I wasn't trying to be bulimic."

"So you really don't know. How late are you?"

I sigh and look at the TV. She stopped on a true crime documentary. *A small town is shaken by an act of violence.*

"Starla?"

"May. The last period I remember was in May."

She's about to speak, but suddenly a herd of elephants is unleashed and making their way down the stairs. Orion and Austin come through the living room, reeking of the skunking smell of marijuana. They confiscate a soda each from the fridge and head out the front door.

"Don't be too late," Sky yells after them.

Sunny stands at the bottom of the stairs looking tentative. "Was that Austin?"

"Him and Orion," Sky answers impatiently. "They left."

Sunny stares at the closed door. "I didn't even know he was here."

"Of course you didn't," I say. "You were too busy blowing chunks to realize it."

"I was in the bedroom, actually," she snaps.

"Whatever. You were in the bathroom when I was up there."

"Like you got a lot of room to talk. Wasn't that you throwing up in the sink this morning?"

"So? I throw up once and suddenly I'm bulimic? Try again, freak."

"Stop!" Sky yells. "You're both freaks." She laughs. "Actually, we all are. Have been since the day we were born."

There's truth in her words, but they don't hurt.

"Where's Ray?" Sky asks quietly.

"At home, I guess."

Ray

Well.

Sometimes there are just things. And sometimes there are things. I need an answer to whether or not life is growing inside the girl I love, but she's tired, not seeing the importance of the matter.

The urgency.

So when I get the call from Trent about a little back to school party, I say I'll pick him up. What I don't count on is Orion showing up after I'd had two beers. He gives me a dirty look, similar to the ones he always gives me. Can't blame the guy. He and I are the same age and I have a sister in ninth grade with Star. I'd be a little protective if she were all involved with him.

But why, when I feel a good buzz, did I approach Orion and tell him how much I love his sister? How I can't wait to be his brother-in-law? He laughed at me and told Trent to take me home.

Now Orion will tell Star. And Star will be mad. And then she won't want to talk to me. And then I might have to wait longer to know if there is life growing inside the girl I love.

Sunshine

It's a desperate move, really. But desperate situations call for desperate measures.

I am tired of being just under Austin's radar, like he doesn't quite remember I exist. My solution is one I have contemplated before. See, Orion and him have a routine on Friday's. It involves drinking and getting high and coming back here to crash.

If I just happen to be in Orion's bed when they get back, Austin will have to notice me, won't he? And depending on his level of intoxication, maybe he'll be interested.

As Sky would say: Pathetic.

It's 1:27 a.m. when I hear his loud pickup pull up. At 1:29 a.m. the bedroom door opens and in comes my brother and Austin. Orion falls to the bed, landing on my arm.

"What the...?" he mutters, but barely looks at me. "Sunny...."

I roll over and pretend not to notice the commotion. I wait for Austin to lie down too, but he doesn't. His silhouette sways slightly in the moonlight.

"Sunny," Austin says. "What are you doing in here?"

I pretend to sleep.

He grabs my ankle and shakes it. "Sunny. C'mon, go to bed. Your bed."

"Mmm," I moan. I roll to my back and look at him. *God, he is gorgeous.* "What?"

"Go," he says.

I stare at him, trying to come up with a reason not to go. "Ray's in there with Star."

He makes a face at me. "No he's not. He was with us."

"With you?" I sit up and move over, making room for Austin to sit next to me. He does.

"Well, he wasn't with us, but he was there. Drunk. Talking shit to Orion." He shakes his head and kicks off his shoes. "It was funny. He's such a tool." He pulls his shirt over his head. "One of these days O's gonna pound the shit out of him."

I contemplate that for about .44 seconds. I don't care about Star or Ray. Not with Austin shirtless next to me. "Where'd you guys go?"

"Out by Oak Point. We didn't know the dude who lived there, but it didn't matter." He looks at me. "Your friend Haley was there."

My heart jumps into my throat. "She was?"

His head bobs. "Yeah. You should've come. There were a bunch of sophomores."

Wow. Did he really just say that? Something like he wished I'd been in the same place he was? Like, maybe there was some possibility he would have looked at me, even with Haley Johnston there?

"I didn't know about it."

"Can you go to bed? I really want to lay down, Sunny."

Anything for Austin.

Sleep doesn't come for a while. My mind races, running laps around the words we exchanged. But the race halts when I wonder this: If Sky had been in Orion's bed, would he have been so quick to kick her out?

I can't dwell on that. I need to focus on the fact that we had an actual conversation. One where he wasn't wearing a shirt. And we were in a bed. Yeah, so, my brother was there too. Whatever. It's my memory. I can spin it however I want it.

My fingers brush across my scabby left thigh. I start to pick, pulling the scabs to let the blood seep to the surface. When I feel the wetness on my fingers, I bring them to my lips and taste the saltiness from my own body. Right now, I feel the need to slice deeper, slice longer, but it'll have to wait.

Austin

Last thing I needed was
    conversation with Sunny.
        What was she doing anyway?
        I'm not blind.
I see how she looks at me.
    I feel her wheat-colored eyes
        fall heavy on me whenever she's near.
Asking Orion if she was
    into me led to nothing.
        Said they don't talk like that.
Sure, she's a little weird,
    but she's smoking hot.
        Maybe she's into girls,
            'cause she sure hasn't ever
                had a boyfriend.
But if she's not....
    Well, nothing.
        Sky is who I want,
            who I'll always want.
Sunny may be hot,
    but she's nothing compared to Sky.
        And I think Orion would get a
            little pissed if I messed with
                another of his sisters.
Okay, maybe more than a little pissed.
            But if he never knew....

Skylar

When I told Jake that my family and I would be at his parents' house the next day to check out the burger selection, all he could do was laugh. I failed to see the humor in the situation. He tried to explain it wasn't even funny, that he was just nervous about it.

"Why?" I asked.

He shook his head. "I'm not sure how to explain it. But, like, when I talk to you, I have to talk to you like you're a student. Which you are, but then again, you're not." He laughed again.

Whatever.

I straighten every questionable looking wave in my hair until all that is left is silky, straight perfection. My eyes were expertly lined, lashes donned with an appropriate amount of mascara. I look good enough to meet my future in-laws. Or, uh, step-grandparents.

Wtf.

I find my dad in his room looking equally stressed about his appearance. He's generally a jeans and t-shirt kind of guy, but today he struggled between jean shorts and khaki slacks he usually wears to his day job at the local AT&T Authorized Retailer (which is the ONLY reason Dad can afford for each of us to have a phone).

"I want to look casual, but not too casual." He faces me. "You know what I mean?"

More than he can fathom. "I say go with the shorts. It's hot out. You'll be sweating and uncomfortable in pants."

He nods in agreement. "Is the shirt okay?"

A green polo, versatile for any occasion. "Definitely."

He is clean shaven, except his goatee, which is neatly trimmed. I can smell the cologne that he reserves for special occasions, and it makes me sad. My poor dad has given up just about his whole life to be Dad *and* Mom to us. He deserves to be happy, but did it have to be with Melissa? Don't I deserve to be happy too? Haven't I been surrogate mom for long enough?

I just don't see how, if things continue to move with the force of gravity, things will work out in my favor.

"Do I look okay, Dad?" I stand so he can inspect me.

"Yes, you do." He frowns. "What about them?" he asks, referring to the kids. "How do they look?"

Geez, why hadn't I thought of that? "I'll go check it out."

Upstairs, I am pleasantly surprised to find my sisters and brother looking like the good kids they aren't.

Trepidation builds inside me the whole thirty-minute drive to the Morris'. I feel as nervous as Dad looks when he parks the ten-year-old Durango on the street in front of a split-level house.

"Please, please, guys, be on your best behavior," Dad says before we get out. He turns to look Orion in the eye. "Please."

Orion smiles, his dark eyes twinkling. "It's not me you need to worry about." With that, he opens the door and steps out, my sisters following suit.

I look at Dad. "I'll keep an eye on him."

Dad pats my arm. "Thanks, Sky. I don't know if there'll be any girls here, but I don't need him hitting on them, alright?"

I nod and get out of the passenger side. I walk side-by-side with Dad to the door, the kids behind us. After a ring of the bell, an older woman opens the door.

"You must be Mike," she exclaims. And then, taking us in, she adds, "And your lovely children."

Dad holds out his hand. "Yes, I'm Mike. And this is Skylar, Sunny, Orion, and Starla."

"Wonderful to meet you. Please, come in." She holds the door open wide. "I'm Linda, Melissa's mom."

She's not what I expected her to look like. I guess I expected someone grandma-ish. I mean, she's older, but not, like, ancient. We step into the house, and I forget about Linda, Melissa, Dad, and anything else.

I'm in Jake's childhood home, and he's around here somewhere. My eyes swallow up the sights, wondering how someone who grew up here could be in love with me, or my dad for that matter.

The furniture is nice, paintings hung on the walls along with tons and tons of family photos. Knick-knacks decorate shelves, and throw blankets are folded neatly on the back of the sofa.

Lost in my thoughts, I don't hear Melissa offering me a drink. "Oh, sure. Yeah, I'll take one."

She nods. "They're in a cooler on the back deck. The rest of the kids are already out there."

I stare at her. *I. Am. Not. A. Kid*. Damnit. *I am not a kid!* But for my dad's sake, I don't say anything at all. I smile and nod and go the way my siblings already had.

I'm hurt as I pass through the patio door, and honestly, I feel like crying. I was thrilled to be here, to be able to spend the day with Jake even if it wasn't how I wanted to be spending time with him. Now I was being shoved off with the kids. Maybe even expected to sit at the kiddy table when we eat.

I step into the thick late summer humidity and slide the door shut behind me, and suddenly being outside doesn't seem so bad. Jake sits at a round patio table with an older man, presumably his dad. Our eyes meet for a nanosecond, but we both look away.

"You must be kid number four," says the older man. "I'm Bob, and I'm pretty sure you know Jake." He chuckles. "Or I guess you probably call him Mr. Morris." More chuckling.

I smile. "Actually, I'm kid number one. I'm the oldest. I'll be eighteen in a few weeks. So, I'm not really a kid anymore either." I want to add that I don't call Mr. Morris Mr. Morris, that I *do* know him as Jake, and sometimes baby, but I keep that to myself.

Bob guffaws. "You got a long way to go until you're an adult. Heck, I still consider Jake here a kid." He winks at me. "What's your name?"

"Skylar. Most people call me Sky."

"Well, then Sky it is." He stands and opens the gas grill and I take the opportunity to smile at Jake. He smiles back and shakes his head, his eyes wandering the length of me, a beer in his hand.

In the yard, there are a few tables set up and I can see Sunny and Star sitting at one looking utterly bored. Orion is in the driveway shooting hoops with two boys who look to be about twelve. There's a scattering of other kids around too, but they're all involved in some activity.

I spot the cooler with the drinks and help myself to a soda. Then I sit down at the table, two seats away from Jake. When Bob sits back down, he asks, "So is it weird being here with your teacher?"

He has no idea. "Mr. Morris is cool." I look at Jake. "Or can I call you Jake now?"

Jake laughs lightly. "Sure, Sky. Call me Jake."

I try not to look too hard at him for fear of Bob seeing through the farce. "Cool. Jake," I say slowly, like I'm testing it out on my lips for the first time ever.

"It's still Mr. Morris at school," Jake says firmly. I bite my lip and nod. As if I don't know that. Geez, but at least if I called him Jake now, or we were seen having a discreet conversation, we could cite the potential of him becoming my uncle.

Later, after burnt burgers are devoured and greasy chips are chomped, I go inside to use the bathroom. When I come out, I go to the front room to check out all those family pics. I am dying to see how cute Jakey (as his mommy calls him) was as a wee one. I'm engrossed in the images spread on the walls, envious of the ocean scenes and ski lifts in the backgrounds. We have only ever taken one vacation. It was to Indiana Beach, which I thought was something special. Hopefully Jake and I can give our kids a life like Jake's parents have given him and not a life like my dad had to bust ass to give us.

"What're you doing?"

Jake's voice floats to me, embraces me like a warm scarf. I turn to see him leaning against the doorway to the kitchen and it's all I can do not to go to him and wrap my arms around him.

"Looking at the pictures." I look around the room once more. "You were a little cutie."

"Are you saying I'm not anymore?"

I smile. "Definitely even more so."

He straightens. "Come here. I'll show you more."

I follow him down a few stairs to the lower-level family room. It's wood paneled with older furniture (but still nicer than ours) and a wood burning stove. One entire wall is lined with three rows of thirteen pictures. The top row is his older brother Ben; the next row is Melissa; the bottom row is all Jake from kindergarten through senior year.

I study his face in each stage of his life, looking for the slightest changes, but his eyes were always the same deep blue, his hair always the same sandy color. He grows before my eyes from a little boy with a toothy grin to a man with a confident smile. Seeing these pictures makes my heart sing.

"What are you thinking?" he asks.

I turn my head to look at him now. "Wondering what our kids will look like."

His eyes grow serious as he walks toward me. His arms slide around my waist, my heart racing as his lips brush mine. "You're coming over later, right?"

"Mmhmm." I nuzzle my head into his chest and wonder if anyone would notice if we just left now. I'm about to voice the thought when we hear footsteps.

"Sky? Are you down there?"

Star, I mouth.

Jake nods and ducks into the bathroom without a sound.

"Yeah, I am." I go to the bottom of the steps. "What's up?"

"What're you doing?"

"Looking at pictures."

She skips down the steps. "Pictures?"

"Yeah. Of Melissa and Mr. Morris when they were kids."

Her eyes barely scan the walls. "Oh. Um, Ray is on his way. I'm not sure what to tell Dad."

I frown. *God, I hope she's not pregnant*. "Tell him you don't feel well. I'll back you up."

Hope enters her eyes. "You will?"

"Yeah. You need to find out so we can figure out what to do next."

She nods.

"Go outside and fake sick. I'll come out and find you and make a production of it."

She leaves and I consider making such a big deal that I can leave with her.

Jake comes out of the bathroom. "Everything okay?"

"She thinks she's pregnant."

His eyes go wide. "Isn't she a freshman?"

"Yep." I take a few steps forward and kiss him full on, leaving promises of later on his lips. "See you outside. I gotta go play mommy."

Jake

She's gotta go play mommy
and
I can't wait for the day she
can
really be a mommy.
That day won't be one we see soon.
I am serious about her finishing school
and
going to college.
Not that I won't love her if she doesn't,
but I really think she would feel better about
herself if she did.
My mom never went to college.
She
regrets it to this day.
She
battles depression, feeling worthless and useless.
Sure her mission in life must be
more
than raising kids.

Starla

Skylar's plot worked well. I faked a tummy ache and Sky suggested I call Ray to pick me up so the whole fam didn't have to go, though I'm thinking O and Sunny would've been content with leaving the gig as well.

Ray arrived, stole me away. Now we're driving across the countryside on our way back home, a stop at Walmart part of the itinerary.

We haven't spoken since pulling away, yet our fingers are intertwined over the center console. It's like we're heading to a funeral, and in a way we are. It's probable the death of our future is looming. Not the future of us - we are solid. But the future of us (me) finishing school, finding a good job, living a decent life was looking quite dim from my point of view.

"How are we gonna do this?" Ray asks as we edge into town.

"Do what?"

"Buy this."

I look at him. That's the least of our problems. See, I'm thinking how are we gonna raise a baby when we're babies ourselves? And he can't even figure out how to buy the preggo detector.

"Well, I reckon we'll walk into the store, locate the E.P.T.'s, pick one out, walk to the cash register, pay, and leave."

He lets out a short huff. "What if someone sees us, smartass?"

"So?"

"Like, my parents' friends? Or someone from school?"

I smile. "We'll say it's for Sky." Yeah, it's wrong to haul my sister into this, but I think she'd play along. Damn. Maybe we should've just had her get it in the first place.

"Does she know?" Ray asks. I nod. "What'd she say?"

"To let her know. She'll help us figure this out."

He parks the Sante Fe and with obvious hesitation, we get out and walk hand-in-hand into the Walmart funeral.

Inside, Ray insists on buying candy, chips, and a video game to try and mask the big-ticket item in our cart. I think it's stupid. Any cashier with half a brain will see us for what we are: A couple stupid teenagers trying to act like we came to Wally World for candy, chips, and a video game and decided, *oh, what the heck, let's get a pregnancy test.* You know, just in case we ever know someone who needs one.

Ray's hand shakes as he slides three twenties to the cashier. If he's shaking like this now, what's it gonna be like later when we're staring at the pee-stained stick? Or worse: When a watermelon sized head is sliding out of my buttonhole body?

Ray

I'm not shaking because I'm scared. My blood sugar is low,
which is why I threw the
Snickers, Skittles, and Starburst
in the cart.

I can handle this. It's just a test.

No, not one I can prepare for and attempt to ace. The fate of
the results is in the hands of some power that isn't mine.
Is it God?

Is this our punishment for what we did?

Well, God, let me make you a deal. If you let Star fail this test,
I will keep my testes in my pants until she says I do.

Well, at least until she's on the Pill.

Sunshine

I have been bored since arriving at this lame cookout six painful hours ago. Star shrugged out, faking a tummy ache. O has been entertained by the orange bouncy ball and whipping butt on some younger kids. Sky actually seems to be having an okay time. I could be wrong, but I'm pretty sure she's flirting with Mr. Morris, which is just *ew*. I mean, he's a little cute, but he's, like, a teacher and *old*.

The worst, though, was when I made my plate. I had half a burger and some fruit salad. Plenty of food to give the aura of eating. Melissa came up behind me and said, "Oh, Sunny, don't be shy. Eat all you want." She heaped some potato salad on my plate. And some baked beans. And some cheesy dip nastiness. "This is the best," she assured me.

I take my plate to the table and sit across from Orion. He looks from my plate to my face and laughs. "Hungry?"

"Apparently hungry as a hippo."

He laughs again and so do I, though it really isn't funny. I go through the process of cutting everything into half-inch pieces. It takes forever and a day because there's so much, but when I'm done, I note the time: 1:14 p.m. Then I choose four evenly sized pieces of fruit. After I swallow them, I feel them building their forever home in my thighs, so I look at Orion. "Want any of this?"

He takes my burger and the potato salad. I swiftly toss the plate in the trash and go to the front of the house and let it all out in a bush.

So when Star leaves an hour later feigning nausea, I wish I would've hurled in front of everyone so I could be saved from this hell.

But things have a way of working out.

"Ready to blow this place?" Orion asks me.

I look at Dad and Melissa. "Don't see that happening anytime soon."

He makes a sound like a buzzer. "Wrong. I have summoned my main man to rescue us."

"Austin?"

"You know it." He gives me a knowing smile.

"Does Dad know?"

"Not yet."

"Is Sky coming too?" My voice sounds like a whine.

He scoffs. "I don't think she's interested in leaving."

We both look across the yard at her. She's sitting on the deck with Dad and Melissa and Mr. Morris. "Is it just me, or is she, like, checking Mr. Morris out?"

"Haven't noticed." He stands. "C'mon let's go tell Dad."

Forty minutes later, I'm on cloud nine. Well, really, I'm sitting between Austin and Orion on the bench seat of the rusty pickup. But to me, it's cloud nine.

"Sunshine, my lovely sister," Orion says. "Why don't you hit up your little BFF Haley and see if she wants to hang tonight?"

Per the request, I text her. "She wants to know what we're gonna do?"

Orion chuckles and tosses the butt of a cigarette out the window. "She's gonna do me."

My eyes go wide. "You really want me to say that?"

He looks at me. "Go ahead. I'll bet she's game."

So I do. She responds: *LOL Okayy. Pick me up.*

I read the text aloud and add, "Wow, she's skankier than I thought."

Austin and Orion both laugh, and I feel like I'm on the outside of some joke. Or maybe I am the joke.

When Haley gets in (wearing a skirt shorter than my shorts) I have to squeeze closer to Austin, not that I am complaining whatsoever, but this truck wasn't made to hold four. The music is loud to drown out the failing exhaust, and the conversation is zero as we wind around country roads. East. North. East. South. West. North. I start to wonder WTF we are doing.

Finally, Austin stops the truck at the edge of a tree line, just over a little creek. Everyone hops out and I follow, trying to seem like I have a clue. Austin opens the tailgate and jumps up. He turns and holds out his hand for me. I take it, allowing him to assist me in getting into the back of the truck. Then he does the same for Haley.

The four of us sit, girls over here, guys over there. I'm directly across from my bro, but his eyes are on Haley's legs sprouting from the bottom of her skirt. Austin pulls full cans of beer from a cooler and passes them around.

I hesitate, but why? Because I don't know how many calories are in this can. I turn it over and over in my hands, seeing the Surgeon General's warning, and then there it is in the smallest possible print. *96 calories.*

"What are you doing?" Haley asks.

"Calories," Orion says knowingly.

I shoot him The Death Look.

Austin scoffs. "I don't think you need to worry about calories, Sunny. One good wind will blow you away."

I smile triumphantly at Orion and pop the top of the can. Need to note the time. Where's my cell? Did I leave it in the truck?

O sighs loudly. "It's a quarter after seven."

"Exactly?"

He holds his cell out for me to see. 7:13 p.m.

"Thanks." I bring the beer to my lips and take a drink of the stinky crap.

"You gonna light one up, A?" Orion asks.

"Sure thing." I watch Austin as he picks up a silver and white foil pack from a backpack laying near the cooler. From that pack, he pulls out a long, brown odd-looking cigarette. It might be a cigar, actually. And of all the things to wonder, I wonder how he gets cigarettes. He's only sixteen. But one whiff of the odd cigarette/cigar and I no longer care how he buys Newport's. That's marijuana. I recognize the smell from Orion's bedroom and from the car he and Skylar share. Strangely, or naively, I thought pot was smoked in a pot of some type.

I watch Austin as he puffs on it, his cute little lips puckering. Then he passes it to O who does the same thing but it's creepy, not sexy like when Austin did it. Orion holds the cigarette toward me.

"I want you to try it, Sunny," he says.

"I, um, I don't know how."

"It's easy," Haley says. "Breathe in. Suck it to your lungs and hold it."

"Watch me again," Orion says.

I watch. And take a nervous drink of piss in a can. "Okay."

See, I'm gonna do this because Austin is here, and he did it. And Haley is here, and I know she's gonna do it (and probably a lot of other things) and I don't want to be shown up by skank-o-rama next to me. The cigarette is in my hand and I am feeling so incredibly self-conscious, like they're all watching me, which they are. Putting it to my lips, I suck in. The smoke tickles my throat and I start coughing.

My eyes are watering when I look up at my brother to save me.

"Try again," he instructs. *So much for salvation.*

I do, and this time I don't cough. I hold the cancer causer in my lungs and hope this is really bringing me steps closer to Austin.

Are there calories in marijuana? I'll have to look into this.

Haley takes the cigarette from my hand as I let out my breath.

When I take a second beer a short time later, it takes me a minute to add 96 calories and 96 calories in my head. Orion sees my concentration and thinks I need the time. He shows me his phone. 8:01 p.m.

"Ninety-six plus ninety-six?" I ask.

O laughs, as does Austin. "Buzzed much, little sis?"

"No," I say, even though I think that may be the malfunction.

"One-ninety-two," Austin says. "Why are you counting calories, anyway?"

"She has a number thing," Orion says. And I love him for it. Better to be a number freak than a bulimic freak.

Haley stands up and jumps off the tailgate. "Are we sitting here all night?"

"No," Orion says. "There's a party I think we can get into later, but there's a five-dollar cover."

"I don't have five dollars," she whines.

"I got you," my brother assures her. He stands and jumps out of the truck. Taking her hand, he leads her away where we can't see whatever they might do.

I watch them go, thinking, wow. Just like that. She *is* skank-o-rific. I laugh aloud at my made-up word.

"What's funny?" Austin asks.

I look at him, the little smirk playing on his lips. I smile back, hoping I look half as sexy as he does. "Nothing. I just made up a word."

"Made up a word?" He raised his eyebrows.

"Skank-o-rific."

He chuckles. "That describes her well."

Our eyes hold and I wish I had a clue how to let a guy, any guy, know I'm interested. I wish I knew how to flirt like Haley and Sky. But I don't. I'm just me and my skills lie in the area of counting calories and cutting skin.

Austin looks away and pulls out another cigarette/cigar. "Wanna smoke another one?" His eyes meet mine again.

I bite my lip and he looks away and smiles. "What?"

He shakes his head and puts the cigarette to his lips. "You. You're one of those girls who doesn't even realize how sexy she is."

My eyes go wide, I'm sure of it. *Did he just say I was sexy?* If I was on cloud nine earlier, then I must've died and gone to heaven because this isn't real. And since it's not real, I take the brown cigar-looking cigarette when he hands it to me.

We pass it back and forth until it's gone, but don't speak again. I don't even know what to say. *"Gee, Austin. I sure think you're sexy too."* I mean, really.

I wish I wasn't me. Or at least that I had the courage of someone else.

I finish the beer and lay back on the dirty truck bed. The sun has set, leaving a residual orange tint in the sky. I'm staring up, debating another beer, but 192 calories plus 96 calories equals...?

"What's one-ninety-two plus ninety-six?" I ask. I look at Austin to answer since it's just me and him all alone.

He is already staring down at me. I tug at the hem of my t-shirt making sure my gut is covered. He grabs my hand and holds it.

I think I'm gonna die.

With his other hand, he lifts the bottom of my shirt and runs his fingers across my stomach. "A girl that looks this good doesn't need to worry about calories."

Oh, yeah. I'm dying. Of embarrassment.

I sit up as quick as I can and pull my shirt down securely over my waist. "Two-hundred-eighty-eight," I mutter. I haven't consumed that many calories in one day in forever.

He holds a beer out for me to take. I reach for it, and he grabs my wrist. Our eyes meet and I wonder if he'll kiss me. But he doesn't. He lets the beer go and sits back against the side of the truck, leaving me breathless and hating myself for being me.

Orion and Haley get back from wherever then, Haley whining about bugs. I open the beer and take a drink. "Oh, crap!" I yell.

They look at me.

"What time is it?"

"Why?" asks Austin. "Are you Cinderella?"

I laugh. As if.

"Eight-fifty-one on the dot, Sunny," Orion says. He's looking at his phone, so I know he's telling the truth. "You better chug it because I want to get over to that party." He looks up at me, then Austin. "I need to find a hot chick to screw tonight."

Haley smacks the back of his head. The guys laugh. I don't get it. What exactly were they doing off in the bug infested woods if they weren't...?

I take a big gulp of the beer and hear Austin say, "You better drive, man. I'm starting to feel it." He stands up. "We smoked a fat one while you were gone."

I'm wondering what Austin's feeling, but I don't ask. And that cigarette didn't seem any fatter than the one before it.

Austin jumps to the ground and looks back. His hand is outstretched, waiting for me. I set my beer on the side of the truck and stand up. Well, I try. The truck is wobbly.

"Oh, hell," I hear Orion say.

I take Austin's hand and jump, or something. I'm not sure what it was. Whatever it was, he caught me. Both his arms around me and my face is, like, a millimeter from his.

Oh, God, Austin, kiss me, kiss me, please.

He doesn't. "You okay?" he says with a little laugh.

I straighten and nod my head. But I'm not. I'm drunk, and I suppose you could say I'm high too. "I don't have five dollars either," I tell O. "For the party." It's my desperate plea to my brother to not take me home first.

"We got you," he assures me.

We cram into the cab of the truck. Austin's arm is around me, his hand sort of rubbing my shoulder. I wish I was sober as I close my eyes and lean into him, breathing in the memory. No, if I was sober, I would never have my cheek on his shoulder, my nose in his neck.

Haley pokes me. I lift my head and look at her, slightly annoyed. "What?"

She leans forward, so I do too. "Did you guys mess around?" she whispers.

I scoff and sit back. Orion's eyes are on me and maybe Austin. He looks frustrated. I close my eyes and forget them.

We get to the party and there's no cover charge, at least not that I noticed. But there's a keg and that's all the guys care about. They go to get beers and I panic.

How will I know how many calories are in *that*?

Well, duh, Sunny. Just go puke. Without a word, I shrug off from Haley and disappear into the shadows, where I find a suitable spot. One tickle to the back of my throat and all the beer nourishes the grass. God, it was a lot. I haven't puked that much in, like, IDK how long. Gross.

And of course, I still don't have my phone, so can't note the time.

I turn back toward the party and wander through a sea of unfamiliar faces. I start to feel panicky, thinking I've been ditched, but no, Orion wouldn't do that to me. Would he? No. He watches out for me. Just like Sky. And Star.

Wow. I'm so pathetic. No wonder I've never had a boyfriend. But, so, if they didn't ditch me, then where did they go?

"Sunny, hey. There you are." It's Austin. He has my hand and a smile on his face.

"What time is it?" I ask.

He pulls out his phone and shows it to me. 9:40 p.m. It's probably been five minutes since I puked, but I can't be sure.

"Can I have a drink of your beer?" I ask. Better to have beer breath than puke breath. Probably. I really don't know. I'll just assume.

He hands it to me. "Want to get your own?"

"No, actually." I don't tell him it's because I can't count calories from a keg. "I do want to sit down though." I smile at him. "Feeling a little woozy." I take a drink of beer and hand the cup back to him.

Still holding my hand, he leads me. I follow without question. I'm surprised when he takes me back to his truck. "What're we doing? We can't leave Orion and Haley."

"We're not leaving. I figured you could lie in the bed until you feel better. We weren't gonna find anywhere to sit over there."

Ok, sensible and considerate Austin. Add that to the list of reasons I love him.

I lay back, and this time, I don't worry about my skin showing. In fact, I hope he touches me again.

"Is this the first time you've drank?" he asks from his spot beside me.

"No, but definitely the first time I smoked."

He laughs. "Uh, yeah. I could tell." His body shifts next to me so he's lying on his side, his head propped by his hand, his body aligned with the length of mine. (Touch me touch me touch me please). "What did you think?"

"It was okay," I say quietly. I'm looking at him and he's looking back. "I'd do it again."

"Really?"

I nod. And that's when he leans forward, kissing me softly, and only once.

He pulls back slightly. "Sorry," his lips whisper.

I shake my head so slightly, but he sees that, knows that I don't mean for him to be sorry, that I mean for him to do it again and he does. Another soft kiss, and another, and another. His lips part and his tongue comes out and wants inside my mouth. I let it in and know for a fact that I am living a dream.

His fingers play with the skin covering my stomach and it's the best thing ever when they creep up and massage my breasts through my thin bra. I turn into him, and he pulls his mouth away from mine. It relocates to my stomach, and God, I hope it really is as skinny as he thinks it is. His hands push up my shirt, and then my bra. I know my chest is exposed for all to see, but *this is Austin*. This is the one I love. And oh, how I want him to love me. His warm mouth is kissing my breasts now, and I make a bold move. I reach up and run my fingers through his hair and wrap one of my legs around his.

He misinterprets. I know this because now his hand is trying to unbutton my shorts. I grab his hand and hold tight. He can't go down there. And it's not because I don't want to give him all of me, but I need to hold on to that one secret.

Orion

What was I thinking

when I invited

Sunny

along for the ride?

I sure wasn't thinking

she'd

Get drunk.

Get high.

Make out

(and who knows if there was more)

with Austin.

And puke on my shoes.

Skylar

When Dad and I finally left the Morris', I was relieved. It's hard putting on such a show. Good thing I don't want to be an actress. Dad rambled on and on all the way home, replaying the highlights of the day. He thought it was a success.

"I really like her parents and her brother. They're good people."

I knew he was talking about her brother Jake because her brother Ben wasn't there. So that was a good thing. If he already likes Jake, hopefully that won't change when he finds out about us.

When we get home, Dad changes his clothes to go to his shift at the bar and I pretend to watch Netflix.

"Sky, hon, how come you never go out with your friends anymore?"

I kinda feel nervous, so I say, "Actually, I was thinking about seeing what Kylee was doing. Thought maybe she'd want to come over." Dad nods, and I add, "I don't know, though. Most of my friends seem kinda immature, you know what I mean?"

Dad picks up his keys. "Or maybe you're just too mature for your age." He sighs. "That's not a bad thing, I guess."

"Well, would you rather me be out there with Orion every weekend?"

"You used to be." He opens the door to leave. "What happened?"

I look at the TV. "Guess I got tired of dealing with Austin."

"Makes sense. See you in the morning."

"Okay, Dad. Have a good night."

I wait until he's gone a full five minutes before getting in the Taurus and driving to the park. I leave the car there and walk the rest of the way to Jake's house. He's just pulling in his driveway when I get there, but still, I go in through the back door and meet him when he comes through the front door. Our lips lock and we move straight to the bedroom.

A while later we're in the kitchen. Jake's warming up some leftovers his mom sent home with him, and I marvel in how comfortable it is to sit here in his kitchen. It's like a preview of the years to come. I smile at the thought.

"What'd Star find out?" he asks.

"About what?"

"You said she thought she was pregnant."

"Oh, yeah! I forgot all about that. I'll text her." I go to the bedroom and get my phone. When I get back in the kitchen, Jake's sitting at the table hunkering down on a burger. I send the text: *Did you take the test??*

I look up at Jake. "I think today went well. My dad likes you."

He starts to nod but stops. Swallows. Wipes his mouth on a paper towel. "Yeah, for now he likes me." He takes a swig of beer. "That'll come to an end."

"Maybe. Maybe not." I steal a Dorito from his plate. "What if we make it look like we fell in love because of them."

He raises an eyebrow. "I think that would be worse. Because then it'll look like I'm some kind of pervert checking out my potential niece."

We ponder that for a moment. "Even so. It's not like we're blood related. Or that you've known me since I was a baby or anything."

"Even if I did, I still would only be five years older than you."

"Exactly."

He sighs and shoves his plate to the center of the table. "No matter what way we handle this, it's gonna take everyone time to get used to the idea."

I cock my head a little. "The *idea*? We're more than an idea, don't you think?"

"I do. But don't expect your dad, or my parents, or Melissa to be excited for us." He sits back and lets out an exasperated sigh. "We still have months before we even get to that point."

My phone vibrates on the table. I look down to see it's a text from Orion. It says: *U home?*

No, I text back.

He says, *Can u get there?*

I want to ignore him. I really do.

"What'd she say?" Jake asks.

"It's Orion." Weird. Star usually texts me right back. "I'm gonna go soon."

He nods knowingly. Knowing I have to be mommy to the kids. "Sometime soon you need to stay all night."

I smile. "Actually, Dad said something about me not hanging around with my friends as much anymore. So I guess I should plan a slumber party or something."

"I wouldn't plan on much slumbering, Sky."

I walk back to my car feeling content with how my life's going. Sure, a lot of it's based on secrets, but I don't mind. I don't think he does either, but he definitely has more to lose than me. So what if I'm the subject of gossip and my dad disowns me.

My phone vibrates in my pocket as I get to the car. It's Star: *Where r u?*

Where r u? I ask.

Home.

Be there soon.

She's waiting for me in the living room when I get there, Ray by her side. I glance at the clock. It's almost eleven. "Don't you have to get home?" I ask, knowing he has a strict curfew.

He nods and looks at Star. The looks on their faces tell me the results of the test, and he's here because they expect me to figure out what to do next. Before I can find and offer a probable solution, we hear the rumble of Austin's truck outside.

"Don't say anything, Sky," Ray pleads with me. "Please."

I shake my head to assure him I won't just as the front door opens. Haley Johnston comes in and holds the door wide open. Orion is next, supporting Sunny's slight weight with his body. I cover my mouth to hide my smile.

This is hysterical.

Orion doesn't seem to see the humor in the situation. He drags her to the couch and Star and Ray jump up as he lets her fall to the couch. She is half-lucid and smells like vomit.

"What the hell happened?" I ask, trying so hard not to laugh as Austin comes through the door.

"Before or after she threw up on me?" Orion yells.

"Sorry, O, sorry," Sunny says from the couch.

I can't contain it anymore. I laugh, and that causes Star and Ray to laugh. And then Haley and Austin are laughing. Everyone is laughing except Orion and Sunny. He pulls his shoes off and throws one at me, the other at Sunny.

"Yeah, real funny! These are the only shoes I have!"

Somehow that's even funnier. Not only are they his only shoes, but he just got them a week ago for school. I have to lean on the wall to hold myself up.

"Why are you still laughing?" He comes closer to me, and I can see he really is angry.

I try to stop laughing, but losing the smile is impossible. *Sunny drunk?* Never would I have thought I'd live to see that! "I'm not laughing at you, O. I'm laughing at her!"

He looks at Sunny passed out on the couch, shakes his head, and storms up the stairs. Austin follows quickly behind, and then Haley. "Haley is *not* staying here!" I yell after them.

"My mom is on her way," Haley says.

I go to the couch and inspect my little sister. She opens one eye and whispers, "Are they gone?"

"Who?"

"Orion and Austin?"

"Yeah."

She sits up and looks around. "He kissed me, Sky."

"Who?"

"Austin! Who else?"

I don't know why, but it's like a punch to the gut. I can't explain it. It hurts. "Why?" I ask.

"Who cares?" Her smile is like none I've seen before, and I want to choke her. *How dare she kiss him?* I've recovered from the punch in my gut and am thinking about punching her in her face.

I know, I know. This doesn't make sense. I have Jake. I love Jake. I want to be with Jake. I really don't even like Austin, not sure I ever did.

But something inside me doesn't want to see him with someone else.

Austin

The sun has a gravitational pull.
Did you know that?
Me neither.
But tonight, I felt it.
The sky is vast and unobtainable.
The sun is condensed and warm.
And so completely naïve.
So, she likes numbers and counts calories.
We all have quirks.
I like her quirks.
I could get used to them.
But will she have to have a beer or three just to talk?
I see her at school, all smiles and conversation.
How come I didn't meet that girl tonight?
It's like she's two different people.
I'm not sure which one I'm supposed to like,
if either is even an option.

Starla

I follow my sisters upstairs, and instead of going to my own room with tipsy Sunny, I follow Sky into hers.

"Don't make me sleep in there with her," I plead. "She reeks."

Sky chuckles. "Yeah, but on the floor." She faces me. "Well, wait. I assume the test was positive."

I look at the floor and nod.

She sighs. "You can have the bed." She slips out of her shorts and into pajama pants. "Do you want to talk?"

I shrug and sit at the foot of her twin bed.

"What do you want to do?"

I shrug again.

"What's Ray want to do?"

"I think he wants me to have an abortion."

"Did he say that?"

I shrug.

"Okay. Star. You and Ray really need to figure out what to do. This is between you guys. I mean, I can tell you what I think you should do, but still it's up to you."

I look up. She's standing across from me, her hands on her hips like the mother of a small, immature child. "What do you think I should do?"

"Have an abortion, Star. You're fourteen for Christ's sake!"

"I know how old I am, Skylar. That doesn't mean I have to kill my baby."

She stands there for a minute before shaking her head and leaving the room. I fold myself in half and collapse on her bed into the fetal position. This would be an appropriate time to cry, but that's not something I've ever done. For as long as I remember, a tear has never fallen to my cheek.

To take my mind off the true issues, I ponder why. I have a pretty good guess, not that I would actually tell anyone, but I think my cries went unanswered when they were my only way of communicating. So why bother with them now? I might be the youngest Hollis kid, the only one with no memory of our mother, but I'm not deaf nor am I blind.

This is what I see: Pictures of my mom, young, but not as young as me, standing tall with long black hair and clear blue eyes. I see my dad every day, hovering over us at more than six feet, with pale hazel eyes and light brown hair. I see Skylar, their original love child, the first mistake, a dead ringer for Mom. I see Orion, a male version of Mom, just taller at six foot even, but with dark brown eyes which match Dad's brother and parents. I see Sunshine, as tall as Sky with Dad's hair and a paler version of his eyes.

Then I see me: My growth has halted me to the destiny of the shortest one in my class forever, my hair is pale blonde and my eyes a dark blue, sort of like denim you could say. My bones are tiny making my frame a shadow of my siblings.

This is what I hear: From as early as I can remember, the whispers were hushed but they were definite. *Are you sure she's yours, Mike?* And *I know she's not mine, but what can I do? What would happen to her?*

So, my theory is that in my infancy, Mom was doped up and Dad refused to acknowledge me. My cries went unanswered, or maybe Sky tried to soothe me. Maybe that's why she feels like my mom. I could see her, three years old, shushing me and maybe trying to give me a bottle. Or maybe she didn't. Maybe I was always lost at sea.

When Ray offered me a life preserver, I clung to it with all I had, praying he would be everything I needed. And he is, I guess. He's a good guy for real, but father material, I don't think so. Not now. Not yet.

What would crying feel like? What would pain feel like? How can I feel that?

I'm pregnant. I'm fourteen. If my calculations are right, I'll be fifteen when I give birth. If I give birth. Maybe that will make me cry. Not the birthing process, but the so logical decision that I don't want to think about.

The decision to be a murderer.

Ray

Murder is likely what my conservative parents will do to me, if not Star, when they find out the following unfortunate facts:

1.) I've had premarital sex.
2.) More than once.
3.) Much more than once.
4.) Apparently enough times to impregnate my girlfriend.

With any luck, Sky will know how to fix this.
There's gotta be a place a kid can go to get rid of a kid without having to alert the parentals.
There has to be.

If not, well, guess their golden boy will be tarnished, forever the black sheep of the family.

Sunshine

I wake with a start, feeling like I'm falling. It takes me a minute, but the memories of last night flower into my mind. I'd smile at the warmness of them, but my head is pounding, and I feel sick.

When I get up, I'm pleased to be alone in the room. I note the time: 5:46 a.m. Star must've slept on the couch. Fine by me. I reek. No need for her to smell that, but oh, God, *did Austin smell that?*

I gather clean clothes and go to shower. I strip, and while I wait for the water to get warm enough, I inspect my body in the mirror. How could I have let Austin touch this disgustingness, let alone look at it? How drunk was he? That beer had settled around my stomach, giving me a sizeable beer belly. And there has to be calories in marijuana because my face looks fat too.

Sonofabitch. I should've known better. I perch over the toilet, gag myself, and watch virtually nothing come out. I will never drink again. I can't keep tabs on my intake and output when I'm inebriated. *This is a disaster*. I'm gonna need a scale.

But I did kiss Austin, let him feel me, didn't I? If my memory is correct, I would've given him all of me if it weren't for those hidden slices.

I shower away the stench, wrap myself in a towel, and go back to my still empty room. Sitting on the edge of my bed, I let the towel fall around me, my fat rolls exposed for anyone and no one. I feel under the mattress for the razor and debate: Left leg or right leg. Neither is healed at all. But I have to do it. *Have to*. Maybe I can find somewhere new.

But where? Where can I slice my flesh where no one will see it? I consider my breasts, but what if Austin wants to touch them, kiss them again? He probably already thinks I'm a prude because I didn't let him explore the land down under. And he probably thinks I'm a freak because I puked on Orion's shoes.

Oh, God. How did I become this mess?

Tears blur my vision, and I don't have any other choice. I dig the razor into my thigh, the inner thigh, between my legs.

One

Two

Three

Four

Four even slices from left to right *one two three four*. I note the time. 6:31 a.m. I watch the fat-laced blood soak the towel. I push on my skin, squeezing out as much fat as would come out. No matter how hard I push, it'll never be enough.

I dress in loose joggers because the chafing of jeans would be too much. I'll hide in my room until I'm sure Austin's gone. What would I say if I saw him, anyway? I need advice, but I'm sure Sky's not awake. In fact, no one is awake, so I creep downstairs and get a glass of water. But I don't drink it. First, I need the scale.

I tiptoe into Dad's room and into his bathroom and latch the door as quiet as I can. I strip again and step onto his scale and watch the numbers tip too far. Tears blur my eyes again as I pull my clothes back on. *Damnit*. Damn beer. What did I need it for anyway? To make Austin like me? To like myself?

As I sneak back through Dad's room, I glance at him in the bed. He's not alone. Melissa's there too. I look away, feeling like I just caught a glimpse of something X-rated even though they are totally covered and sound asleep.

In the kitchen, I dump the water. No need for extra intake. Not today. Today it will be zero caloric intake. Maybe even a workout. One of those high-powered ones that makes your muscles burn.

As I round the top of the stairs, Sky is coming out of Orion's room, looking like she just woke up. "Hey," she mutters. She goes to the bathroom, and I go to my room and look out the front window. Austin's truck is definitely parked there.

I cover my hand with my mouth. Why was she in Orion's room?

I go back to the hall and push the bathroom door open. "Did you sleep in there?"

"So what if I did?" She pushes the door shut again.

I wait, anger pumping through me. How dare she? *Who does she think she is?* She opens the bathroom door and stands face to face with me. "What, Sunny?"

"Why?" My voice comes out like a desperate whine.

She rolls her eyes. "What? Do you think because he kissed you that he's gonna fall in love with you, or something? He's a prick and was using you because you were drunk. I hope kissing was all you let him do. Because if you lost your virginity that way, you'll regret it forever." She shakes her head and goes around me. "I told you to stay away from him."

Austin

I wish I hadn't awoken when Sky left the room. Because then I would've missed the exchange between her and Sunny.
I don't know why Sky came in Orion's room last night, or why she played with my hair from her spot on the bed while I sat on the floor, which is also where I slept. She hadn't looked twice at me in nine months, and now she inserts herself into the same room with me and places her claws on me.
It wouldn't by chance have anything to do with what happened with me and Sunny, would it?
Jealousy, maybe?
I need to talk to Orion about Sunny, see where he stands.
But will it matter if Sky wants to try us again?

Skylar

After I kick Star out of my bed, I cover my head and pretend I didn't say what I said to Sunny and pretend I didn't give false hope to Austin just to keep him on a leash where I like him.

Eventually sleep wins and guilt loses.

When I stumble into consciousness again, it's almost noon. Crap. I never sleep this late. I jump up and contemplate a shower. I probably should since I didn't take one after coming back from Jake's last night. No need for Dad to suspect, but then again, Austin was here and there's always that assumption to be made.

And now I remember how Austin and Sunny apparently messed around last night, the words I said to her, and the time I spent in Orion's room.

Fuck. I don't have time for this childish drama.

I go downstairs and find Dad and Melissa on the couch watching a movie. Weird, but okay. "Where is everyone?"

"Hey, sweetheart," Dad says. "O left with Austin a little while ago. Star went to Ray's and Sunny must still be sleeping." He smiles at Melissa. "Lazy teenage girls."

I scoff. "I never sleep this late, Dad, and you know it."

Neither does Sunny. I better go check on her. And apologize. Maybe. If I apologize, will she think Austin is free rein again? It was one thing when she was crushing on him like the hopeless freak she is, but this, this actually doing something about the crush cannot happen.

When I go in her and Star's room, she's lying on her back staring at the ceiling. She doesn't look at me as I approach. Or when I sit on the edge of her bed. I notice blood on the inside of her sweatpants near her crotch.

"Your tampon leaked," I tell her.

"I don't have a tampon in."

"Fine. Your pad, whatever."

She sighs and reaches between her legs. Her fingers go to the exact spot where the blood is, like she knew it was there. She touches it gingerly, looks at her fingers and then touches it again. Then she brings her hand to her mouth and licks the blood off her fingers.

Oh. My. God. How. Fucking. Gross.

"Did you really just do that?" I ask.

Her head snaps to the side, her eyes narrowed at me like I'm the devil incarnate. "Did you really do *that*?"

I have no clue what she's talking about. "Do what?"

Her eyes focus on the ceiling again. "Whatever you did with Austin last night."

I laugh. "The only action Austin got last night was from you, Sunny. Though God only knows why, you nasty freak." I shudder at the image of her licking her blood-stained fingers.

"Get out of here," she mutters.

"I really hope that's period blood and not blood from losing your virginity last night."

She draws her legs up and kicks me, causing me to lose my balance. I start to fall off the bed but catch myself with my hand. I stand and look down at Sunny, the wetness on her cheeks.

"What kind of nasty person licks their period blood?"

"I don't have my period, Skylar! Get the hell out of my room!" She sits up and throws her pillow at me. I throw it back.

"He didn't even say goodbye to you this morning, did he?"

"Go!"

I start toward the door. "Of course he didn't. You know why? Because he's in love with me."

She lets out a blood curdling scream, her eyes squeezed tight, hands clenched at her sides. I leave the room before her head starts to spin.

I'm about to slip into the bathroom for a shower when Dad comes up the stairs, concern furrowing his brow.

"What was that?"

I shrug. "Sunny, I guess."

Even with the bathroom door shut, I can hear Dad consoling her in the next room. She doesn't answer him no matter how many times he asks what's wrong.

No answer for Dad. It might mar his image of his best, perfect, most accomplished daughter. If he only knew. If everyone only knew the hell Sunny lived in. But I don't feel sorry for her. She puts herself there.

I'm about to step into the shower when I remember to look in the trash for a tampon or pad wrapper. Nothing.

Which leaves only one rationale for the blood on Sunny's pants.

She lost her virginity.

To Austin.

Just. Like. Me.

I don't know why this makes me cry, but it does. I sit at the bottom of the shower and sob, but for no good reason other than every now and again, a girl needs a good cry.

Mike

Something's bothering my Sunshine.
She won't tell me what,
and I'm not a mind reader.
Sometimes girls just need a good cry,
so that's what I let her do.
Having Melissa around will be helpful,
because I am clueless with these
daughters of mine.

Orion, though, I can read him.
He's too much like me when I was that age.
Maybe
I should be scared.
Maybe
I should put my foot down.
But truth be told,
I too often forget he is even around.
Maybe
because he's usually gone,
but more likely because my daughters
consume me with confusion.

Starla

"So, did you and Sky talk?" Ray asks from the driver's seat.

"Not really."

He frowns. "I thought you said she was gonna help us figure this out?"

"That's what she said, but she was preoccupied with Sunny last night and she was still sleeping when I left."

"Text her and ask her to meet us somewhere."

I roll my eyes and send the text. I wanna ask Ray if he's ever heard the phrase 'man up', but I don't. No need to fight. "Are we actually going somewhere, or are we just gonna drive around all day?"

He sighs. "I guess we could go to my house." His eyes look my way, but not at me, at my stomach.

In aggravation I lift my shirt. "Still flat as ever."

"Sorry. I'm freaking out that they're gonna notice." He looks out the driver's side window and exhales loudly. "What'd you do with the test?"

"Left it on the kitchen counter with a note for my dad letting him know I'm pregnant."

The look on his face is priceless. Something between shock and panic.

"I'm kidding. I shoved it deep in the bathroom trash and then took the whole bag out to the garage."

"And the only one you told was Sky?"

"Yes."

"Okay. Sorry. I'm just--"

"Freaking out. I know." I look at him. "Don't you think I'm freaking a little too?"

"You don't seem to be."

Yeah. That's the problem with a complete lack of emotion.

My phone chimes to let me know I have a text. "Sky," I say. "She says sure. Where?"

"Where do you think, baby?"

I roll my eyes. Partly at his indecisiveness, partly because he called me baby when I'm carrying a baby and a baby is the problem and the reason we have to meet with my sister in the first place is because we are a couple of babies.

"Somewhere with air." It was a steamy first day of September, that's for sure.

"McDonald's?"

"McDonald's it is."

An hour later, me, Ray, and Sky are sitting in a booth at the back of McDonald's. Ray and I are both eating, but Sky said she's not hungry.

"Like I told Star last night, I think she needs to have an abortion."

Ray just stares at her.

"You guys are too young for this."

Ray nods.

"I'm not sure I want to be a murderer," I offer.

"But are you sure you want to be a mom at fourteen?" Sky asks.

"I'll be fifteen by then."

"Oh, well, that changes everything, doesn't it?" She laughs. "Gee, if you're gonna be fifteen, then why are we having this conversation at all? Every fifteen-year-old has their life together and should have a baby. I mean, look at Sunny. Maybe she should have a baby, too." She stops, puts the back of her hand over her mouth and looks away.

"I'm nothing like Sunny. Don't compare us."

"Actually," Ray interjects, "Sunny does seem pretty together."

Sky and I exchange glances, but don't contradict him. That's not why we're here.

Sky sighs. "What about adoption?"

Ray looks out the window and I know he wishes he were anywhere but here. So do I, actually.

"I don't know," I say slowly. "What would it be like to give it away after it grew inside me?"

"But that would be giving it a chance at a decent life, don't you think?" Sky asks. "I mean, you don't want it to have a life like ours, do you?"

"It wouldn't. Why would you even say that?"

Ray clears his throat. "It's just a thought, but what if when the baby came, it lived at my house. Like, then my mom could take care of it."

We stare at him. It seemed like a viable option, except, "You think your parents will go for that? Really?"

"We don't know until we tell them."

Just the thought of that makes me want to crawl into a hole and never come out.

"I like that idea," Sky says.

I do too, but it's not realistic. Ray's family is Catholic. Abstinence until marriage is what they're expecting, not for their sixteen-year-old to be a father.

"Okay. How about this plan," Sky says, taking charge as usual. "Monday is a holiday. So, Tuesday I will make you an appointment at Planned Parenthood. I suggest we don't tell any parents until we make sure the test was right, and if it was, we need to know how far along you are."

"How soon will the appointment be?" Ray asks.

"Do I look like the appointment desk?" Sky snaps.

I giggle.

"I just thought maybe you had an idea," Ray says.

"Why? Because you think I've done this before?"

"Well, no...."

Sky looks at me. "Are you good with this?"

I nod.

She stands and frowns at us. "I'd say something like 'stay out of trouble', but I guess it's too late for that."

I lean on Ray as Sky leaves, closing my eyes, wishing I wasn't stuck in this mud. Wishing I could shed my shoes and leave them behind. If I'd seen the mud in front of me, could I have stepped around in time? Would I have pulled Ray in with me? Or maybe he's the one who pulled me in?

He wraps his arm around my shoulders. "I love you."

I look up at him.

Ray

When she looks at me, I melt.
She is my kryptonite.
The problem with that is that it makes me weak.
I can't imagine telling my parents about this baby.
But I don't want to be the accomplice to murder either.

Is it really murder?
I mean, when does life become a life?
From the moment of conception, or is it later when the heart is beating?
Would we be killing our child, or saving it from a life of misery?

I guess what this really comes down to is this:
    Who do I fear more?
            My parents or Star?
    Who do I love more?
            My parents or Star?
    Who can I manipulate easier?
            My parents or Star?

Sunshine

Lying in bed all day is counterproductive. It's not helping me burn any calories, in fact, it may be adding some. I'm not sure if that's possible, but I'll have to look into it. That wouldn't be good. If you gain calories or weight by lying in bed, then I'm going to have to figure out how to get by with less sleep.

The house is quiet and I'm thinking I might be the only one home. That would be ideal.

I go into the bathroom, sit on the toilet, and wait. And wait. No number 1 and no number 2. My fingers tickle the back of my throat to see if there's any reaction. I gag, but there's nothing coming up. I do it again just to be sure.

My fresh cuts are still bleeding. It was a bad idea to put them there. Every time I take a step or move my legs, it's painful. Every movement rubs them, keeping them raw, open, and oozing. I wipe the blood with my finger, and then lick it clean. Sky thought it was gross, but only because she thought it was my period blood. That *would* be gross.

See, there's a reason for this weirdness. I don't eat much, but I'm smart enough to know I need some kind of nourishment.

I cover the cuts with Band-Aids (twelve of them to be exact (twelve is divisible by four)), go back to my room and change my sweats before going downstairs. Dad and Melissa are there, cuddled on the couch, watching TV.

My mind flashes to the pictures of me and Austin last night, his arm around me like Dad's arm is around Melissa, and I bite my cheek to make myself think about something else. It doesn't work, even though the blood rushes onto my tongue, salty and warm.

"Hey, Sunshine," Dad says. "Feeling better?"

I nod. "I think I'm gonna go for a run."

Dad nods and Melissa smiles. "I love running," she says. "Maybe we can go together sometime."

I fake interest and a return smile. "Yeah, maybe."

Dad looks concerned now. "It's pretty hot out there. You sure you want to wear that?"

My joggers go to just below my knees and I'm wearing a bulky hoodie. "I'll be fine. I have a t-shirt underneath," I lie. Well, kinda. I have a cami on with a built-in bra. Not something I'd be seen in public in. Everyone would see all my fat rolls. "Besides," I add, "the more I sweat the better."

"You won't have to move a muscle out there to break a sweat today," Dad says.

"Some rain would be nice," Melissa says.

"Yeah, this summer has been too dry," Dad adds.

I leave them to discuss the weather and walk out the door. Dang, it is hot out here. I stand in the driveway and stretch my upper body, afraid to flex my legs.

Get over it, Sunny. Suck it up. You did this to yourself, so now you have to pay the price. Besides, Austin definitely doesn't want some fat girl. And if you just keep standing here, you're gonna keep getting fatter and fatter and fatter.

Stop! Don't think about Austin. Don't do it. Think about anything else.

I start to jog down the drive, taking a left and heading toward the school. I'll run the track there.

Man, it really is hot. Must be, like, one-hundred degrees at least. Oh, crap! I forgot to see what time it was when I started. Wait. Where's my phone? I never found it, did I? What if Austin has tried to get in touch with me? Now he's thinking I'm ignoring him. He's gonna hate me. Whatever sliver of chance I had is gone.

Stop! Stop! Stop! Stop thinking about Austin. He doesn't love you and he never will. He loves Sky and will always love Sky.

Rainbows.

Beaches.

Sunsets.

Sunrises.

Waterfalls.

Whirlpools.

Slipping.

Falling.

Drowning.

Dying.

My thoughts are all over. My entire back is drenched in sweat, and I am ignoring the pain shooting down my leg and all into my groin. I need water, but I have to keep going. I'm almost to the school. Maybe if I concentrate on my feet hitting the pavement, I'll feel better.

One. Two. Three. Four. One. Two.

"Sunny!"

I think I hear someone calling my name, but I'm not stopping.

Three. Four. One. Two. Three. Four. One. Two. Three. Four. One. Two. Three. Four. One. Two. Three. Four. One. Two. Three. Four. One. Two. Three. Four. One. Two. Three. Four.

"Sunny! Stop!" Someone grabs my sleeve, and I don't have a choice but to stop. It's Orion. There's sweat on his forehead and concern in his eyes. "What the hell are you doing? It's a hundred degrees out here!" He tugs on my shirt. "Take this off. You're sweating like a hog."

I pull away from him. "Stop. I am a hog, that's why I'm out here."

His eyes narrow slightly. "Are you crying? Or is that sweat?" His hand is nearing my face and I back away. With both hands, I wipe all the wetness from my face.

"It's just sweat."

"Take the hoodie off. And get in the car." He pauses. "C'mon." When I don't move, he reaches for the hoodie again.

"I'm fine, O. I'm just gonna go to the school and run the track a while."

He frowns. "Sunny. I will pick you up and put you in the car if you don't get in it yourself."

We stand there on the sidewalk, facing off in the humid air, for several sweaty moments.

He speaks first. "You're gonna die out here. Is that what you want?"

I stare at him, so mad. Mad because he would think that, or mad because he knew I had actually thought that? I can't be sure.

Now the wetness on my cheeks is definitely tears. Orion pulls up on my hoodie and I let him. I shrug out of it and the hot sun feels cool on my saturated skin. I look up at my namesake and damn it to hell.

Why does it have to be so bright when I am so dim?

"You need to stop this shit, the puking and not eating." He pokes at my ribs. "I can see your bones through your shirt, Sunny. You don't need to lose any more weight." He starts toward the car, and I follow.

The icy air conditioning hits my wet skin when I get in. I shiver, but in a way it feels nice. Orion pulls away from the curb and asks, "Is this because of Austin?"

I look out the window.

"There is no guy worth all this."

"My jogging has nothing to do with him."

"Well, what then? And I'm not just talking about the running."

I don't answer because I really don't know. I can't explain something that is so logical. I mean, what is so strange about watching my diet and exercising?

"You're bleeding," Orion says. "A lot."

I look down between my legs. The entire crotch of my pants is blood stained. I know why, but Orion assumes the same thing Sky did.

"Here," he says. "Sit on this." He hands me my hoodie, which is red, and I slide it under me. He hands me a bottle of water. I reluctantly take it. "Drink it," he says. "There's no calories in water."

"So they say," I mutter. I look at the in-dash clock. 3:14 p.m. "Do you know where my phone is? I never found it."

"No," he answers. "I'll have Austin look in his truck." He glances at me. "Drink the water."

I do. I take a sip; just enough to wet my palate. It tastes good and it's like my body is crying out for more, so I give in. By the time we're home, half the bottle is gone.

"I'm gonna shower," I announce when we walk in. When I get in the bathroom, I don't even take off my clothes before I stick my finger down my throat and lose the water my body had so desperately cried out for.

When I walk out of the bathroom after my shower, Orion calls for me from his room. I go to the doorway, still in my towel, blood dripping down my leg.

"Come here," he says. "Sit down." He's sitting on his bed, the laptop in his lap.

"Um, I'm not dressed."

"I just wanna show you something real fast."

I sigh and walk over there. He points at the screen, and I see that he's looking at our mom's Facebook page.

"Read her status from today." He points to it.

I'm off today spending it with my family. Tomorrow I work 12-730, so skip the cookouts and come leave me big tips LOL!

"Family," I mutter.

"Look past that, Sun." He looks at me. "She's working tomorrow."

"So? Am I supposed to feel sorry for her?"

"No. Geez, Sunny. I think we should go there."

"Where?"

"To TGIFriday's. To see her."

"No freaking way! Are you serious?"

He shrugs and looks at the computer screen. "Why not?"

Why do I want to go to TGIFriday's? Not for the

    Good food

    Good times   or

    Good friends.

But to check out the woman who

    Gave me life

    Gave me up   and

    Got her own life.

Then maybe I'll

    Get closure

    Get high   or

    Get a gun.

Skylar

When I told Jake I wanted to get out of the house, this wasn't what I had in mind. I guess that's because I haven't lived a whole lot, or perhaps my expectations are low.

When I said *let's get out of here*, I thought maybe a walk around the mall or a dinner out. But Jake exceeded anything in my dreams.

We've just walked into a hotel room that was designed for romance. More romance than I've ever known, that's for sure. Jake is staring at me, a smile playing on his lips. "Well?" he asks.

I smile back. "You are so bad, Jake Morris." I drop my purse on the floor and walk toward him. "What charge will this add to your rap sheet? Kidnapping?"

He chuckles. "At least we didn't cross state lines." He takes my hands in his. "You like it?"

"I love it," I say, taking in the sun-drenched room. The king size bed is covered with a plush comforter. The mahogany wood furniture makes the room feel elegant.

He kisses me then, soft and sweet, but he stops, leaving me wanting more. "What's bothering you?"

"Why would you say that?"

He sits down at the little desk and faces me. "You've been pretty quiet. Hardly said anything the whole ride here." His hand reaches out for me. "Is it Star?"

I sigh and take his hand. He pulls me to his lap. "It's Star, it's my dad, it's Melissa. And Sunny, and...." I trail off, not wanting to confess that Austin has been on my mind all freaking day.

"The rest of it I get, but what's with Sunny?"

I lay my head in the crook of his neck. "That's why O needed me to come home last night. She was drunk." Jake chuckles. "She's a little different, you know? So it's weird that she would even drink. But then she apparently messed around with Austin Spencer." I pause to see if Jake says anything. We've never talked about my thing with Austin, but it's not exactly a secret. "She was a virgin," I add with a quiet sigh.

"Oh," Jake says. Then a moment later, "What about that bothers you exactly?"

I sit up, look straight into his eyes. "Austin's a worthless loser. Sunny can do so much better than him, but she gives herself zero credit. She's gonna regret what she did for the rest of her life."

"Do you regret it?"

I draw my eyebrows together. "Regret what?"

"Austin."

"What do you know about it?"

"Only what I'm privy to as his coach."

"Such as?"

He shakes his head. "It doesn't matter."

I get up. "It does to me. What did he say?"

"Guys talk a lot of crap. I don't know what's true and what's not."

"But you know something."

"Skylar, don't get mad. I'm not one of those guys talking shit, okay?"

"I'm not mad at you," I snap. "I'm mad at myself for ever being low enough to mess around with someone like that. Like I didn't think enough of myself to aim higher. Do I regret it? Yeah, I regret all of it. If I could do it over, I would have never touched him. And since he's Orion's friend, he's always there. Like a damn cockroach. I can't get rid of him!"

I sit on the bed. Jake comes over and places a comforting arm around my shoulders. "He just aggravates the crap out of me, and now seeing Sunny all hung up on him just makes me so mad! What can she possibly see in him? I mean, really?"

"Did you ever see anything in him?"

"No. He was just there. So it was easy to just...."

"Well, I'm not a girl, but I think Austin's an alright kid." Did he just call Austin a kid? If Austin's a kid, then what am I? "He pulls decent grades, stays out of trouble. He's respectful. Decent baller. Maybe you just see him as bad because of the way you guys broke up."

"Ha. Now tell me what you know about that." *This* I have to hear.

He chuckles. "You blew him off. Stopped talking to him."

"Do you know why?"

"I do." He pulls his arm back and I face him. "He was really struggling at practice one night, so I pulled him aside. He told me his girlfriend was pissed at him and he wasn't sure what he'd done. Said he couldn't think about anything but trying to figure out how to make things better. I told him sometimes girls just need their space. The next day, he came up to me in the hall and said, and I quote, 'Sky blew me off again last night.' Something about you said you'd be home when he got there but weren't. He waited around and when you got there, he said he could tell you were with someone else." He paused. "You were at my house. I was the someone else. Then he asked me what to do. I had no idea it was you until then, or that you had a boyfriend when we started...well, you know."

"So what'd you say?"

He shrugged. "What else could I say? I told him that no woman who cheats is worth keeping around."

"Is that really how you feel?"

"Well, yeah."

"But--"

"I know, I know. But this is different. I didn't go into this looking for love." He smirks. "Does that make me some sick pervert who sleeps with his student just because he can? I hope not, because it's way beyond that now. But I didn't plan on things turning out this way."

"So then why? Why are we here?"

"Skylar, I fell in love with you. You know that."

"But if you were just looking for a good time, how did it turn into this?"

"I don't know. Do you? I mean, why did you go for this?"

I shrug and look at the floor. "I mean at first, it was like, whoa, is he flirting with me? And then, I was like, okay, well, he's cute." I look up at him. "I don't know."

"What did you think you were getting into when you came to my house?"

He's talking about that first time during Christmas break last year. I'd run into him at the store while I was picking up milk and bread.

"Hey, Mr. Morris," I said. "I didn't know teachers ate."

He laughed. "Some teachers are aliens, but not me. I'm human and need human food."

"Good to know." I started to walk away. "Have a good Christmas."

"You too." His eyes sparked and held mine for a moment too long. "Hey, you got plans over break?"

"Not really." I turned back to him, curious as to why he would ask. "Sleeping, eating, opening presents."

He nodded and looked to be mulling something over. "Well, okay."

I started to walk away again, grasping to make sense of the whole awkward exchange.

"Hey, Sky?" he called again. I faced him. "Maybe, um, if you need help with your math...." He looked at the gallons of milk in the cooler. "I don't know. Maybe I could help you if you need it." He looked back to me. "I don't really have much going on."

"Um, okay."

Now I was really uncomfortable. At first, I thought he was just being polite, then maybe I detected a little flirtation, then it got really strange. I mean, I had an A- in algebra. Why would I need help?

"Let me give you my number," he said.

I handed him my phone. He called himself so that his number was in my phone. Also, he now had my cell number. I was so blown away by the whole thing that I planned to tell Austin and Orion about it when I got home. But in the fifteen-minute drive, my curiosity got the best of me, so all I said was that I'd seen Mr. Morris at the store. And I saved his number in my cell as Math Help Desk.

I didn't call because I didn't need help with algebra. But the Friday before we were due back at school, he called me. He said he could use help grading papers and asked if I'd come over. Mere curiosity was why I went, why I didn't tell anyone where I was going had nothing to do with curiosity.

In the week or so since I'd seen him at the store, I was sure he'd been trying to flirt with me. But it was awkward due to the teacher-student relationship. I had replayed the encounter over and over in my mind, nearly obsessing over it. Austin noticed I was distracted, and suddenly he looked like a little boy (which he is) in comparison to someone like Mr. Morris.

By the time Jake called, my mind was made up. If he wanted more than just help grading papers, he could have it.

I look at Jake now, in this beautiful hotel, offering me a beautiful future. "What did I think I was getting into when I went to your house?" I smile. "I was hoping for something like this." He grinned and tucked a strand of hair behind my ear. "What were you hoping for when you invited me?"

"Honestly," he whispered. "I was hoping that I wouldn't try to kiss you, but that if I did that you wouldn't freak out and call the cops."

"Wow. So I totally let you down."

He shook his head. "Well, you didn't call the cops."

"It actually never occurred to me."

After being at his house for a few hours, legitimately grading papers at the kitchen table, I excused myself to the bathroom. When I came out, he stood near the kitchen table. He came towards me and thanked me for my help. I smiled and said it was no problem, that I'd had fun. Then he leaned down and placed his mouth on mine.

At first, I was frozen, disbelieving it was actually happening. Then I came out of the momentary daze and pushed him away.

"What are you doing?" I yelled. "Are you insane?"

"No, Sky, no." He looked completely panicked, the color draining from his face. "Oh, my God, Skylar. I am so sorry. Please. I am so sorry."

I went to the living room and grabbed the keys. He followed.

"Skylar, I am so sorry. I didn't mean to. It's just that I... That you... Oh, God, Skylar. I am so sorry."

I left there thinking he was some kind of sicko. I was pissed. At him and at myself. But on that first day back to school, I was over it. In fact, I walked into his classroom before the first hour and said, "Sorry, I overreacted the other day. I really had a nice time."

The rest is history.

Jake

On the first day of my professional career as a high school math teacher, I was overwhelmed by the students. In fact, my third hour Algebra I class was so horrid that I regularly relied on a student to take control. That's how she first caught my eye. She took charge and wasn't afraid of anyone. She always had the answers, and her homework done. A star student with a beautiful smile and an excellent body, I started to appreciate more than just her academics.

Was it wrong to look at her that way?
Of course.
Was it wrong to think of her as more than a student?
Of course.
Was it wrong to give her my phone number?
Of course.
Was it wrong to invite her to my house?
Of course.
Was it wrong to corner her and lay my lips on hers?
Of course.
Was it wrong to invite her back?
Of course.
One more question:
How many wrongs does it take to make a right?

Starla

Tuesday seems like forever away when it's really only tomorrow. On Tuesday, things will seem somewhat normal again. I can go to school and let my mind be there, not here. Here is where all I can think about is this damn mistake growing inside me.

Tuesday is also the day that Sky is making the Planned Parenthood appointment. I'm with Ray on this; it better be soon.

That doesn't mean I've made any kind of decision. This isn't easy. I mean, for one, I'm fourteen. What business do I have trying to raise a kid? But on the other hand, I'm fourteen. Old enough to know better. And then there's that whole murder thing.

No matter which way the cards fall, there's no easy solution.

But today I get to put on a smile and a swimsuit and head over to Ray's to celebrate Labor Day with his family. Labor Day. Hmmph. Am I the only one who sees the irony in that? How many months until my labor day?

From my bedroom window I see Ray's Sante Fe pull up. I dart downstairs and out of the house before he can even make it to the door.

"Hey," he says with a laugh as I jump up, wrap my legs around him. "What's with this?"

I kiss him once and let myself slide down. "Nothing, really. Just trying to make things feel normal."

His eyes that had looked playful for that brief moment suddenly transformed back into the dark, serious ones I had come to know too well over the past few days. "Oh, yeah." He takes my hand. "Normal would be nice."

"Do you wish I wouldn't have told you?" I ask when we're pulling away.

He doesn't answer right away. "No, it's not that. I'm glad you did." He slows as we reach a stop sign. "I just wish this wasn't happening." He looks at me, his baby blue eyes as soft as a cloud. "I love you. And I know no matter what we decide that we'll get through this."

Those words all but erase the turmoil we're in. Everything had felt so uncertain, but I was right. We are solid. His feelings for me are the same as they've always been.

"I love you too," I say. I lean toward him as the car stops. He meets me over the console and our lips lock, signifying the strength in our bond. I sit back as he pulls away and say, "Today I think we need to forget about this pregnancy thing. Like completely. Let's just be us and have fun." I lift my shirt a little. "I'm wearing my suit."

He smiles. "Think we have time for a little detour before we go?"

I smack his arm. "No!" Like I really want to show up at his family cookout stinking like s-e-x.

"On the way home?" He glances at me. "It's been, like, two days, Star."

"Oh, my God. You're just gonna die, aren't you?"

"You never know. I might."

I roll my eyes and laugh. "I'm pretty sure no one has ever died from lack of s-e-x."

He turns down his street. "Are you ever going to be able to say that word?"

"What word?"

"Sex."

I scrunch my nose. "I've said it before."

"Not that I've heard. You always spell it."

"Do I?"

"Yeah. Not that it matters much to me. As long as you know how to do it."

"Which I definitely do, as the test results have proved."

"Hey," he says, pulling into his driveway. "Remember? No talking about that."

I nod. "Right. Today we're just Ray and Star, your average teenagers."

He clears his throat and shuts the car off. "Who've never had s-e-x."

I can't help laughing. It's going to be a wonderful day. Probably the last great one we'll have for a long time.

S is for sin.
E is for eternal damnation.
X is for (e)xcellent (e)xperience.

For our sins we face eternal damnation, so was the

        (e)xcellent (e)xperience

                      worth it?

Sunshine

So this is what I did about the bleeding problem:
- I found an X-Large Sterile Gauze Pad under Dad's bathroom sink.
- Couldn't find medical tape, so I used masking tape to hold it over my slices.

Now:
- It keeps rubbing me in places I won't mention.

And:
- I don't think this tape is gonna hold.

Orion and I are on our way to TGIFriday's. I'm not sure this is a good idea. You know, since curiosity killed the cat and all.
"Have you asked Austin about my phone?" I ask.
"Yeah, I mentioned it. He said he'd look."
"When?"
"Expecting a call?"
"No, it's just that...." How do I explain this? "I don't wear a watch, you know."
He chuckles. "You're gonna eat when we get there, right?"
I don't answer.
"Sunny. Do not waste my money. I have less than a hundred bucks and I'm forgoing a new pair of shoes, and I won't mention why I need them, to do this."
"I didn't ask you to do this, O."
"You didn't say you didn't want to do it either."

True, I suppose. "Whatever. I'll eat, but I'm not promising anything more than that."

He rolls his eyes and turns the music up. I wonder what it would be like to eat whatever I wanted. To pick up a roll at a restaurant, slather it with butter. To eat a hunk of red meat and carb-filled potatoes. Wash it all down with some decadent chocolate cake and a scoop of creamy ice cream. God, I barely remember what chocolate tastes like. Or ice cream.

"Hey," Orion says when we pull into the parking lot. "Follow my lead when we get in there, okay?" I nod. "Nervous?"

"A little. What if she recognizes us?"

He exhales loudly. "I don't know. We'll figure that out if it happens, I guess."

I follow my brother inside, feeling very apprehensive. I wish I'd brought my razor. I've never cut anywhere except on my bed, but I'm really feeling the need to do it now. My nerves are going nuts.

Or maybe it's just me going nuts.

"Two, please," Orion tells the hostess. "And last time we were here, we had this great server." He glances at me, "What was her name, hon?"

I almost laugh but follow along. "Gosh, I don't know. Something with an A, maybe."

Orion snaps his fingers. "That's right." He looks at the hostess. "Amy? Do you have an Amy?"

She smiles. "We have Amy Jo."

"Amy Jo," we say in unison.

The hostess looks down. "It'll be about ten minutes. Can I get your name?"

"Spencer," Orion says, using Austin's last name.

We walk to the row of seats near the door and sit down. He sits especially close, and I scoot away.

"We're supposed to look like a couple. So stop."

I giggle and scoot so I'm leg to leg with my brother. "Do we need fake names too?"

He smiles. "Sure. I'll be Austin."

"Haha, jerk. Fine. Then I'm Haley."

He raises his eyebrows, "Well, if you insist on being a nasty...." He's looking across the restaurant and I follow his eyes.

It's the first time, to my memory, that I've seen my mom. She doesn't look that much older than us, but we know better. We watch her move from table to table, checking on her customers. Her smile comes easy, and her laughter can be heard from where we sit.

"I don't want to do this," I say. "C'mon." I stand up, ready to leave.

"Spencer?" the hostess calls out.

Orion stands and takes my hand. "It's fine. She won't recognize us."

We follow the hostess to our table. "Amy Jo will be over soon."

"I don't like this, O. Let's go."

"Shut up. And if you call me Orion, she's gonna know who we are, *Haley*."

I'm about to argue more when Amy Jo appears. "Hey, guys! Welcome to TGIFriday's! Can I get you started with some drinks?"

We both turn to stare up at the woman who brought us into this world. And I think I'm gonna be sick. Like, seriously.

Orion, though, holds it together. "I'll have a Coke, and she'll have water."

She looks at me, "Lemon in your water, hon?"

Hon? Did she call me hon when I was a baby? I shake my head.

"Okay. I'll be back to get your order in a few minutes."

We watch her walk away.

"She even walks like Sky," Orion says.

Our eyes meet. "She looks just like her," I say, even though it's obvious.

"Wow," he says, shaking his head. "Okay. Figure out what you can eat off here. A salad or something."

I scan the menu, knowing I won't eat anything on here. But for Orion and his crazy desire to be here and keep up appearances, I will order the least caloric thing on the menu. I wonder if they sell lettuce by the leaf.

"You know, I could order a beer. Then she would card me and see my name. I'm fairly sure I'm the only Orion Hollis in existence."

I look at him, wide eyed, as she returns with our drinks. "Have you decided?" she asks eagerly.

Orion smiles wide at her, a smile that looks like Dads. *Oh, God. Please don't let her see that.*

"I'll have the Jack Daniels Burger with fries," he says confidently.

"How do you like your burger?"

"Medium-well, please."

She pauses, her eyes lingering on his face. Then she blinks and faces me. "And for you, hon?"

Again with the hon. "Um," I say without looking up. "Friday's House Salad. No croutons."

"What kind of dressing?"

"None, please."

She finishes writing and reaches for our menus. "Are you guys heading to a cookout later on?"

"No," O says. "This is it." He looks at me. "It's kind of our anniversary."

"Anniversary? How long?"

"Six months," he says. He smiles at me. "Right?"

"Right," I say. "Six months."

"Awe. That's so sweet." She smiles at us both, her eyes studying Orion more closely than me. "I'll get your orders in. Let me know if you need anything."

"Maybe I should make her a list," O says when she's gone.

"A list?"

"Yeah," he says with a chuckle. "She said to let her know if we need anything."

He gets me to smile and excuses himself to the bathroom. That's a good idea, actually. I unroll my silverware and eye the steak knife's blade. I'm not sure it's sharp enough, but I won't know unless I try. I slip it into the waistband of my jeans and wait for Orion to return.

I see him come out of the bathroom. He passes by Amy Jo and she pauses and watches him walk. Then he looks back at her, like he could feel her eyes on him. She looks away, and he looks at me.

"Think she knows?" he asks when he sits down.

"She's thinking something. I can fake sick, and we can leave."

"No. We drove all the way here. If she figures out who we are then so be it."

I sigh. How did I get myself into this? "I have to go to the bathroom."

"You haven't even eaten yet."

I narrow my eyes. "I do know how to use the bathroom like a normal person, you know."

He snickers. "True."

When I pass Amy Jo, she doesn't look twice at me. Guess she doesn't remember me like she remembers Orion. Maybe if I was Sky, she would be staring at me.

I lock myself in the handicapped stall and pull out the steak knife. Running my fingers along the serrated edge, I contemplate whether I really want to do this. More importantly, where am I gonna do this?

I pull my pants down and inspect my legs. No way. Unless I go lower, but then I eliminate wearing shorts. And with no air conditioning at school that would be disastrous. Since I haven't given up hope of spending more time with Austin, I really didn't want to mutilate my stomach or anything else on my torso.

Why hadn't I worn long sleeves? Then I could cut my arms.

Why is deciding so hard? And why can't I wait until the other ones are healed? Why do I have to do it now?

I look at my thighs. They're so fat and disgusting. But even worse than them is my stomach. My stomach is the real problem. Maybe if I cut the fat off from there....

I didn't think it through. No, because if I had, I would have realized that it would bleed and being pressed against my jeans, well, that's not proving to be a great way to heal slices.

And the worst part is that this stupid steak knife isn't even sharp enough. The slices are jagged and uneven, bleeding in thready spots. This makes me mad. They're supposed to be straight.

Even.

Perfect.

Left

to

Right.

One. Two. Three. Four.

But these stupid slices are a mess.

A mess like the body they are decorating.

I coat the oozy blood spots with toilet paper, wipe the evidence from the knife blade and leave the stall. I've been crying, not that I noticed in the stall, but the evidence is all over my face. I splash cold water on my temples and wash my hands before leaving the room.

Back at the table, the food has arrived, and Orion's mouth is full. He swallows as I sit down and says, "What the hell took you so long?"

I shrug and pull the knife from my waist band and start cutting up my salad.

"Why did you take the knife to the bathroom?"

I shrug.

"Sunny," he hisses.

"Just shut up and eat your damn burger, *Austin*. This is our anniversary, remember?"

He glances around. "What's with the knife?"

"Don't worry about it, okay?"

He drops it. And after I chop my salad to smithereens, he sets his phone on the table for me to check the time. But I don't. Why? Because I didn't check while I was in the bathroom and those slices are an uneven mess and so what does it matter if I note the time now. It's all out of whack and I have lost complete control of my body, my life.

After four bites, I excuse myself to the bathroom again. Orion grabs my knife when I stand.

"I don't need it this time, for your information," I assure him. I could be wrong, but he looks scared. Like, scared of me.

I go through my routine as best I can in the handicapped stall. I know it doesn't sound pretty to whoever else is in the bathroom, but I've lost all control, so what does it matter anyway?

Deciding against checking the new slices, I come out of the stall. Amy Jo is checking her reflection in the mirror. I almost go back in, but she says, "Feeling alright, hon?"

I shake my head and go to the sink to wash my hands.

"That's too bad, on your anniversary and all. Was it the food?"

I shake my head again and look at her reflection in the mirror. She stands even height with me and studies me like she studied Orion earlier.

Then she faces me, her hand covering her mouth.

Oh, crap. What the hell do I do now?

"Skylar?" she asks.

I look her in the eye, this Skylar look alike who gave birth to me. "No," I say. "My name's Haley." My voice is surprisingly even.

"Sorry." She waves her hand in the air. "Sorry. You just reminded me of someone I haven't seen in years."

I nod and walk out, my hands still wet. Orion is watching for me. He stands as I approach and starts to say something.

"Let's go," I say.

I get to the car and wait for him to join me.

"I saw her go in there," he says when he gets in the Taurus. "What happened?"

I scoff. "She wanted me to be Skylar." He stares at me long enough that I say, "Can we go before she catches on and comes running out here?" I look down at my gut. "And we need to stop at Walmart. I cut myself. Need a Band-Aid or something."

It seems my mom

    recognized me,

    remembered me.

It seems my sister

    lost her lunch,

    lost her mind.

                      Who slices themselves

                        with a steak knife in

                        TGIFriday's bathroom?

It seems it's time

    to talk to Dad about Sunny,

    because Skylar sure isn't doing

    anything to make things better for her.

It seems I

    didn't find closure

                or anything else

                I thought I was missing.

Skylar

I won't say why we got a late start to the day, took advantage of late check out, but we did. And if it weren't for the primal need to eat, we'd still be at the hotel.

"There's a TGIFriday's right over there," Jake says. "How's that sound?"

"Eating a meal in public? I thought we'd go through a drive-thru."

He chuckles. "I think we're far enough from home."

I consider that. He's right. "Okay. Sounds fine as long as you're sure."

When we pull into the parking lot, Jake says, "That looks like your car over there."

I spy the green Taurus. "Pull by it."

"It's not yours, there's a million green Ford Taurus'. It probably wouldn't even make it this far."

"Just pull over there."

He does and as we creep down the row, I see Sunny sitting in the passenger seat. "Oh, crap!" I duck down. "Go!"

He slows, inspects the situation, and then hits the gas. "What the...."

"Did she see you?"

"No, I don't think so. What is she doing here?"

I sit back up. "I have no idea. Orion must be with her, but that doesn't really make.... Why here? There's a TGIFriday's closer. A lot closer. And O's more like a Burger King kinda guy."

We exchange confused looks as we pass through a green light and I'm about to add how this whole adventure was a bad idea and that we should have just stayed home when we're suddenly spinning in circles. The only sounds I hear are of rubber grinding into the ground and then there's a crash that makes me scream.

My scream is cut short by the airbag deploying in my face. When it deflates, I scream again. My window is gone, the windshield is shattered, and Jake is leaning into his airbag.

It seems like eternity before he opens his eyes. Behind him I see people getting out of their cars and coming toward us. By the time they reach us, Jake is sitting up, talking to me, reaching for me.

And then it's all fading. The sounds are in the distance, the people are moving in slow motion. "Jake," I say, or at least I mean to.

"There she is!" someone says. "She's awake."

Jake is in front of me now, the passenger door to the car open. There's a crowd of people standing behind him staring at me.

"Hey, Sky. Are you okay?" Jake says. I hear sirens in the distance.

"What happened?" I whisper.

"That guy blew the red light, broadsided us. You passed out." He reached toward the right side of my head without actually touching it. "Your head's bleeding pretty good. Probably from when you hit the window."

"It hurts," I whine.

He smiles gently. "I'm sure it does, babe." He kisses my cheek. "The airbag smacked you pretty good, too."

Two paramedics appear and Jake moves out of the way. It seems like they take forever removing me like hand-blown glass from the car and laying me on a stretcher. I insist that I'm fine, but Jake tells me, "You're bleeding from your head, and you lost consciousness. You need to be checked out."

"How are we gonna get home?" I ask as they stick me in the back of the ambulance.

"Don't worry about it, okay?"

Things move fast when we get to the hospital. Nurses, doctors, technicians, monitors, blood work, CT scan, and admitting.

"What insurance do you have?" the lady with the clipboard asks.

"Um, I have a public aid card."

"Do you have a copy?"

I shake my head.

She looks at Jake. "Do you have a copy?"

"No," he says. "You know what? Just put me down as responsible. I'll pay the bill."

She looks from him to me and back to him. "Who are you?"

"Jake Morris."

"Your relationship to Skylar?"

"Her boyfriend."

Lady with the clipboard pauses, then continues to gather pertinent information from Jake. Then she rounds it out by saying, "Skylar, we're gonna have to call your parents. For a couple of reasons. We have to have their consent to treat you since you're seventeen, and also, because you're seventeen, we have to release you to your parents."

"But I came here with him," I argue.

"Sorry," she says. "What's your mother's name?"

"I don't have any parents!"

"Sky," Jake says gently. "It's okay."

"No, it's not. We're screwed." I look at clipboard lady. "Do you really have to do this?"

"Her dad's name is Mike Hollis," Jake says. He has my phone in his hand and proceeds to give away my dad's number.

"What are you doing?"

"It's fine," he says.

"Thank you," clipboard says before she ducks around the curtain.

"Why, Jake? Why'd you tell her? We could've made something up."

"No, we couldn't. What would that have done? Bought us time? They'd figure it out."

"But I love you," I whine like a baby.

"I love you too." He touches my cheek. "We're just gonna have to come clean. Whatever the consequences."

"No! You can leave. I'll make up a story for my dad."

He shakes his head. "It's okay."

Tears wet my cheeks and I do nothing to stop them. Why should I? Jake is everything to me. Everything I had ever wished for in a man and now it's over. All over.

"Hey, it's not that bad. You'll be eighteen in a few weeks, and I'll quit teaching. Okay?"

That doesn't help. It just made the tears fall more. He sits on the edge of the bed, and I lean into him, crying until the well goes dry.

When Dad arrives nearly two hours later, Jake is sitting on the bed with me, his arms around me as I rest my head on his chest. Dad pulls back the curtain and stands there, his face placid. I sit up and Jake gets off the bed and moves to the side. I'm about to tell my dad that I can explain when the curtain draws back again, and Melissa comes in.

"Jake?" was all she gets out before the doctor comes in.

"Okay, now that Dad is here," the doctor says. "Looks like a mild concussion. She should be okay, just keep an eye on her for the next twenty-four to forty-eight hours. She'll probably have a couple black eyes, but that'll go away with time." He steps to Dad. "Just need your signature here." While Dad signs, the doctor adds, "I'll have a nurse come in and unhook you from the monitor. Then you're free to go."

As soon as the doctor turns away, Dad speaks. "Somebody tell me what's going on. Now."

I look at Jake, but he looks away from me. I look back to my dad, seeing the anger in his eyes, his set jaw. "Daddy...." I don't really know what to say. There's no uncomplicated way about this.

"Let's try this, Skylar. I'll ask questions, you answer. Why are you all the way out here, so far from home? I thought you were at Kylee's."

I stammer, look at Jake, but he's facing the wall. Melissa is at my dad's side, probably trying to figure out how her brother plays into all this. "Um, we were gonna have lunch, I guess," I finally manage to say.

"Who? You and Jake?"

I nod.

"I don't understand," Dad says.

Melissa speaks up. "When they called, didn't they say she was with her boyfriend?"

"They did," Dad says thoughtfully. His eyes penetrate into Jake's backside. "They did."

"Jake," Melissa says, her voice coming out higher than normal. "Why are you having lunch with Sky?"

Jake takes a deep breath and faces his sister. I've never seen him look so upset. It makes my heart ache and I start crying all over.

"God, Melissa," he starts. "What do you want me to say?"

Melissa covers her mouth.

Dad exhales. "You're kidding me, right?" He laughs, but it's definitely not because he thinks this is funny. "You're kidding." He looks at me, steps closer to the bed. I draw my legs to my chest. "Is he the boyfriend you were with? Your teacher? This guy?" He laughs that evil laugh again. "How old are you?" he asks Jake.

"I'm twenty-three, Mike."

"And do you know how old she is? Well, of course you do. Because, for one, she's not old enough to check herself out of the hospital, and for two, she's your student!"

Dad lets out a stream of swear words while pacing between the curtain and the bed. "I have so many questions that I don't even want to know the answers to. Like, did you really go to Kylee's? I'm guessing not, which makes me think you were with him. So then I have to wonder if you slept together. I'm guessing you have. At least I do know you're on the Pill." He stops pacing and steps right in front of Jake. "What the hell is wrong with you? She's a little girl, man."

"I love her," Jake says quietly.

"What?"

"I love her."

"You love her. Is that some kind of joke?" Again with the nasty laugh.

"Daddy," I start, "I love him too. And we've been together for a long time."

He scoffs. "A long time? Really, like what? Two weeks?"

"Almost nine months."

That stops my dad in his tracks. I can see his mind reeling with the past nine months, questioning my every move, wondering about my motives. "I need some fresh air."

With that he walks out. Melissa is left looking between the two of us. She shakes her head. "Why didn't you tell me, Jake?"

"What was I supposed to say?"

She throws her hands up. "I don't know. What the hell are you thinking? How did this even happen?"

"None of that matters now. What's important is that we are in love and nothing else matters. We don't care if I lose my job or go to jail or nothing. We're gonna be together no matter what anyone thinks."

Dad comes back into the room, a nurse right behind him. "I suppose I have to give you a ride home, too, huh?" he asks Jake.

"I can wait for my insurance to set me up with a car."

My dad meets Jake's eyes. "You're coming with us."

Jake nods once and there's no more conversation on the matter. Dad makes me sit in the front seat of the Durango, Jake and Melissa sit in the back. The ride starts with Dad grumbling to himself, and I wonder how much of his anger is being controlled since Melissa is there. Not that Dad has a hot temper or anything, but this is good cause to be plenty angry. Or maybe he's coming to terms with it.

Yeah, right.

Twenty minutes into the ride, Dad starts in on me. Going on and on about how proud he was of me, how he brags about me and how mature I am, how I look out for the other kids so he's not so stressed.

"I cannot even put into words how disappointed I am in you, Skylar. I'd expect this crap from Orion, but not you. I hold you to a higher standard than this." He scoffs. "This, this is like something your mother would've done. And I thought you were a good role model for your sisters and that's why they were doing so well, but maybe you should've been looking up to them."

Now I'd pretty much kept quiet so far other than to give my weak defense. But for me to look up to Star and Sunny? *I don't think so.* "You know, Dad, you don't know those girls as well as you think you do. Did you know that Star's pregnant? And that Sunny is bulimic and only eats four bites at any meal, and then purges it all as soon as she can? Did you know that, Dad? You're gonna be a grandpa? What do you think about that? Do I still look like the worst kid in the world?"

Mike

It's not funny how life can go from mundane to mind-boggling in a matter of an hour. I expected to find Austin at the hospital with Sky. Instead, I find out my baby girl is in love with her teacher.

Then to take the spotlight from her own lifelong grounding, she pulls the wool away from my eyes. I guess I should've done more parenting and less partying. Because when I take stock of my kids this is what I find:

Star is pregnant.

Sunny is bulimic.

and

Sky is dating her teacher.

Oh, yeah, don't I have a son? Has anyone seen Orion? At least I don't have to worry about him.

Thirty-five is too young to be a grandpa. Even stranger than that, Sky and Jake have been together longer than me and Melissa. And I've been thinking wedding,

but what now?

Starla

I'm playing Marco-Polo in the pool with Ray's two brothers and his sister Tessa. After we'd eaten BBQ ribs from the grill, their parents made us wait the requisite thirty minutes before jumping in, you know, in case anyone got debilitating stomach cramps. Now the sun looks to be slipping lower on the horizon, but not quite ready to retire for the day. My skin feels dry and achy, new sunburn atop the one that had just started to think about fading.

"I'm gonna go get more food," Ray told me minutes ago when he got out. "Come with me?"

"No," I said. "I'm fine."

He gave me a weird look, but I ignored him and called out *Polo* to Tessa's *Marco*. She got me, and now I'm wading through the water with my eyes closed saying *Marco*, trying to decipher where the giggling little boys are. Tessa, being the same age as me and the closest thing I have to a friend, is a little more discreet. But not Dylan and Lucas. They think it's funny to watch me stumble around with my hands outstretched.

"Marco!" I call.

"Um, Star?" Tessa says. "I think your dad's here."

I open my eyes and see my dad at the edge of the yard. Mrs. Douglas is approaching him, smiling, probably offering a plate.

"Hey, Mike," Ray calls from the patio. He's gnawing on a rib, BBQ sauce around his lips like someone had finger-painted it on.

My dad nods at him and turns back to Mrs. Douglas. I'm worried something is wrong. Why else would he show up here? I make my way to the ladder, ignoring Lucas begging me to finish this round.

Grabbing a towel, I jog over to my dad. I start to wrap it around my waist when he says, right there in front of Mrs. Douglas, "Well, you sure don't *look* pregnant."

I don't know what my face shows, but I know I feel like dying. "I-I-I'm not."

Mrs. Douglas is looking between me and Dad. Why is he doing this? I have no doubt Sky told him, but why? What is this going to help? Wasn't it Sky's idea *not* to tell the parentals until we decided what to do?

"Are you sure about that?" Dad asks.

I take a step back and look at Ray licking his fingers on the patio. Dad and Mrs. Douglas follow my eyes. Mr. Douglas comes onto the patio, spots us, and calls out, "Mike! I didn't know you were stopping by. Come make a plate."

Dad shakes his head. "I don't have much of an appetite, actually, Ray. But I was hoping we could have a chat since I'm here."

My Ray looks up from his sauce, finally detecting there might be something wrong.

"Sure, sure," Big Ray says. "Should we go inside?"

Dad looks at me. "That'll work."

Mrs. Douglas's hand is covering her mouth and I'm sure she knows what's going on. She's much nicer and more understanding than Mr. Douglas. Mr. Douglas has a pretty bad temper. I've seen him hit Ray before, and Ray has told me several times about the fights his parents get in. Maybe I should've told my dad about these facts. Maybe then he wouldn't be here now, dropping this bomb on them.

Dad grabs my shoulder and guides me to the house. "Star and Ray need to come inside too."

"I'm sunburned, Dad," I say, hoping he'll take his hand off me.

"That's nothing. Just wait," he says snidely.

Mr. Douglas's face changes at Dad's announcement that me and Ray need to be part of this chat. "Get inside, Junior," he says flatly.

As soon as I walk into the cold air, I start shivering. Ray goes to the kitchen sink and washes the BBQ sauce from his mouth and hands. I try to go to him, but Dad won't let go of my shoulder.

"Let's sit in the dining room," Mr. Douglas says. "Angela, get Mike something to drink."

Mrs. Douglas looks at Dad. "Would you like some tea?"

"Yes. Thank you."

Mr. Douglas looks at Ray. "Follow me, Son." My dad and I follow Mr. Douglas and Ray into the dining room. Dad pulls out a chair for me; I sit, and he sits beside me. Ray moves to take the seat on my other side, but his dad says, "I don't think so. Over here."

Ray lowers his eyes and goes across the table. Before he sits, he says, "She's freezing. Can I get her a blanket?"

"Ang?" Mr. Douglas calls out. "Bring a blanket for Star."

I try to look at Ray, read his eyes, send some sort of silent S.O.S. to him, but he won't look up. He's studying his hands like they're some sort of complex anomaly. I know he's scared. He's told me enough times. But this, this happening right now like it is, is scarier than anything I've ever experienced. So I know he's freaking out. He should be. His parents (dad) are much stricter than my dad. I'll be in trouble, he'll be in T-R-O-U-B-L-E.

Mrs. Douglas comes into the room with two glasses of iced tea and a blanket. She sets down the tea (one for my dad, one for Ray's dad), and drapes the fleece throw over my shoulders.

"Thank you," I whisper, though I'm still freezing.

She takes the seat between me and Mr. Douglas and folds her hands in her lap, looking expectantly around the table.

Mr. Douglas asks, "What can we do for you, Mike?"

Dad clears his throat. "Well, Ray, I, uh, have it on pretty good authority that Star is pregnant."

No one looks surprised. No one moves. No one speaks. The only sounds come from the pool outside. I close my eyes and call out *Polo* in my head, wishing I could be found.

When I open my eyes, Ray is finally looking at me. He's crying. I have to look away. I can't see that. Why is he crying? How does he cry? I've never seen him do that before.

Now I think I'm scared.

"Is this fact?" Mr. Douglas asks.

Well, if it wasn't, wouldn't we have denied it by now?

"Raymond! I asked if this is a fact!" he yells.

Ray lets out a little sob and nods his head. *Why do I want to roll my eyes?* God, why does he seem like a little kid now, when he should be trying to act like a man?

"Oh, what the hell?" Mr. Douglas mutters. He stands, his hand to his forehead. "What's wrong with you guys? Are you stupid?" His eyes fall on me. "How old are you? Fifteen?"

I don't answer, so Dad does. "She's fourteen."

My eyes look at the wood grain on the table. It's like a little maze, and *oh how nice would it be* to get caught in there.

"So you've had sex," Mr. Douglas says. "Didn't we just talk about this, Ray? Didn't you just sit there a few weeks back and promise me you weren't having sex with her and that you'd both vowed to wait for marriage?"

"Yes, sir," Ray barely said.

"You're a lying piece of shit, Son. I'll never trust another damn thing you say."

This makes Ray cry harder. *God*. He's probably embarrassed to be breaking down like this in front of me. He should be. I'm embarrassed. *What the hell is his problem?*

"When did all this start? How pregnant are you?" Mr. Douglas's fiery eyes fall on me now. I'm not answering him. He's not my dad and he doesn't scare me. I stare back at him.

"Answer him, Starla," Dad demands. "I'd like to know this too."

"I don't know," I say.

"You don't know when you had sex?"

"I don't know how pregnant I am." I look at dad. "I just found out Saturday."

"Well," Dad starts, "when did you guys do it?"

I shrug and return to the wood grain maze.

"It was only a few times," Ray lies.

Now my dad stands. I can feel anger radiating from him. He stares at Ray's lowered head. "Only a few times? Do you think that justifies it? It's okay because it was only a few times? Are you so damn stupid that you don't realize it only takes *one* time?"

Mr. Douglas grabs Ray by the hair and jerks his head back. "Look at him when he's talking to you. And answer him."

Ray's face is red splotched and tear stained, and I'm overcome with the need to go to him and be comforting. I push my chair back but think better of it.

"No, sir." Ray's voice is strained. "It's not okay."

My dad stares at him while I readjust the blanket to cover the length of my body. "What about you? Did you think it was okay? Why didn't you guys use protection?"

I look up and realize everyone's looking at me. I shrug.

"Don't you have anything to say?" Dad asks. "You're as responsible as he is for this mess."

"We didn't think we needed to," I say.

"Needed to what?"

"Protection."

"Why not?" Mr. Douglas asks.

"Because, like, well, we were never with anyone else."

My dad chuckles and looks at Mr. Douglas. "They are that stupid."

"Apparently," Mr. Douglas says.

I steal a glance at Ray's mom. That must be where he got his crying gene. Silent tears roll down her cheeks. I feel bad for her, but it fades when Mr. Douglas's backhand hits Ray in the face.

Ray falls off the chair, letting out a cry of pain. Mrs. Douglas stands, lets out a gasp. Dad stands back. I stare at the table.

"Get up here like the man you are now, Raymond!" his dad yells. I can't look as Ray struggles to get to his feet. He grabs the back of the chair, but his dad pushes it away. "You stand here. You look Mike in the eye and apologize for what you did."

Ray is struggling to find any spark of composure. He's not a man, he's sixteen. I don't want him to be a man. I want him to be my Ray; my sixteen-year-old boyfriend. I just want to be a kid. We're *so* not ready for adulthood, let alone a baby.

"Sorry," Ray says softly.

"Try again. Address him properly. And state what you're sorry for," Mr. Douglas yells.

It takes him several long moments, but he gives it another try. "I'm sorry, Mr. Hollis. For getting Star pregnant." His voice starts strong but wanes at the end.

"That's not all you're sorry for, Son. Go on."

Ray swallows hard. "I'm sorry, Mr. Hollis, that I had unprotected sex with her."

"With whom?" his dad asks.

"With Star, sir."

Mrs. Douglas sits again. My dad nods once at Ray and also sits, along with Mr. Douglas. Ray doesn't move, tears still falling from his eyes. He's shaking.

"Have you guys discussed what you plan to do now?" Mrs. Douglas asks quietly.

I wait for Ray to say something, but he doesn't. So I say, "Yeah. But we aren't sure."

"Well," Mr. Douglas starts, "Abortion is out of the question."

Dad nods. "I agree."

Part of me feels relieved. Part of me doesn't.

Dad continues, "I don't think they're ready to raise a baby."

"Well, no," Ray's dad says. "Not if they're stupid enough to get pregnant in the first damn place." He looks at his son. "Dumbass. I really thought better of you. This is over the top, Raymond."

It's pissing me off how hard he's being on Ray, like this is all his fault and his fault alone. "It was my idea," I say.

"What was your idea?" Dad asks.

"To do it."

"To get pregnant?"

"No. The s-e-x."

"The s-e-x? Did you just spell it?" Dad is staring at me with eyes that are telling me I should've just kept my mouth shut. "You can do it, but you can't say it?"

"That doesn't matter," Mr. Douglas starts, "though I'm fairly sure you're just trying to save your stupid ass boyfriend. Even if it was your idea, which I'm sure it wasn't, Ray is two years older than you. He should know better." He looks at his son, still standing paralyzed next to him. "He does know better, don't you, Ray?"

"Yes, sir."

"So what do we do now? She needs to go to the doctor, right?" Mr. Douglas and Dad look to Mrs. Douglas.

"Um, yes. She needs to go in to be examined and find out when she's due." Her soft eyes find me. "When was your last period, hon?"

"Um, in July," I lie. I'm afraid if I tell them the truth it will just open season for a whole new round of screaming.

Mrs. Douglas nods. "Okay, so you're not very far along." She looks at my dad. "What about health insurance?"

"She has a public aid card. I can't afford health insurance for the kids."

She smiles softly. "I'll call my doctor and see if they accept that. I've been going there a long time, so maybe if I explain…. At any rate, if we find an adoptive family relatively soon, they'll probably pay for the prenatal care."

"And do you know of somewhere to call about that?" Dad wants to know.

"Yes. I know of a couple different ones."

"Um," Ray sputters. We all look at him. "Don't we get a say? Me and Star? I mean, it *is* our baby."

My heart swells. Standing there red faced, acting like a man, has apparently caused him to grow some balls. I'm impressed, and so furiously in love.

But why is he saying that?

His dad stands, looks him dead in the eye. "Are you kidding me? You got a lot of nerve, boy. Do you think you're actually capable of raising a kid? How? On your seventy dollar a week paycheck from Taco Bell?"

Ray doesn't back down. "I was hoping you and Mom could help, you know, until we finish school and get jobs...."

His dad shoves him back. "You're stupider than I thought. How the hell did I end up with such an ignorant ass son?"

"Dad, I'm not stupid. Me and Star, we have rights."

"The only right you have is to shut the hell up." He brings his face so close to Ray's that I'm sure Ray can taste his spit. "This baby is going to people who are mature enough to raise a child. You'll never see it, never hold it, never even know if it's a boy or a girl. You got that?"

Ray is shaking again. *God, his dad is so mean.* I'm lucky, I guess. I've hardly gotten yelled at. Guess they don't believe I'm the vamp who caused Ray's little s-e-x, uh, sex, addiction. I'm just the one housing the unfortunate side effects of premarital s-e-x.

Ray

When Star left with her dad, I wasn't allowed to give her a goodbye kiss or hug. I called out that I loved her, and she called out the same. I watched them get in her dad's Durango and turned to face the music.

Unfortunately, the song my dad played was an asswhooping in the den. Now I have a black eye, a busted lip, and probably a broken rib. Mom just checked on me, probably to make sure I'm still alive.

Living in this house, I have no rights. Or phone, laptop, or car. Grounded until I'm twenty-one, they say, sequestered to riding the bus the rest of high school.

Oh, and let's not forget.
Forbidden to have any contact with Star.

Well, Dad, I got news for you:
   Okay, I really don't. Other than I will still see her at school.
                       They can't prevent that. Can they?

Sunshine

Orion must feel sorry for me because we've been playing Xbox since we got back from our disaster at TGIFriday's. I don't remember the last time he was this nice to me. It's actually going well and I'm having an enjoyable time. I haven't thought about Austin, my mom thinking I'm Skylar, my fat rolls, or my slices in, like, at least twenty minutes.

After I stocked up on XL Sterile Gauze Pads and medical tape at Walmart, I doctored my slices in the bathroom. When we got home, I changed out of the jeans and t-shirt I'd been in and removed the bandages. They need to air out so they can scab. I put on a sundress, one that's fitted on the top but loose and flowy on the bottom.

"That looks good on you," Orion said.

I took it with a grain of salt. For one, he's my brother. And he's probably trying to make me feel better after dragging me out to see Mom.

"Boo-yah!" he yells. "Kicked your butt again!"

"Whatever," I say with a laugh. "I let you win."

"You wish!" He shifts his weight on the floor. "Play again?"

"Sure," I say. Before he can reset the game, though, we hear the front door open downstairs.

"No," Dad says firmly. "Both of you. Sit on that couch. Now." Orion and I exchange a glance and jump up to go see who's in trouble. As we're leaving the room, Dad yells, "Sunny! Are you up there?"

"Yeah," I call out. We start down the steps.

"Get down here. Now."

What did I do? I glance at O and he shrugs. In the living room, we find Sky and Star sitting on opposite ends of the couch. Dad is in the kitchen pushing buttons on the microwave. I follow Orion around to the front of the couch. I gasp when I see Sky. Her eyes are bloodshot and her whole face is red, bruises starting around her eyes.

"What happened to you?" Orion asks.

"Your older, more responsible sister," Dad says as he comes into the room, "was in a car accident with her *boyfriend*."

Austin comes to mind, and I take a step back. "Boyfriend?"

"Yeah," Dad says. "Jake Morris? Maybe you know him?"

Whoa. What? "Mr. Morris? Melissa's brother?"

"That's him."

"Wow." I look at Orion, who's looking at Sky, who's looking at her fingernails.

"And your little baby sister," Dad goes on, "is knocked up."

My eyes go wide, but really, it's not all that surprising. "Really?" I look at Star. She's shooting daggers at Sky, not that Sky notices. The microwave beeps and Dad goes back to the kitchen.

"You're pregnant?" Orion whispers.

Star shoots him the evilest look she can muster.

"I'm gonna kill him." He's still whispering as he glances into the kitchen. "You know that, right? He's dead."

She huffs. "Yeah, sure. If his parents don't kill him first."

"Star! No talking." Dad comes to the doorway. "Come here, Sunny." I follow Dad into the kitchen. "Sit down."

"Why?" I'm drawing a blank as to what I've done wrong. Lost my phone?

"Sit down." His tone tells me I better just do what I'm told, so I sit. He slides a TV dinner in front of me. "Start eating."

"What?"

"You heard me. Eat."

I stare at the food (if you can call it that) in front of me. Looks like some deep-fried, sauce coated chicken, some instant mashed potatoes, corn, and...is that a brownie? No freaking way am I eating any of this. "No. This is disgusting."

"You will sit there and eat every bite, Sunshine."

Orion is standing in the doorway. I shoot him a desperate look.

"Dad, we ate out earlier."

"Yeah, and from what I hear, she probably puked it up after she ate it. Right, Sunny?"

I shake my head. It doesn't matter who told Dad; he knows. And he is pissed. He thinks the solution is to make me eat this fattening mess. "What makes you think I wouldn't throw this up?"

"Because I will be on you all night. When you go to the bathroom, I'll be right there outside the door."

That's okay. I can lock it and he won't be able to stop me. Whatever. I'm not eating it, so it doesn't matter. "What does it matter if I throw up? Star's pregnant!"

"I've dealt with Star. Now I'm on to you."

"What's the big deal? So I want to lose a little weight. Who's that hurting?"

"Sunny, I bust my ass every damn day so you guys can have food on the table. Then I come to find out that you're *wasting* everything you eat. My hard-earned money literally being flushed down the toilet."

"Dad," I start. "We get food stamps. It's not your money."

Probably not the right thing to say. He slams his fist on the table and yells, "Start putting that food in your mouth before I come over there and feed you like the baby you are!"

I stare at him, tears spilling from my eyes. My dad usually keeps a pretty even temper, so I'm kinda taken aback. Plus, I don't want to be fed like a baby. I pick up the fork and go for the least harmful thing: Corn. I put one kernel in my mouth, squish it between my teeth, and feel the starch coating my insides.

"That's not a bite." Dad takes the fork and cuts the chicken in half. He spears one half and shoves it at my lips. "That's a bite."

I shrink away and look at Orion. He looks as freaked out as I feel.

"Open your mouth, Sunny!" Dad yells.

"No," I say through clenched teeth.

"Dad," O says finally. "Don't do this."

Sky comes up behind him. "She needs help. Like professional help. If you make her eat that, her body will reject it anyway. She's been eating like this too long."

"Well," Dad says, "maybe if you guys would've spoken up sooner about this, it wouldn't be so out of hand!" He shoves the fork at me again. "Eat it!"

"Sky's right," Orion says. "And so are you. We should have said something." He looks at me. "Sorry, Sunny, but I have to." And I know what he has to do. "She cuts herself too. On her legs. They're all cut up."

Dad looks at him and falls back into his chair. "Cuts herself?" His eyes shift in my direction, the fork still in his hand. "You cut yourself? Like, to die?"

My silent tears are no answer, and I don't think I know what to say anyway. I don't have any secrets. Everyone knows everything.

"No, like, self-mutilation, Dad," Sky says. "She needs help, not food shoved down her throat."

Dad looks from me, to Sky, to Orion. "I'm an idiot. I thought I had some good kids. What I have is four out of control disasters." He huffs and shakes his head. "Well, regardless, I need your phone, Sunny."

"I lost it."

"Fine. I'll just have it shut off." He stands up, tosses the fork onto the TV dinner tray. "All four of you are grounded until further notice. No phones, no Internet, no going out, nobody over. No Ray. No Jake, or whatever you want to call him. No drinking, no pot smoking." He looks at me. "No knives."

As if a knife would really work.

"Now eat that food while I Google places to take you for help."

"What about Star? Don't you need to Google something for her?" I ask.

"Mind your own business, freak!" Star calls from the living room.

"Ray's mom has that under control," Dad says.

I look at Orion and Skylar as Dad leaves the room to get the laptop. I back away from the table and creep behind them, through the living room, and out the front door.

I ran at first, but when I realize no one is following me I slow to a walk and start cutting through yards. I don't have far to go. And it's the last place anyone will think to look for me. Austin only lives a few blocks away in a little ranch-style house with his mom and younger sister. I arrive there within five minutes and knock on the door.

He opens it and smiles. It makes me feel lighter. "Hey," he says. "Here for your phone?" I nod, even though that's not why I'm here. "Come in. It's in my room."

I follow him through the house, saying hi to his sister Sierra as I pass her in the living room. His room is little and dimly lit by the video game paused on the TV. A twin mattress lies on the floor, along with clothes, books, and video games.

"Sorry. It's a mess in here," he says. He sits on his bed and fishes in his backpack for a moment before pulling out my phone. "Figured I'd see you at school tomorrow."

"Thanks," I say as I take it.

He smiles and stands back up. "No problem. It was just lying there on the floorboard."

I nod and open my mouth to thank him again, but I change my mind and shut it again.

"What?"

I shake my head.

"No. You were gonna say something, Sunny."

I frown. "It was nothing. Thanks, again," I say holding the phone up.

"Aren't you gonna see if you have any missed calls?"

"No one ever calls me," I confess. Except family, but what good are they when they can't keep your secrets.

"Really?" he asks.

I'm so sick of secrets. So this time when I open my mouth, this is what comes out: "Austin, I love you. I really do. I know it's stupid because everyone knows you have a thing for Sky, but I don't care. I think about you all the time, like, non-stop. It kinda drives me crazy."

He's staring at me, the teasing that was in his eyes moments ago is gone. He looks serious, very serious.

"I'm gonna go," I say and start to turn away.

But he grabs me, pulls me to him, and kisses my lips. I melt in his arms and start to cry. *Cry?* Really? *Why am I crying?*

He pulls away and gazes into my eyes, sees past the tears. He reaches behind me and closes the door, leads me to his mattress on the floor. I sit on the edge and wipe my eyes. He moves behind me and wraps me in his arms, holding me, hugging me.

"I'm sorry," I whisper.

"Shh," he says as he moves my hair away from my neck and starts kissing me there. It feels so nice, much like what I'd imagined so many times before. Except this time it's real. He pulls my face toward his and now he's kissing my lips. His hand slips away from my face and falls to my chest. I don't mind, even though I am completely sober.

I have loved him so long that this is all like a dream come true.

We keep kissing, his hands exploring my upper body for a while. He feels so good. I could stay this way forever. Then his hand tugs on my dress pulling up the loose skirt of my sundress. I pull away from him and readjust my dress.

"You don't want me to?" he asks. His voice is so gentle, like rain on a spring day. "I won't do anything you don't want me to. I'll stop when you say." He kisses my neck again.

"Turn off the TV," I whisper. I'm scared, and this sounds like more than what I intended when I confessed my feelings.

He shuts the TV off, making the room almost completely dark. This is safer. I would just die if he saw my thighs. He's next to me now, guiding my body back so I'm lying on the bed. I'm not crying anymore, but I feel like I should be.

When he starts kissing me again, the trepidation fades away. I love Austin and I love that he's kissing me. Why should this be scary? I'm tired of hiding truths. If he sees the slices, then he sees them. I shouldn't be ashamed of who I am.

So, why when his hand tickles my thigh and slides under my dress do I freeze? He notices and whispers, "Do you want me to stop?"

I shake my head. "It's just...."

"I know," he says.

How does he know? Did Orion tell him already? I want to be mad, but before I can decide if I should be, the tip of Austin's finger brushes over the slices on my left leg. I jerk my leg away, but he pulls it back, rubbing over the same spot. His mouth stops moving on mine as he feels the scabby lines.

Fresh tears nip my eyes, but he resumes kissing me, his fingers moving on to a new spot- a spot that makes me forget I have things I need to hide. He starts to tug on my underwear and lifts the dress up to my hips. He stops kissing me to concentrate on trying to move my underwear, looks down at my body.

There's just enough light in his room that he can see something. It seems he forgot my underwear and the possibilities that lay ahead. He's staring. He can see my slices. The questions are in his eyes.

I tug my dress down and start to sit up. *I have to get out of here.*

He lifts it back up, stares at me, at my imperfection, at my self-destruction. I watch his face as his fingers trace over my injuries. When he looks up at me, I look away. "Why?" he asks.

Silent tears fall from my eyes. I don't have an answer for him. There's no explanation. Other than I'm a mess. Stupid mess. "You said you knew," I whisper. "Why are you looking at me like that?"

He shakes his head, lowers my dress. "I knew that you never...."

Oh, great. So he knows that I'm a virgin too. *Wonderful.* Sitting up, I hide my face with my hands. Wait. Was he going to.... If I let him? It's too much to comprehend. I need to get out of here, but I can't go home. That would be worse than this.

Recalling the drama at my house an hour ago, I look over to him. "I really don't want to go home yet and--"

"Stay as long as you need to." He moves next to me, draws me in his arms, his soft lips a siren song on my neck. "My mom works until midnight."

Austin

When she came to my house and confessed what she did,
I
was so overcome with memories that
I
didn't know what else to do.
I
had said those exact words to her sister at least once, if not more. All
I
wanted from Sky when
I
spilled my heart was for her to return the feelings, share them with me.
I
wanted her to love me.
Sunny gave me her heart and
I
wasn't sure what to do with it. So
I
did with it what
I
wanted done when
I
was the one handing out feelings.
I
don't know if that's what she wanted.
Confusion is a familiar feeling, one
I
know well. But one thing
I'm
not confused about is why there are cuts up and down her legs and across her waist. That,
I
know, is a sign that she is not right.
I
don't know if
I
made it better. Or if what we did made it so much worse.

Skylar

Orion was able to easily talk himself out of being grounded, saying he hadn't actually done anything wrong and pointed out how he'd brought to light Sunny's fetish with a blade.

I think Dad felt more than defeated. His eyes were tired and moist; the lines around them making him look older. Maybe that's why he didn't go after Sunny when she covertly slid out the door.

Then Melissa showed up. When we'd gotten back to town earlier, we'd dropped her and Jake off at our house, where Melissa took Jake home in her car. I wasn't allowed a goodbye, just a look of longing that went unreturned. Dad and I continued on down the road, snaking across town until we reached Ray's house.

When Melissa got to our house it was nearly ten o'clock. We had school in the morning and Dad had work, but that didn't stop me and Orion from sitting at the top of the stairs, straining to hear the conversation below.

"What are you guys doing?" Star asks when she comes from her bedroom, pajamas and a towel in her hand.

"Shhh," I hiss. "Listening. They're talking about you." She rolls her eyes. "Don't you want to know what he's saying?"

"I already know." She ducks into the bathroom.

I tune back into the voices downstairs. First, they talked about Sunny taking off. Melissa suggested Dad give her time to come back, seeing as she was so upset. Then we were privy to hearing about what went down at Ray's. It didn't sound like a pretty situation.

"Where were you when all that was happening?" Orion whispers.

"In the car sleeping."

He nods and we focus again.

"Well," Melissa says with a heavy sigh. I figure she's getting tired and about to leave. I'm wrong. "I talked with Jake, Mike." Her voice is gentle. "He is beside himself over all this."

"He should be." Dad's voice came out hoarse. Several seconds pass and I wonder if anything more would be said on the topic.

"He wants to talk to you," she says. "Man to man."

Dad chuckles. "I should let him talk to the cops."

My stomach lurches. *Oh, God, no.*

"Mike," Melissa says calmly. "You know, I don't want you to think I'm saying this because he's my brother, but Skylar is going to be eighteen in less than a month. I doubt the cops will do anything. All that'll happen is he'll lose his job and will probably never find another one. Not teaching at least."

"A sick freak like that doesn't need to be teaching."

"Okay, well, now I will speak because he's my brother. He is not a sick freak. He loves her. I don't doubt that one bit."

Orion looks at me, a weird look on his face. Kinda curious.

"What?" I mouth.

He shakes his head and looks away.

"Just hear him out," Melissa says.

"I don't want to hear anything he has to say."

The silence weighs heavy. I'm not even in the room and I can tell.

"He's my brother, and if our relationship has any future, then you and him are going to have to work through this, whether he and Skylar have a future or not."

"How could he sit there at your parents' house the other day and act like everything was fine? Like he wasn't screwing my daughter?"

"She told him you guys were gonna be there. He was prepared." She waits for Dad to respond. "Skylar is very mature. She carries a lot of responsibility on her shoulders. That much is obvious to me, and I just met her. Jake told me that anytime one of the other kids calls, she drops everything to do whatever they need. Mike, that's what a mom does, not a seventeen-year-old girl."

"Are you staying or going?" Dad asks with a yawn. "I am exhausted, mentally and physically." He waits for her answer. "It's been one hell of a day."

"What do you want me to do?"

"Stay."

The downstairs goes dark, and we hear footsteps padding down the hall to Dad's room. Apparently, he forgot Sunny hasn't come back. Orion and I get up and I follow him to his room.

"Dad will be lucky if he doesn't have a heart attack by the time he's forty because of you girls," O says. He sits in his beanbag chair and turns on the Xbox.

"Oh, yeah. Because you're so innocent."

"Hey," he says with a laugh, "today I am."

I can't help but laugh. Orion has seen his share of trouble, nothing ever too serious. He's been caught smoking and drinking by Dad and by Austin's mom. He's been caught having sex more than once. And there have been other rumors.

"Remember when Rachel Cotter's mom called the cops on you?" I ask.

He laughs. "What made you think of that?"

"Thinking of how you're not so innocent."

"Yeah. That was hysterical." He shakes his head. "Wonder what happened to her."

"Her parents probably sent her to a convent."

We both laugh. Rachel and Orion dated last school year when he was a sophomore, and she was a senior. The way he tells the story is that she was a little on the freaky side. And one fine Saturday afternoon, her mother and younger sister, who's a freshman with Star, came home to find Orion and Rachel in the kitchen. Let's just say they weren't cooking. Her mom freaked out, covered the younger sister's eyes. Orion says he got dressed and took off. An hour later cops were at our house looking for him. Nothing more ever came of it. Well, except the rumor that Rachel got pregnant. But it was just a rumor, I guess.

Star comes into the room, her hair wet. She sits next to me on the bed. "What's Rachel Cotter's sister's name?" I ask her.

"Emily."

"Yeah. Emily. Do they still live here?"

"Yeah. Why?"

"We were just talking about how Orion never does anything wrong."

She laughs. "Okay. Sure."

We stare at the TV screen, watch O annihilate some zombies. "So, Star," O says. "You're pregnant?"

"I guess."

"And you're going with adoption?"

"That's what they tell me," she says with a sigh.

"That's good, I guess. I really wouldn't want my niece or nephew to grow up without a father." He jerks his controller to the left. "We know what it's like to have only one parent and it sucks."

"Ray wouldn't ditch me."

Orion shakes his head. "You don't understand. I'm gonna kill him. I'm gonna wrap my hands around his pathetic little throat and choke the fucking life out of him. Okay?"

She kicks the back of his head with her little foot. "Oh, but you don't care about Sky and Mr. Morris, or about Sunny messing around with Austin? Why don't you kill them too?"

He pauses his game. "Sky is a big girl. If she wants to make a big ass mistake like screwing her teacher, that's on her. And Mr...er, Jake, he's a grown man. If he wants to spend the next five or so years in jail, well, that's fine by me. And nothing happened between Sunny and Austin. She might *wish* something happened, but it didn't."

"That's not what she said," Star says. "You might need to check your best friend, Orion, because he's lying to you."

"Austin wouldn't lie to me. Sunny probably lied to you to try and make herself look less pathetic."

Star and I exchange a look as I contemplate the likeliness of this. Orion's phone is on the floor beside him. I grab it and say, "Let's just text him and see what he says."

"Go for it," he says.

I text: *Hey. It's Skylar.* And I wait.

After a while, Orion asks, "What'd he say?"

I look at the phone. "He hasn't answered me."

"I'm going to bed," Star says. "I know Sunny's telling the truth." She walks out of the room, only to return a moment later. "She's here, laying in her bed sound asleep."

"I didn't even hear her come in," I say.

"Should I let Dad know?" she asks.

I shake my head and lay back on the bed with the cell phone still in my hand. My body is feeling stiff. "If he cared, he'd still be up."

Once again, I stayed up to make sure everything was safe and sound, even though I was the one almost killed in a car accident earlier.

Once again, I'm playing mom while Dad's downstairs screwing my boyfriend's sister.

If he's even still my boyfriend. This might be too much for him. We thought we were prepared for being discovered, but now, faced with the reality of it, it may be too much for him. He might want to call it quits. At least until I graduate.

I make myself as comfortable as I can and the phone vibrates. It's Austin: *Yeah??*

Heyy. What u doin??

Goin to bed.

Same. I say. *Hey, what's with you and sunny?*

His answer takes a long time to come. Maybe he's changing his clothes or something. *Why do u want to know.*

O wants to know. It's not a complete lie.

Nothing

Really??

Really

K.

I don't completely buy his answer. I think he's trying to hide something from Orion. Besides, well, let's just see what happens.

Me: *Heyy. Still there?*

Ya

I just want to say sorry

Long wait. *For what*

For how things ended

Long wait. *It's all good*

Me: *It's not. I'm sorry*

No answer.

Do you forgive me?

Him: *Sure*

Me: *Do u still think about me??*

Long wait. *Why u askin?*

I been thinkin about u and kinda miss us

Why u textn on o's phone?

Grounded

For what?

Now I pause. Will Orion tell him the truth? I answer: *Got in car accident. Dad's pissed.*

R u ok?

Sure

K

I'm done texting him. He's not confessing anything. And I've said just enough to get inside his head.

There's one last text he sends: *Honestly I don't want to hurt your feelings but I don't really want to talk to you right now.*

Orion

The only boy with three sisters comes with great responsibility.
        To protect and serve.
Fourteen is too young for sex, not to mention childbearing.
        (not that I have room to talk)
Just maybe I should've been more observant, offered Ray some
        protection
Because now there's a good chance I'm gonna have to
        serve
                some hard time.

Sunshine

We spot the rusted truck on the way to school, pulled haphazardly to the side of the road. Austin is standing in front of it, the hood open.

"Stop," Orion instructs Sky.

"Fuck that."

"Don't be a bitch. Just stop." He eyes me in the backseat. "She's just pissed because he blew her off last night."

She glares at him as she pulls to the side of the road. "I am not."

My heart made a home in my throat. "Blew her off?"

He sneers at Sky. "She was texting him on my phone wanting to know what happened between you guys."

"At the party?" I try to swallow, but my throat is too thick.

Orion opens the car door. "Need a ride, loser?"

Sky watches me in the rearview mirror. "Don't listen to him, Sunny."

Orion tosses his phone into the backseat. "See for yourself."

"Okay, really, Orion?" Sky turns around. "You guys all know that there's nothing between me and Austin. I have Jake now."

I read through the text stream as Austin approaches the car. "Then why did you tell him you miss him?"

Austin opens the back door, Star scoots closer to me. "Thanks for stopping. I'm about to burn that piece of shit."

I toss O's phone back to him and look past my pregnant baby sister to the boy I love. His eyes are on me, and I smile. He smiles back.

In his last text, he totally blew her off. That's why I'm smiling.

That and, well, because the fact that he's looking at me with his smile and I'm easily and eagerly offering him mine has me believing that last night wasn't about nothing.

Who knew I ever had a chance?

Who knew if I pulled down the iron curtain and let someone cut the red tape that I could feel, *dare I say, happy?*

"What's wrong with it now?" Orion asks.

"Not totally sure. Fuel pump maybe." His baby blues are devouring my heart.

"I'd help you tonight, man, but I gotta work."

"Why do I feel like I'm in the middle of something?" Star asks.

Orion turns around. I narrow my eyes at him. His gaze shifts to Star. "Must be a side effect of being knocked up."

"What?" Austin guffaws.

O gets comfy in the passenger seat as we pull up to the school. "Oh, yeah. Dude's going down."

"Shut up, O." Star kicks the back of his seat. "Just leave him alone. It's not just his fault."

"Yeah, I'm so sure the fucker was all like, *no, Star, I really don't think we should.*" Everyone laughs, even me. Except Star, she's definitely not laughing. "Did his dumb ass even have enough sense to pull out?"

Sky pulls into the student parking lot as I focus on Austin again. He gives me his lopsided grin as he flips his cigarette butt out the window and I knew, just absolutely *knew*, this was going to be the greatest day of my life.

I walk slowly toward the school, waiting, hoping, and yep, sure enough, Austin shrugs off from Orion and falls into step next to me. "Hey," he says.

"Hey."

"How are you?"

I want to be all *OMG this is the best day of my life*, but instead, "Fine. You?"

He shoves his hands in his pockets. "Well, my truck's dead on the side of the highway, so it's been a crappy morning. But I had a good weekend. And last night was really good."

I giggle. I didn't even know I could giggle. "Really?"

"Yeah, you?"

"Me?"

"Did you have a good night last night?"

I nod and look at my shoes. "I suppose I did." When I look back at him, his eyes are still on me.

He smiles wide and looks away. "Who knew?"

"What?"

"Nothing." He shakes his head. "After I fix my truck, can I pick you up?"

"Pick me up?"

"At your house? O will be at work."

My smile fades. Back to reality. Back to where my brother will flip his shit if he knows what happened. Back to where my older sister will flip her shit if she knows what happened. "I hate secrets."

He nods. "Me too." We step into the school, drowning in a sea of familiarity, and stop, standing face to face, and oh-so-close. Close enough that I can't help but hope he kisses me. "We can talk about it tonight. I'll text you."

I groan. "My dad took my phone. And I'm grounded." I don't mention that Dad said something about intense counseling for 'people like me' and maybe even a lengthy stay at a place for 'people like me'.

"Maybe I'll just show up and see what happens." He cocks his head to the side, diamonds glittering in his eyes.

"Works for me. You know how my dad is."

He reaches out and electrocutes me with his touch. "I want to kiss you."

My cheeks catch on fire, and I look down, smiling bigger than I ever thought I could smile. He drops his hand and steps back.

"I'll see you later."

I watch him go, leaving me standing there like a love-struck statue in the hall. And when he looks back at me, I know. I know this is the beginning of something.

What I don't know is why, when my feet began to function again, they lead me to the bathroom, where, of course, I perch over the toilet and gag nothing into the porcelain.

When I step out of the stall, Haley Johnston is there, a knowing look on her face.

Austin

No regrets.
Not at all.
And it meant something.
                        Not just to her, but to me too.
                        She's the kinda girl that guys like me
                              only wish they could get.
Off limits is what she should be.
You'd think I would've learned a
lesson or two after dating O's other
sis, but no, guess not.
                        I can look past the slices
                        that decorate her otherwise
                                 perfect body.
I can play along when she
counts her calories
and checks the time.
                  Can't I?
          How hard could it really be?
             It's not like she's crazy.

        Besides, any girl who lets me
           be her first deserves a
            fair shot at something.

Starla

Ray wears a few black eyes and a busted lip to school on Tuesday. He looks like a lost little boy when he spots me from his position in front of my locker. It takes every iota of strength inside me and this fetus not to roll my eyes at the sorry sight waiting for me.

"You got a story?" I ask him.

"A story? For what?"

"For why you look like your dad tried to murder you yesterday."

He looks past me. "Not really."

I follow his eyes. Orion is down the hall glaring in our direction. He's running his index finger along his throat, a threat of certain death. "Oh, yeah. O plans to kill you."

Ray sighs, looks down at me. "That's not necessarily a bad thing."

I close my locker. "Yeah, being dead is better than being a dad." I shake my head. "Jesus, Ray, fucking grow a pair."

What a joke. I leave him standing there, knees shaking and all, and head to my first educational experience of the day. It takes a good five minutes before I feel bad for what I said, but I can't text him because, of course, I don't have my phone.

Dad jumped off the deep end last night. I mean, well, he barely stuck a toe in the shallow end compared to Ray's dad, but still. It's only once in a blue moon that Dad implements a punishment. And even when he does, it only lasts a day or so. Seems serious this time. Like all us kids had secrets that were unveiled at once (thanks Skylar), throwing Dad into parenting with hurricane force.

I don't see Ray again until lunch. He's waiting for me by the door of the cafeteria. "I got called to the guidance office second period," he says as we fall into the lunch line. Today, the school cafeteria features a delectable selection of pizza or chicken sandwiches.

"Why?" I let the hairnet wearing lady with the mole on her chin slide a slice of grease on my tray.

"They wanted to know what happened to me." He looks back at me. "Should you eat that?"

I roll my eyes. "What'd you tell them?"

We're standing at the cashier now, Ray dolling out cash, while I flash my free lunch card and swipe some extra napkins. I follow him to a table towards the back of the cafeteria, seeing Orion shoot daggers at us the whole way.

"What'd you tell them?" I ask again after we sit.

"The truth," he says as I pile napkins on top of my slice to soak up the pools of grease.

I don't look up. I'm making sure I have every last drop of the slick liquid off the so-called food. "Really? What'd they say?" There's a mound of orange-tinged napkins next to my tray now. "Did you tell them about me?"

"No, I didn't say anything," he starts. "Star."

I look up at him, and behind the swelling and the bruises I see my Ray. But I have to look away because I can't stand to see him like this. It hurts me that I was a piece of the puzzle that, when complete, made him look like this.

"I really think my ribs are broken." His voice cracks even though he's barely audible to me. I look into his eyes. "I probably need to see a doctor." He looks down at his own oil-slicked pizza. "I told them the truth." His eyes find mine again, and I swear to God, if this dude starts crying. "They called DCFS. And they'll probably call the cops."

I narrow my eyes, way too familiar with child services. I can't even count how many times they've shown up at our house for stupid things like Orion playing basketball in the street or our house being too dirty. "Why would they call DCFS?"

He shrugs. "He said they're required to. I'm a minor. It's child abuse."

What else am I supposed to do? I laugh. I snort. I laugh some more because I snorted. Ray actually smiles. "This. Is. Hysterical."

He shakes his head. "It's really not."

I lean forward. "They're saying you're a child, but yet you are able to make a child."

He glances around. "Even so, I'm sixteen. I'm still a minor and it's illegal, what my dad did."

I smile and shake my head. "This is ridiculous." He really needs to grow a pair. "You're pissed at your dad. That's why you told."

"Yeah, Star, I'm pissed. I mean, look at me! You think this is okay?"

"No, I'm not saying this is okay. What I'm saying is maybe it's time you grow up a little."

He shakes his head. "You know, I'm kinda getting pissed at you."

"Nice." I shove my tray of inedible trash across the table. It hits his. He shoves it back. "I suppose this is all my fault."

He sits back in his chair, crosses his arms over his chest. "It's just as much your fault as it is mine."

I nod. "Sure is. Damn. Guess the next time I plan to get knocked up at fourteen, I need to make sure I get someone who has picked up his man-card already."

"Ray, got a minute?"

We look up to see Orion standing over us. "No, O. Sorry," Ray says "I'm kinda in the middle of something right now."

"I really don't give a fuck."

Ray looks at me; I shrug. "Really, Star?"

I look at Orion, see the menacing look on his face. As I open my mouth to suggest an alternate meeting locale and time, Ray rises, standing face to face with my big bro.

A hush washes through the cafeteria at our small school. All eyes are on Ray and Orion. I can hear people muttering, saying O already kicked his ass once over the weekend.

"What's done is done," I hear Ray say. "If I could undo it, I would in a heartbeat."

"Too bad you can't, huh?"

"I really don't think you have room to talk. I mean, have you seen Rachel Cotter's baby?"

Yeah, probably not the right thing to say to Orion. I stand to get between them, but my reaction time is a little too late. Orion shoves Ray backwards. Ray reacts and comes back toward Orion.

Fists start flying. I back away, stopping when a wall touches my back. Sliding down its cold concrete, I watch my bro take the upper hand. Ray is on the ground, barely defending himself at this point.

Broken ribs. *Stop*, I say in my head. *Stop. Stop. Stop. Stop.*

Ray

Breathe in   Out

               In   out

Don't go to sleep.

               What feels so warm covering my face?

               In   out

Well, Star said he was planning my demise.

               Didn't think she meant literally.

               In   out

Skylar

"Are there papers I have to complete to drop out, or do I just stop coming?"

The guidance counselor looks at me through his thick glasses. "Why do you want to drop out, Skylar?"

"Oh, I'm gonna get my GED and start college in January."

"You can't do the GED until your class graduates." He frowns. "I don't understand why you need to drop out. You're a senior, you have decent grades." He crinkles his brow. "Is there something going on at home?"

I shrug and let out a sigh. "Well, I don't really want to say anything, but yes."

He raises his eyebrows. "Your dad will have to sign the papers too."

Well, that'll never happen. "He does? What if I'm eighteen?"

"Are you eighteen?"

"I will be in a few weeks."

He's giving me a hard look, trying to make me uncomfortable. Trying to make me cave. He mustn't have any idea how strong I am. "Let's set up a time to talk, Skylar. Figure out what your options are."

I cock my head to the side and smile. "I know what my options are. I'm not choosing the one that keeps me locked up in this hell for the next one-hundred-seventy-eight days."

"How about tomorrow? What's your free period?"

"Mr. Brookfield?" I turn to see a panicked woman standing in the doorway. "You're help is needed in the cafeteria." She glances at me. "There's a fight."

There is something, in the briefest moment of eye contact the woman gives me, telling me to get to the cafeteria too.

When I get there, the fight is over, but the evidence is still present. Ray is lying on the floor, not moving, two teachers kneeling over him. Orion is cornered by several staff, pacing, running his hands through his hair.

Scanning the room, I spot Star, sitting with her back against the wall near Ray, looking pale and scared. I start towards her, glancing around for Sunny, and run smack into Jake.

"Excuse me." His tone is hasty, and our eyes meet. "Sky." He shines a half-smile and starts to walk away.

"Mr. Morris."

He pauses, looks briefly at me, and then glances nervously around.

"Don't. Just get out of here."

"What?"

I raise my eyebrows while I walk away, still seeing Jake surveying the scene. Orion has stopped pacing. His angry eyes have set their sights on me and Jake. My heart thumps in my chest, I'm so freaked out, and as I get closer to Ray, all I see is blood. His face isn't even his. If it weren't for his blond hair, I'd think it were someone else.

Sitting next to Star, I reach out to her, but she pulls away. "Hey," I say softly.

"Is he dead?"

I stare at Ray's body and wonder the same thing. He hasn't moved. I've never seen a dead body before, and neither has Star. How much would it suck for her if her brother just killed her boyfriend and the father of her unborn baby?

Tears nip at my eyes. I cover my mouth. And then I see it.

"He's breathing," Star says. "I see his chest moving."

That's not what I see. I see Sunny near the cafeteria door, Austin beside her. His arm is around her.

Sure, she looks distressed, her hand covering her mouth. And yeah, we've known Austin forever. So what if he's our bro's bestie. He's not supposed to be *hers*.

"Ok, everyone out!" The principal's voice booms through the silent cafeteria like a bomb. "Go to the gym until the bell." No one moves, so he adds a resounding, "Now!"

Bodies scurry from the cafeteria. Sunny and Austin are gone. O is leaning against a wall, his eyes closed. I start to stand so I can go talk to him, but Star touches my arm.

"When I was a baby, did I cry a lot?"

"What?"

"It's like, I feel like I want to cry, but I never do." She looks at me. "I don't remember ever crying."

The principal stalks our way. "You two, go."

I open my mouth to argue, but Star speaks first. "Is he dead?"

His brow furrows. "What?"

"Ray? Is he dead?"

My eyes find Orion. He's watching us. Can he hear Star? Can he hear what she's asking? Does he realize how much this hurts her?

"No, hon," the principal says. He's new this year. Doesn't know our family. "You girls need to go to the gym."

"Did you call an ambulance?"

"Yes, an ambulance is on its way."

"Can I please stay?" Star is pleading, begging, like a five-year-old wanting a cookie, not a pregnant fourteen-year-old with a half-dead baby daddy. "He's my boyfriend."

The principal frowns and starts to tell her no, but I speak up. With a nod in O's direction, I say, "And he's our brother."

"You're sisters?" I nod. "And he's your brother?" I nod again. He focuses on us. "What happened to you?"

"What?"

"Your face. You're bruised."

Damn. I keep forgetting about that. "I was in a car accident yesterday." No sooner than I say it do I wonder if he knows Jake was in a car accident yesterday too.

He nods. "I'm sorry, but you'll need to go to the gym."

Jake

Fight, fight I hear from down the hall.
As a dutiful teacher, I take off that way, never imagining I would see what I did.
Orion, the semi-decent kid brother of my love, has all but disfigured some kid on the floor.
What I don't know, and why I didn't get Sky's warning, was that it was Ray Douglas laying there bloodied.
Did Sky think Orion would do that to me?
Did she think I couldn't defend myself in a fight against her little bro?
The real question is:
>Would I
>Jeopardize our relationship?
>Melissa's relationship with their dad?
>Risk jail time for hitting a minor?

Oh, who cares? I am one wrong move away from the end of my life as I know it anyway.

Sunshine

I have the house to myself after school. Sky barely slowed down for me to jump out of the backseat, in a hurry to get a solemn Star to the hospital to assess if Ray is still capable of breathing.

"Dad's still at the police station," Sky told us. "It's not looking good."

"How'd you get O's phone?" I asked.

"He gave it to Jake before he left."

I always knew there'd be a day when I'd watch my brother get hauled away like a common criminal. But I never banked on my older sister hooking up with her teacher, or my little sister harboring an unborn child in her womb.

When considering all that, I don't see why Dad gives a crap about me and my self-destruction. I mean, who really cares? So what if I need to release some stress with a razor, or diet with my finger down my throat? Dad never noticed anything I did before, but this is what he wants to make a grand production out of? Where was the hoopla when I was voted class president? What's my reward for never ever never getting even a B?

'People like me' blend into the wallpaper until they don't.

'People like me' aren't the pride and joy until they're really not.

'People like me' know they'll never be good enough for themselves.

'People like me' try to be the best someone else they can be.

'People like me' don't even know who they are.

I watch the blood glisten on the edge of the blade as it glides across my arm. Note the time: 3:44 p.m. That hurt more than I expected, but I needed a new place. No more sleeveless shirts for me.

One. Two. Three. Four.

They are even. Perfect. So the opposite of what I am.

When the four slices are in place, I wipe my life from the razor and hide it away. It's nearly four o'clock, and I seem to recall that a certain boy (!) is due to be here soon. I fan the slices, urging them to dry.

Nearly an hour and a purge later, when I had pretty much decided Austin wasn't coming over and am debating if it's time to slice my other arm, I hear his truck pull up the street. My empty stomach tightens up.

All day, every time my mind had a free moment, I remembered (last night, him, me, so close, so connected, so something, so I can't believe that really happened, so what I'm not a virgin anymore). And my stomach would get this tight feeling. I'd stop breathing and close my eyes, taking myself back there (was it heaven? or the highway to hell? maybe bliss-land, maybe not).

I feel that and so much more now knowing he's going to smile for me in

Four

Three

Two

One

"Hey," his smile says as he walks in. "Turns out I was just out of gas." He holds up his hands. "I'm gonna...."

I watch him go to the kitchen, hear the sounds of him washing, and smell the roses.

"Any word on O?" he calls out.

"No," I say as he comes back to the living room. "Sky said Dad was at the police station and it wasn't going well."

He nods. "Is anyone here?"

I shake my head. "Sky took Star to the hospital."

"I never saw O lose it like that." Austin sits beside me on the couch (not that I left him any choice- I sat in the middle). "It was like he was possessed." His baby blues look me up and down. "Did you change your clothes?"

I nod.

He leans towards me, his lips pulling me into him. Lips, tongue, the whole full-on kissing experience lasts for about 15.4 seconds (so what if I counted). "I have been waiting all day to do that."

My newly obtained giggle escapes, and I feel heat in my cheeks.

Turning his body, he faces me. "What do you think is going to happen?"

"With what?"

"O. And Ray. I mean, he looked really bad."

"I don't know." I shrug. "Where's your phone? Sky has O's phone. She'll probably know something about Ray by now."

His eyes light up and my heart goes dim. He digs his phone from his pocket.

"Orion showed me the texts she sent you last night." I say it so softly that I wonder if he hears me.

"Yeah, that was weird. Totally caught me off guard." He meets my eyes. "What's your dad's number?"

Calmness washes over me as I tell him the digits.

He's holding the phone to his ear. "Hey, Mike, it's Austin. I stopped by and Sunny's the only one here. We're both wondering what's going on."

I watch him nod and say uh-huh and okay for a few minutes. My mind is blown that he called Dad instead of Sky. But I guess he cares more about what happens to Orion than Ray.

He hangs up. "They're not letting him leave. He's being charged with battery and has to stay at least until he sees a judge."

I raise my eyebrows. "Wow. This is serious."

Austin looks at his phone. "Your dad's on his way home." His eyes find mine. "Before you call Sky, what're we doing?"

I crinkle my brow. (Before *I* call Sky? He's not willing to talk to her?) "Us?"

"Oh." And then I remember. "Haley saw us this morning. In the hall."

"And?" His fingers snake into mine.

"She thinks there's something going on."

"And?" He leans forward.

"I didn't know what to tell her."

"And?" His soft lips brush mine.

I don't answer, because he's all in my face again, letting me taste his tongue and lips and his hand rubs my thigh and my entire body fills with warmth and euphoria and elation and OMG.

Austin

So, I think it's odd that on the day I decide that just maybe I will give things a try with my BFF's other sister, my BFF decides to beat the crap out of another sister's boyfriend.

I mean, well, he knows we kissed and that's about it that night we were all together, but he knows not a thing about her running away to my house last night.

About me inviting her into my room, into my bed.

About me discovering her secrets.

About me realizing that imperfection is perfection.

About me tracing her pain with my finger.

About me uncovering her soul.

About all the blood.

Starla

I tell myself I feel fear, but I really don't. I know that's what I should feel, but I don't know what it is to feel anything, really. Never did I think anyone would be so mad that I accidentally started growing a tiny human inside me.

It wasn't like I planned it. I said it was an accident. Accidents happen. *Oops*, I tripped. *Oops*, I spilled the milk. *Oops*, I'm pregnant.

What wasn't an accident was when Big Ray knocked my Ray to the floor last night. And even though I wasn't there, I'm fairly certain that the aftermath when we left wasn't an accident either. I really doubt Big Ray said *Oops* at any point last night.

Orion premeditated what he did. There was no *Oops*, sorry sis, I beat the fuck out of your boyfriend. Nothing. He didn't *accidentally* walk up to us in the cafeteria without fully intending to do exactly what he did.

Sky and I are sitting in the emergency room waiting area. They won't let us go back there. They won't tell us how he is, or if he's dead or alive. The only reason I'm sure he's here is because Ray's mom's minivan was spotted in the parking lot when we arrived. Sky finally convinced the gatekeeper to let the family know we were here.

Orion's phone rings in Sky's hand. "Hey, Dad."

I tune her out and stare out the window, contemplating a few accidents I might arrange for Orion when I get home tonight. Like revealing his stash. *Oops*. Or cutting the crotch out of all his jeans. *Oops*. Or texting Rachel Cotter from his phone. *Oops*. Or replacing his cologne with ammonia. *Oops*. Or all of the above. Double *Oops*.

"He's not coming home." Sky looks at me as if I give a shit. "He has to see a judge."

Mrs. Douglas enters the waiting room, surveying the crowd. I stand and she sees me. It's a frown she wears on her way to me. The mud that seems to always hold me back has my feet planted.

"Star." She touches my arm. "Are you okay?"

I nod and hold my breath. Sky stands beside me. "They won't tell us anything."

Mrs. Douglas nods. "He will be fine. Eventually." She takes a deep breath, looks past me, focusing on something on the other side of the window. "He's being moved to the ICU." She looks from me to Sky and then back to me again. "I should've called the police last night. Then it wouldn't be this bad."

I wonder if that qualifies as an *Oops*.

"So what's going on?" Sky inquires. "Why the ICU?"

Mrs. Douglas shakes her head, like she's trying to wake up from a bad dream. "Four broken ribs, punctured lung, three facial fractures." Her wet eyes find mine. "I'm not even sure what's from last night and what happened today."

"Orion was charged with battery," Sky informs. "He's not being released yet."

"I'm afraid he's not the only one being arrested," Mrs. Douglas says and I know she's talking about Big Ray. She wrings her hands and tries to smile. "As wrong as this sounds, I wish someone would've called DCFS or the police years ago."

I exhale. "You know?"

"Know what?"

"That Ray told?"

"I don't care who told. I'm just glad someone did." She takes my hand.

"Can I see him? Please?"

She shakes her head. "Sorry, Star, family only."

"Can't you say she's Tessa?" Sky asks.

Mrs. Douglas and I look at Sky. What an amazingly brilliant idea.

"That could work," Mrs. Douglas says. "It could." She looks toward the gatekeeper of the ER. "I've always thought you and Ray looked like you could be brother and sister." *Okay, weird.* She tugs my hand. "C'mon." I walk with her, leaving Sky behind. "Can I get a pass for my daughter?"

The gatekeeper barely looks at me before handing me a VISITOR sticker. I apply it to my chest and am home free. Next stop: Ray.

When we get to the tiny room, crammed with monitors and bags of fluids and my love, I hold my breath. I don't even think we have the right room. The person in the bed looks nothing like Ray. He looks like a, well, I don't know.

A freak? Someone completely disfigured in an accident? Someone born with a strange facial abnormality?

This is not my Ray.

But it is. And I know it is. And I feel like I'm gonna vomit.

"Ray, honey." Mrs. Douglas creeps next to the bed. "Star is here."

"She is?"

And that's his voice, little and scared and I go to be next to him and try to look past what I see on the surface and look for what I know is inside. "I'm right here," I whisper. I don't really know what to say or what to do. "How do you feel?"

"I don't, really. I might be dead."

"He's on medicine for pain," Mrs. Douglas says.

"Orion's in jail." I take his hand in mine. It's ice cold.

"For what?"

"For, well, this, I guess."

"My dad did this, Star."

I look at Mrs. Douglas. She steps closer. "Ray? What's the last thing you remember before being here?"

"Star's dad came over, Dad got mad, Star left, and now I'm here. Orion, he wasn't even there."

Ray

Her hand was so warm in mine.

    I couldn't see her with my eyes.

        I could hear her sweet little voice.

            I wished I could wrap myself around her.

                I can still catch a whiff of her if I dream.

                    I can't seem to move.

                        Breathing is tough.

                            Living is a priority.

                                I'm raising that baby.

                                    Fuck my dad.

Skylar

"What the hell is he doing here?" Austin's sorry ass excuse for a vehicle is parked in front of my house when Star and I return from visiting Ray on his not quite death bed.

"You know exactly what he's doing here," Star says. It's the first thing she's said since we left the hospital. "I told you something's going on with him and Sunny."

"I think you're wrong."

"Well, I didn't really want to say anything, but she was bleeding the day after she came home drunk." She looks my way. "I just think she doesn't remember."

I remember the blood. And her licking it from her fingers. "Or maybe she doesn't want to remember." I shudder. "Wish I could forget." We get out of the car and make our way to the front door.

"What if they did get together? I mean, would you be okay with that?"

No, I definitely would not. I'd rather have my eyeballs clawed out by a rabid cat than to see Austin with Sunny. Maybe some other girl, but not my damn sister. I mean, really? "She can do better than him."

"I agree, but she has zero self-esteem. I mean, why do you think she's anorexic?"

"Because she's nuts." I pause when I step onto the porch. "I think she's bulimic, not anorexic."

"What's the difference?"

"Bulimia is when you purge all the time. Anorexia is, like, not eating because you don't want to get fat."

Star screws up her face. "She does both."

I swing the front door open. Sunny and Austin are sitting on the couch together. Too close, but really it's not all that close. Dad is sitting in the recliner, a bottle of beer in his hand. I point at Austin. "You can leave. Orion isn't even here."

He flashes his eyes at me. "No shit."

"He'll be home tomorrow hopefully," Dad says.

"Hopefully?"

Dad closes his eyes. "What the hell did I do wrong? All four of you are fucking up your whole lives." He opens his eyes. "Didn't you learn anything from me?"

"And I'm out," Austin says. He stands, his eyes lingering on Sunny a microsecond too long.

"One kid's in jail, one's knocked up, one's screwing her teacher, and one is anorexic." Dad stands. "Sometimes I can't help but wonder if I did the right thing raising you guys alone."

Austin is staring at me. Process of elimination left no question as to which one of us is screwing her teacher, as Dad so eloquently put it.

"Dad," I say. "Really?"

He shrugs. "Oh, is it a *secret*? You afraid Austin's gonna tell everyone your secret?"

"I'm not gonna say anything," Austin says.

"Go ahead," Dad says. "Tell whoever you want. Shit, after what O pulled today, I doubt anyone would be surprised at anything my kids would do."

"Dad," I say. "Stop. It wouldn't just affect me. It'll affect him too."

"You think I give a *fuck* about some twenty-three-year-old asshole that's screwing my underage daughter?"

Austin moves toward the door. Sunny stands up and watches him with a sideways glance at Dad.

"I am barely underage," I argue. "And it's consensual."

"Whatever."

"He'll still lose his job. And then what? What good is that for me?"

Sunny creeps toward Austin. His hand is on the doorknob.

"Skylar, you'll be the next one knocked up, so you'll be fine. Welfare and government housing are right around the corner for you. At least Jake has a job. That way you'll get child support." He huffs. "More than I ever saw from your whore of a mother."

Well, now. Let's pause. Thank you, Dad, for recognizing Jake by name in front of my ex-boyfriend. But there's something else. How would he get child support from our mom if he doesn't even know where she is? For a nanosecond, I debate dwelling on this, but I don't. Why? I don't want to know if he knows where she is. I don't want to know where she is. Because I swear, if I ever saw her, I would have to utilize my skills as a professional cat fighting bitch.

The door opens, Austin slips out. Sunny darts behind him. Star lies on the couch, watching me and Dad face off.

"Aren't you gonna say anything?" I ask.

"About her leaving?" He shakes his head. "Why should I? Maybe she'll go get knocked up too."

"What is wrong with you, Dad?"

He stalks from the room, and I look at Star kicked back on the sofa, remote in hand. "I think he's losing it," she assesses.

She could be right. I sit at her feet and remember I have Orion's phone in my pocket. As I reach to pull it out, Dad reenters the room.

He drops three cell phones on the floor. "Do whatever the fuck you want. Sky, you're about to be eighteen, so start packing your bags. Star, you're having a baby. Better find a place to raise it." He looks toward the door. "And when she gets back, let her know that some inpatient treatment is in her future. And Orion? He can fucking rot in jail for all I care."

Star and I watch Dad leave the room again. She looks at me and says, "He didn't even ask how Ray was."

I give up.

No, seriously.

I give up.

Sunshine

I stare at the ceiling, feeling blissful, and replay the movie in my head. At least it seems like a movie because it cannot be real.

Austin moves around the kitchen, sending microwaves through some food, pouring some liquids. "Can I get you anything?"

"No, thank you."

He carries his plate to the table and sits beside me. "Anorexic, right?"

I can't respond. What would I ever say? Deny it and be a liar, or admit it and, well, admit it.

His eyes hold mine. "I'm not judging, just repeating what your dad said."

Feeling judged, I look away. How does he know I'm the anorexic one? Maybe I'm the ~~pregnant one, the one in jail, the one screwing her teacher~~.

Okay, yeah, I'm the anorexic one. "I don't think that's so bad compared to my siblings."

Smiling, he melts me. "Definitely not." His cell phone rings; he pulls it from his pocket, looks at it and sets it on the table. "Well, looky there. Skylar is calling me." He looks at me. "Wonder what she wants." He swipes the screen, pushes the button to put it on speaker. "Austin's answering service. How can I help you?"

I bite my lip and smile.

"Bring my sister home."

He grins. "Sorry, who's this?"

"Don't be stupid, just bring her home."

"Who exactly is your sister?"

I cover my mouth to keep from laughing. Sky doesn't see the humor in this. "Look, Austin, I don't know what the hell is going on with you two, but you just need to keep your distance from her. She needs help, and not the kind you can give her."

It's always nice to find out exactly how your sister feels about you. I reach over and press End on his phone, hanging up on my bitch of a sister.

Austin smiles at me. "Is there something I can help you with, Sunshine? Or are you beyond help?"

No one ever calls me Sunshine. No one. *Ever*. My cheeks are on fire. I surprise myself when I say, "Do you think I need help?"

And he surprises me when he says, "Only if you need help finding somewhere to put those lips."

Sky didn't stop calling. Not only did she call from her phone, but she called from Orion's and mine. Austin answered when she called from my phone, just to keep up the game. "Seriously, Sky, I don't know where she's at. She didn't come with me."

And then she showed up. When we see the headlights flash across the kitchen, Austin jets to the living room. "Sky's about to knock on the door," he tells his sister, Sierra. "No matter what, do *not* say that we are here."

"Whatever," she says.

"I will pay you," he adds.

Her smile seals the deal.

When Sky knocks on the door, Sierra answers. We stand out of sight in the hallway, his fingers intertwining with mine.

"Hey, is Austin here?"

"No, he's not."

"Um, well, his truck is here. So I'm guessing he's hiding from me."

"No, he left a while ago. Someone must've picked him up."

Sky lets out an over-exaggerated sigh. "Well, was my sister with him? Sunny?"

"I'm not sure. I don't think so."

"Well, gee, Sierra. Thank you for all your help."

Sierra chuckles. "Anytime." The door slams heavily. "Pay up," she says as she drops back onto the couch.

"Yeah," Austin says as he leads me to his bedroom. "I get paid Friday. You know I'm good for it."

There was lots of kissing, some touching, and a whisper that will haunt me and now he's asleep next to me. It's four-thirty in the morning. I think I slept earlier, but I can't be sure. His arms hold me tight, his breath warm on my cheek. I squirm in his arms, trying to shift so I can stare at him as he sleeps.

"Mmm," he breathes. "You're still here."

"Is that okay?"

Somehow, he pulls me tighter. "Most definitely."

And his whisper comes back to me. "I don't what this to just be about sex. I want it to be something."

Yes. Yes. Yes. *Yes.*

Austin

>Jumping in with both feet.
>No backup plan.
>No life-preserver in sight.

She doesn't need help.
She needs someone to notice her.
Someone to care about her.
She needs to be the sunshine in someone's life.

>My life.

She can outshine me.
She can always be the bright spot.

>I won't stop her.

Maybe if she hadn't spent her life
living under the sky and looking after the stars,
she would see that she is worth more
than gold and not need to slice her flesh and
count her morsels.

>Jumping in with both feet.
>No backup plan.
>No life-preserver in sight.

Skylar

I can't believe I fell asleep. Before my eyes are even fully open, I'm halfway up the stairs. Having never found Sunny last night, I'm a nervous wreck. It was well into the morning hours when I fell asleep on the couch. Jake talked to me on the phone for a while, but when he started yawning, I let him go, succumbing to mind-numbing television.

The shower is running; I open the door, seeing the shorts and t-shirt Sunny was wearing when she left. "Where the hell were you?"

She peeks around the shower curtain. "What're you talking about?" Her eyes are narrowed at me.

"Where'd you go when you left here?"

She shuts the curtain. "I have no idea what you're talking about."

"Bullshit, Sunny." I stare at her dirty clothes, tempted to inspect them for evidence she was with Austin. Maybe even some DNA left behind on her underwear. "Were you with Austin?"

"Just let me shower in peace, Sky. What the hell does it matter to you anyway?"

"So you were?"

"Leave me alone!"

I stand there for a few short moments before walking out. I feel like I'm fighting a losing battle. There's gotta be a better angle to go at this. One with less resistance. One with more leverage.

Star meets me in the hall. "She was never in bed." She nods into their bedroom, and I take a look. Sunny's bed is made, which is completely normal.

"How do you know she didn't already make it this morning?"

She walks to the bed and pulls back the comforter, revealing Sunny's cell phone. "I put it there so she would find it when she got home."

An hour later, Star and I are walking out the front door. Sunny stays put on the couch, her phone in her hand, texting. "Um, let's go, Sunny."

She barely glances at me. "I have a ride. Go ahead."

"Who?" Star asks. "Because none of your friends drive."

"Don't worry about it. I'll be at school."

"It's Austin," I say matter-of-factly.

Now she glares at me. "So what if it is? You guys broke up months ago. And, if memory serves me right, it seems you have a new *man* in your life."

Her words vibrate through me. An admission. Not a guilty one, but not a not guilty. I don't respond, just walk right out the front door to the car. I will not let her get to me. Besides, where did she suddenly find her backbone?

Star gets in the passenger seat, and I start the car. As I'm sliding the shifter into Reverse, Austin's old truck pulls up. Sunny comes out of the house, doesn't even look our way as she walks through the yard to get into his truck. She's smiling big and cheesy, a smile that actually means something for her.

"That cannot seriously bother you?" Star interrupts my thoughts.

"She can do better."

Sunny was always the overachiever among us. Always pulled straight A's, joined every club, played all the sports, had all the friends. She has more potential in her right hand than the rest of us have all together. Her focus has always been on success and her future. Never on boys. I mean, we all knew she had this weird little crush on Austin, but we all thought she'd end up with a male version of herself.

Austin is a loser who barely coasts by in school. He plays basketball, but he isn't even that good at it. I don't even think he knows what he wants in life. He's not even allowed in the same playing field as Sunny, let alone sharing a base with her.

Sunny doesn't see herself like most people do. Sure, I see her as the freak she really is, but most people don't know about the purging and the slicing. But Austin, well, he just may be close enough to our family to know she's a weak little fawn.

When I get to school, I go straight to Jake's classroom. There's a student sitting in a desk, but I go up to Jake anyway. "So, I fell asleep and have no idea when she actually got home. But we know that when she did, she didn't go to bed." I pause, glance at the kid in the desk. "She was in the shower when I woke up."

"What'd your dad say?"

"I don't even think he knows."

Jake nods. "Any word on Ray this morning?"

I shake my head as Austin walks into the room. He chuckles. "I should've known." He takes a seat. "I should've known." Another chuckle. I glance at Jake, his brow furrowed. "Well, I think, Skylar, that you will mind your own business from now on."

"What is he talking about?" Jake hisses.

I look at him; see the weight of the world in his eyes. "Um, my dad may have said something in front of him last night."

"Something like what?"

"Something like everything." I glance at Austin; he has his phone out and is texting. "I figured you'd be more worried about Orion than me anyway," I say to Austin.

He shakes his head. "O actually likes me, and cares about Sunny, which is more than I can say for you."

More students start to enter the room. "How dare you say I don't care about Sunny? You don't even know what you're talking about."

"I know more than you think I do," he says, looking up at me, then to Jake. "More than I should. Things you would hate for other people to find out."

Maybe he does. Maybe he's just an asshole.

Jake

Was that a threat just issued by the sixteen-year-old ex-boyfriend of my girlfriend?
        Yes, I think it was.
Would he really out us if Sky doesn't let him date Sunny?
        This is getting tricky.
        This is getting deep.
Maybe if I try to reason with him.
        "Hey, Austin?"
He glances over his shoulder as he leaves my classroom, grins, and says,
        "I think a B will work."
        "What?"
        "You want my silence. I want a B."

That little jackass is a manipulative fuck.
But what choice do I have?
Break things off?   No.
Tell the truth?   No.
        Fuck.
        It's all coming down to something.

Starla

After school, Sky drops me off at home, promising to take me to the hospital to see Ray as soon as she takes care of something. The house is silent. I'm alone.

I busy myself loading the dishwasher. It hasn't been done in a few days, and smells disgusting. You'd think we'd all be mature enough to rinse off our plates. When I grow up and have my own house, I'll never let things get out of control like this.

When I grow up.

Dropping the last spoon into the dishwasher, I feel a lump form in my throat. *When I grow up.* The fact that I can even think that tells me I'm not grown up. I'm not old enough to handle the kind of responsibility a baby brings. Ray, all swollen and bruised, enters my mind. How can I even be sure he's the one I want to spend my life with? I mean, I love him now, but will I love him always?

My self-loathing is interrupted by Orion coming through the front door, Dad following. They come into the kitchen, O going straight to the fridge. I skirt around him and sit at the table. "How's the daddy-to-be hanging in there, sis?"

If I could shoot daggers from my eyes, now would be the time I'd do it. "Barely breathing, no thanks to you."

"Just fulfilling my responsibilities as a brother."

"More like an asshole." I grit my teeth as he shoves a handful of chips in his mouth. "I hope you got raped in jail."

He laughs, and I want to throat punch him. "It was juvi, genius, not real jail. I fuckin' sat there and played Uno. Nobody even checked out my butt."

"Where are your sisters?" Dad asks.

I shrug. "Sunny's probably with Austin." Glaring at Orion, I add, "I'm pretty sure she spent the night there last night."

O shrugs, swallows his food. "Whatever. At least Austin's smart enough to pull out."

Dad clears his throat. "And Sky?"

"I don't know. She said she had something to take care of and then she'd run me to the hospital."

"You know, Star," Orion starts. "I've never liked Ray. Ever. Him knocking you up just finally gave me a reason to kick his ass."

I open my mouth to speak, but Sky walks in, comes to the kitchen and drops the mail on the table. "O, I'm glad you're here. Austin and Sunny are together. And he said if I don't leave him alone about it, he's gonna tell the school about me and," she glances at Dad, but he's thumbing through the mail, "well, you know."

Orion shakes his head. "I couldn't care less if Austin is with Sunny. He's a decent guy. You know that, otherwise you wouldn't have been with him yourself." He smirks at me. "Plus, he knows how to have safe sex."

"Apparently he's the only one," Dad says. He holds a letter toward Orion.

"What's that?"

"You've been ordered to take a paternity test."

I smile. I can't help it. The timing is too damn perfect. Kudos to you, Rachel Cotter. Kudos to you.

Orion takes the letter from Dad. "What the fuck?" He looks up and gone is the cocky asshole brother. He's been replaced by a young, vulnerable sixteen-year-old boy who just found out he's a father.

"Wow," I say. "I so wish Rachel had an older brother to beat your ass."

"Go to hell, Star," he says.

"I'm already there. It's just hilarious how the tables have turned, isn't it?" I shake my head. "Two minutes ago you were Mr. Tough Guy going on about safe sex, and now you're having to take a paternity test." I laugh. "Did you forget how to pull out, O?"

"That's enough, Star," Sky says. She looks over Orion's shoulder at the letter. "I just thought it was a rumor."

"So did I," O says. "I haven't seen her since, well, you know."

"This is great," Dad says. "Just great." He starts towards his bedroom but stops. "And, of course, I have to work at the bar tonight, so I will continue to have no control over any of you. So, Sky, please, go get yourself pregnant tonight. Someone text Sunny and Austin, make sure they're working on it, too. And O, you can't technically leave the house, so feel free to have over a handful of chicks. Make sure you knock them all up too." He laughs, but it's definitely not a happy laugh. "You know, a week ago, I had never even thought about grandkids. Melissa wants kids of her own still. But now that just sounds ridiculous. I mean, who has two grandkids and then has more kids of his own?"

Orion

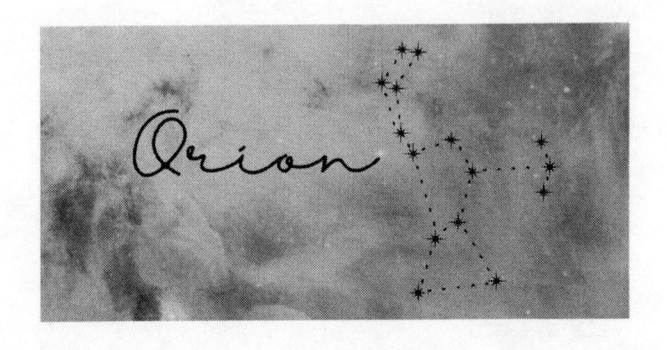

                                        Juvi wasn't that bad.

Coming home wasn't that good.

                                        I don't want to go back.

I don't want any kids.

                                    My punishment is undecided.

My paternity is undecided.

                                            Future: Uncertain.

Future: Bleak

Sunshine

"O's home," Austin says. "Let's go to your house."

I shake my head. We're at his house, facing each other on his mattress on the floor. I like it like this. Our own secret little world.

"Why not?"

"I don't know," I say. "Is Sky there?"

He looks at me, reaches out, brushes my jaw line with his fingers. "Don't worry about Sky."

My skin sizzles from his touch. "What if O is mad?"

"O's not gonna be mad." He looks down at his phone. "I said something to him yesterday morning." My eyes widen. He looks up and sees the panic on my face. "Not about that," he says with a smile. "I told him I kinda liked you and wanted to hang out."

I raise an eyebrow. "Kinda?"

"Maybe a little more than kinda." He leans forward and kisses me.

I giggle. This giggling, it's, like, the result of some new emotion, some new feeling. *Something.* "Why can't he come here?"

"Good idea." He looks down, texting again. When he looks up, his baby blues lock into my gaze. He shows me a half grin and shakes his head. "I told Sky if she has a problem with this, then I will let the school know about her thing with Mr. Morris."

I'm taken aback. "Really?"

He's looking at his phone again. "Really. And O says he can't leave the house." He texts something again. "Sky took Star to the hospital to see Ray. Your dad's at the bar."

The whole time he's talking, my mind is spinning. What *exactly* does Sky have a problem with? What is *this*? I want to ask, but I'm afraid to. I'm afraid this won't be what I want it to be. I'm afraid that my heart is way too vulnerable for finding out. *I'm* too vulnerable. But if he's pretty much extorting Sky, then this has to be worth something to him. He doesn't want this to just be about sex, that he's told me, and proved to me by holding me tight in his arms and dousing me with sweet, warm kisses.

"What's the matter?" He sets his phone aside and scoots closer to me. Loose hair falls into his eyes. I want to brush it away, but I don't. He rests his forehead on mine, kisses the tip of my nose. "What's the matter?"

"Nothing," I say. "I'm fine."

"Are you sure?" He pulls back from me, looks deep into my eyes.

I look away. "Yeah." I start to get up and he takes my hand.

"We don't have to go right now." He pulls me back down, his lips sealing mine. I fall into him, all my weaknesses succumb to whatever this is that's happening.

I want to say I'm truly falling in love, but I really have no clue. It's not like I've ever been loved before. It was a while back that I convinced myself I loved Austin, but can you really love someone you don't have? Even so, that love, as I called it, was the reason I easily cashed in my virginity the night before last. Everything since then has just been an added bonus I never expected. Kinda like winning the lottery.

So, then, tell me why all I can think about is going home and finding my razor.

We drive the few blocks to my house and are greeted by my brother at the door. They hug each other, like they haven't seen each other in years, talking about Orion's arrest and whatnot, and I fade into the background. Which makes it easy for me to slip upstairs to my room.

I see Austin's face centered in my mind as I go through the motions. The routine, perfect and simple. Last night, as we lay in his bed, his fingertips found those horrible, jagged, totally messed up slices on my stomach. I shoved his hand away, but he put it right back. He traced them over and over and over and over again. "This doesn't bother me," he said. "I feel like I know you better because I know they're there."

He hadn't discovered the ones on my arm. And now the other arm will match.

One.

Two.

Three.

Four.

They are beautiful. Perfect. Even.

Controlled.

5:15 p.m.

Orion opens the door as I'm pulling my shirt back on. "C'mere," he says, barely looking at me. "I need to talk to you."

My heart leaps to my throat. Austin said O was fine with us being, uh, doing, yeah, I really don't know what this is, but he said Orion was okay with it. Whatever it is.

Trepidation is what I feel as I walk across the hall to his bedroom. Austin is sitting on the floor in front of O's bed as I've seen him so many times before, scrolling through Netflix. O is sitting at the head of his bed, a paper in his hand. I stand in the doorway, unsure where to go, waiting for someone (Austin?) to notice me.

Orion looks up first. He looks from me to Austin, and back to me. "Sit down somewhere."

I sit at the foot of his bed. Austin turns around and smiles at me; I smile back.

Orion clears his throat. "So, as if being locked up overnight wasn't bad enough, I come home to this."

I'm staring at the back of Austin's head, so I totally think he's talking about whatever this is me and Austin have created.

Austin looks at Orion. "You said you were cool with this."

Orion rolls his eyes at Austin. "Not you guys." He holds up the paper in his hand. "This." He lets it fall to the bed. I reach to pick it up as he says, "Apparently the rumors about Rachel were true."

Austin grabs the paper from me. "What are you talking about?" He sits beside me and holds the paper at an angle so I can see it too.

"I'm being asked to do a paternity test."

"Damn." Austin lets the paper fall back to the bed.

I smile. "That's a little ironic."

"No, it's not. Rachel is eighteen. Star is fourteen. That's a huge difference."

I shake my head. "No, you're sixteen. Ray's sixteen. You guys did the exact same thing. And look what happened to him."

Orion glares at me through narrowed eyes. "You are no longer my favorite sister."

I scoff. "Never knew I was in the first place."

"Have you met your competition?"

It's small, but it makes me feel good. I guess O has always had more tolerance for me than my sisters have.

"So what're you gonna do?" Austin asks. "Do you think it's yours?"

Orion nods. "Yeah, probably. I mean, I guess." He picks up the paper from the bed. "Says she was born July eighteenth." He looks up at Austin and me. "The last time we were together was around Halloween." He shrugs. "Seems about right."

My brother looks tired. Defeated. I scoot across the bed and hug him. He hugs me back, and I swear I hear him sniffle. But when he pulls away, he looks no different.

"A week ago my biggest concern was getting laid and partying. Now I've got an ass-ton of legal problems, and apparently a kid."

"You'll be fine," I say. "It'll all turn out."

"At least I know I don't have to worry about you getting knocked up." He pushes my arm, grinning. "It'll be a long time before you melt enough to let that happen."

Austin

When, exactly, is the right time to tell your best friend, the one who just found out he may or may not be a father, that you've stolen something from not one, but two of his sisters?
Does he even need to know?
What impact would it have?
Now is not the time.
Definitely not.
Not with his own life drama burning on both ends.
Here's what I know:
    Falling happens without warning.
    It doesn't hurt unless you're alone.
        I see the weakness in her eyes.
        I feel the fear etched on her skin.
            She may not be perfect.
            But she's perfect to me.
                Imperfectly.

Skylar

After I take Star to the hospital, I drop her back off at home and run by Jake's for a bit. I figure I need to get in as much time with him as I can because who knows what the future holds. What was our little secret only days ago was now known by my whole family, Melissa, and now Austin. Someone's going to leak the facts to the wrong person and it's all going down in a blaze of glory.

Okay, well maybe not a blaze of glory, but I can't help but think there'll be flames involved.

Jake is relaxed in his recliner, a bottle of Bud Light in his hand, when I arrive. His eyes are glazed over and he's staring at the TV. He doesn't even glance at me when I come in.

"Hello? Are you in there?" I lean down, putting my face in front of his.

"Not really," he says with a sigh.

I plop down on the couch. "What's wrong?" Some reality crime solving show is on TV. He loves watching these. Once he told me he'd wanted to be a cop when he was little.

He takes a drink of his beer. "I gave my landlord a thirty-day notice today."

"What? Why?" I jerk forward and face him.

"Just think I should probably get out of this town."

My heart is thudding in my chest. "Are you serious? No one will say anything, I swear."

His eyes shift in my direction finally. "Calm down, Sky." He licks his lips while I will my heart to pump at a more manageable pace. "If I live in a different school district, then you can live with me and finish school online." The TV caught his interest again. "After you're eighteen."

Well, that didn't help my heart rate. Now it's racing in a happy run, like a puppy that just spotted a mud puddle. My face breaks into a smile. "Seriously?"

He shrugs one shoulder. "I don't know what else to do."

I draw in a deep, cleansing breath. "That's not where I thought this conversation was going."

His chuckle warms the cold corners of my heart. "What it comes down to is I don't want you to drop out and I don't want to lose you." He sighs. "Anyway, I think you should go. I feel like the spotlight is on us. Me more than you."

Normally, Jake suggesting I get lost would upset me, but in light of his recent change of heart, I'm fine. Happy even. With so much falling to crap with my family, it feels good to know Jake still has a brain in his head.

When I get home, I'm anxious to tell Orion what Jake suggested, but first I have to pee.

The bathroom door is locked so I start banging on it. "Sunny! I gotta pee. Hurry up!"

Nothing. I know she's in there because Star is downstairs on the laptop, and I can hear an Xbox game in O's room.

"Sunny!" I peek into Orion's room. "Is Sunny in the bathroom?"

"I don't know."

I bang on the door again. Nothing. I stick my head down the stairs. "Star? Do you know where Sunny is?"

"No."

"Is she even home?"

"How the hell would I know?"

I let out a huge puff of air and head downstairs to use the bathroom in Dad's room. "Did anyone make anything for dinner?" I ask Star as I rummage through the fridge after using the bathroom.

"No."

Settling on a delectable PBJ, I gather the goods and start slathering the PB on the bread.

"You know what?" Star says. "I think Sunny is home. Austin left a while ago and she wasn't with him."

"Well, I don't know. The bathroom door is locked, and she didn't answer me."

"Did you look in the bedroom?"

I glance at Star. "No."

She gets up from the table and walks to the stairs. "Orion! Did Sunny come out of the bathroom yet?"

He yells something but I can't hear what he says.

"Can you check?"

He must've said no because Star starts up the stairs. I can hear her bang on the bathroom door and yell Sunny's name.

I will be so glad when I can move the hell out of here. No more dealing with this immature, childish crap.

"Sky!" Star calls out. "I'm calling her and can hear her phone ringing in the bathroom!"

Panic sets in like a nuclear explosion. Taking the stairs two at a time, I'm standing in the hall outside the bathroom door in 2.3 seconds. Orion gave up his game to evaluate the situation as well. We can hear the distinct ring of Sunny's phone on the other side of the door.

"Sunny!" We're all screaming and pounding on the door.

"Move, move," O says. He backs up and lunges toward the door with all his weight. The door barely moves.

"Call 911," I tell Star.

She looks at me with her big blue eyes, so young, so scared, but she calls. While she's doing that, I call Dad's cell. Orion tries to break down the door again.

"Dad," I say when he answers. "Something's wrong with Sunny. She's locked in the bathroom and not answering."

"What do you mean she's not answering?"

Orion is kicking the door now.

"I don't know. We can hear her phone ringing, but she's not answering it and she's not answering us. Star's calling 911." I can hear her stating our address into her phone. "And O's trying to break down the door."

"You're sure she's in there?"

"Yes!"

There's hesitation when he speaks. "Okay, I'll be there as soon as I can."

It seems like an eternity before anyone shows up at our house. But Orion doesn't stop trying to bust down that door.

First, it's a police officer who arrives, but he also can't get the door open.

Then a fire truck arrives, and thankfully they have equipment for breaking down doors. While I watch as they break through, I wonder how much it'll cost to replace. Will Dad make us pay for it? What if Sunny's not even in there?

Oh, but she is.

My beautiful sister is lying on the bathroom floor in a heap. There's blood on the floor near her face. Star is screaming. Orion is screaming. I'm staring.

My life pauses and I think about all the times I was mean to Sunny, the times I made fun of her, the times I worked hard to make her life hell. How I fought with her. Micromanaged her. Criticized her. Hated her for being someone so unlike me.

I see her little, us playing house. I'm the mom. There's no dad. She's the big sister and Star is the baby. Orion is the dog. Then we're playing in the sprinkler, squealing with pure childlike joy.

"She's breathing," someone says.

Mike

Being a single dad has never been an easy job. Especially when I had to start working a second job a few years back. Any control I had of those kids was lost when I started disappearing four nights a week. But someone had to pay for all those clothes and shoes that teenagers have to have.

When Skylar called and told me Sunny was hiding or whatever, I figured she was overreacting. Sunny was being dramatic. Someone pissed her off and now she was disconnecting herself from everyone else.

I was wrong, as I've been a million times before in my attempt to raise these kids.
Sunny's diagnosis:
        Initially: Dehydration.
Then: Heart Arrhythmia.
        Then: Severe Depression.
And, of course: Obsessive-Compulsive Disorder.
        Oh, I almost forgot:
                Anorexia Nervosa.
It would be two months before she would come home.

Part Two

Austin

"There has to be something wrong with your heat in here," Sunny tells me. She is sitting over my heat vent, her legs pulled to her chest. "It's blowing cold air."

I don't say anything. She rests her head on her knees, faces me, and meets my eyes. The scar on her cheek bone from when she nearly died has faded to a salmon color. Each time it catches my eye, I'm reminded of how fragile she is.

"Aren't you going to do something?" she asks. "I'm getting hypothermia."

From my cozy spot on the bed, I don't see the urgency. "Come over here," I say. "It's warm under the blankets."

She looks away from me and groans. "Maybe if you come over here, and we drape the blanket around us, it will keep the heat in."

You can't blame me for trying. We've been together for five months. There was that one time, before we were anything official. That time that was her first, her only. Then she was gone for two months, but she's been back for three now, and she shuts down every time things seem to get serious.

"What have you eaten today?" I ask, knowing the reaction I will get.

She glares at me. "Leave me alone."

"I'm just thinking, if you haven't eaten, that could be why you're so cold."

"Don't worry about what I eat. How many times do I have to tell you that, Austin?"

"I can't help worrying."

She stands up and walks across the room. I sit up, my body tense, thinking I've ticked her off and she's leaving, but she opens my closet instead. My muscles relax as she pulls a hoodie from the top of my closet. She is hasty and knocks the shoe box next to the hoodies to the floor. I hear the pill bottles spill from the box.

Sunny's curiosity makes her inspect what fell from the shelf. Kneeling, she picks up a bottle. "What are these?"

I lay back against my pillows. "Pills."

"No shit. What are they for?" She shuts the closet door, comes to the bed, and sits beside me, leaving the hoodie on the floor.

"ADHD." I rest my hand on her thigh. She immediately brushes it off.

"You have ADHD?"

I shrug. "Maybe."

"Why do you have so many bottles?"

"I don't take them. My mom thinks I do."

"Why don't you take them?"

She's studying my face. This wasn't something I wanted her to know. I'm already so much less than her. I already know I'm not good enough for her and everyone knows it. They talk about it. They talk about us. About how Sunny cracked, lost her mind, and started dating me. About how she's giving up on herself because she's with me. About how she's really, truly lost her mind.

"I don't like how they make me feel."

"How do they make you feel?"

She leans against me. Why? Because she knows I don't want to talk about this. What she also knows is if she gets closer to me, pretends she feels more than she does, I will open up.

And it works. Every. Damn. Time.

"Numb. Like I'm a zombie just going through the motions."

Her eyes find mine. "Numb?"

"Not my body. Like, if you touched me, not that that ever happens, I would feel that. But, like, I don't have feelings or opinions." Looking away, I shrug. "I don't like it."

"So you're just letting your mom think you're taking them and hiding them in the closet? Why not throw them away, or flush them?"

"I've thought about selling them."

She looks at me like I'm insane. And maybe I am. I mean, she is. Maybe it's rubbing off on me. "Sell them? Who would buy them?"

"Lots of people. People get high with them."

"Seriously?"

Finally. Something I know that she doesn't. It feels good, even if it is just the fact that there's a market for Adderall on the street. "Seriously."

She opens the bottle and looks at the pills inside. "What do you think would happen if I took one?"

"Nothing probably. You don't have ADHD."

"Who needs ADHD when you can have OCD?"

She means it as a joke but it's not funny. Since she doesn't cut herself, tries not to count every calorie, or purge every morsel that passes her lips, she has found other devices to pass her time. Sometimes I wish she was the girl she was before she almost died.

"Do they have calories?" she asks.

"You're not taking any." I try to grab the bottle from her hand.

She jerks her hand away and hides it under her. Then she plants her lips on mine, kissing me softly and slowly. In those rare moments, I forget whatever is going on. I forget she is breakable. I forget she needs to be coddled. I forget her history of decision making is poor. I forget that I know she is manipulating me, because the only time she comes near me, or God forbid, kisses me, is when she wants or needs something.

When she pulls back, she leaves me with a chill on my lips. Before I return to reality, where the Sophomore Class President is dating the Special Ed Junior, I watch her slip an orange capsule into her mouth.

She smiles because she knows there's nothing I can do. I smile back because I wouldn't change a thing.

Sunshine

I never thought my life would be this way.
All I ever wanted was
                perfection,
but all that is blundered now.
                Who cares?
My life is what I've made it.
Perfection doesn't buy happiness.
Who is Austin,
                anyway?
I'll tell you.
He's as crazy as me.
He has to be.
Who else would allow themselves to be
manipulated
by a nut case like me?
Then there's the fact he seems to

      actually

                enjoy it.

Ray

Starla's itty-bitty body has morphed into something alien-like. At any moment, I swear, she will rip at the seams and my baby will fall out. Her skin is so stretched; I'm not sure how much more it can take.

"Can I get you anything?" I ask.

She's lying on her side on the couch in her living room, a pillow propped under her belly. Shaking her head, she says, "A time machine."

"Let me just run out and grab one really quick," I say.

It makes her smile. "If you did have a time machine, where would you go?" she asks. "Back in time or to the future?"

I look at her, the bags under her eyes, her puffy cheeks. If we went back in time, we could prevent her getting pregnant in the first place. But if we go to the future, we will know if we make it through this. Also, if we go back in time, I would have another chance to convince her that we could raise the baby.

The front door busts open, and Orion clamors in. I look at the TV, trying to stay off his radar.

Doesn't work.

"Ray," he says. "I see you were just leaving. Good to see you, bud. Don't let the door hit you in the ass."

I wait for Star to speak up and defend my presence, but she doesn't. "O? Will you get me some water? Put some lemon juice in it too, please."

I glare at her (not that she notices). *Didn't I just ask her if she needed anything?*

Orion disappears into the kitchen. I debate leaving. O's not going to leave me alone, and I doubt Star cares if I'm here anyway. But if I leave, then it's like they win this imaginary battle in my mind.

Truth is: I've lost every battle I fought in the last five months. I let my dad kick my ass. I let Orion kick my ass some more. And I'm letting my baby be adopted.

That was the most meaningful battle.

Sure, we're young, but teenagers have babies all the time and it doesn't ruin their lives. I mean, just look at Rachel Cotter. She's going to college and raising her baby. Why couldn't we?

Orion appears with Star's water, hands it to her, all the while staring at me. I can feel his dark, beady eyes burning holes in my soul. I want to shout, "WHAT THE HELL DO YOU WANT FROM ME?" but I doubt that will end well.

"What are you guys doing?" O asks as he sits by Star's feet.

"Baking a damn cake," Star says. "What the hell does it look like?"

He scoffs. "I thought I smelled something sweet. Then I realized it was Ray's pansy ass."

Star smiles.

I clench my jaw and shake my head. I swear to God, if she wasn't eight gazillion months pregnant, I so would have broken up with her by now. Pregnancy has turned her into a total bitch, and she pretty much seems to hate me now.

It's not like I did it on purpose.

The front door opens again, and in comes Sunny, followed by Austin. They're laughing and holding hands. That used to be me and Star.

I wonder if Austin knocked up Sunny, would Orion beat the shit out of him too?

"Anyone cook anything?" Sunny asks as she disappears into the kitchen.

Austin sits next to me on the arm of the chair. "What's up?" He says it more as a formality than as something he actually cares about.

"Damn, stranger," O says to Austin. "Where you been hiding?"

"I could say the same to you."

Orion shakes his head. "Responsibilities, you know. Gotta have a job to support the kid, then I gotta see the kid, seven hours a day in school. Oh, and don't forget the community service I got for doing something I should've done a long time ago."

Austin looks down at me, but says to O, "Yeah, that'll keep you busy."

With all the shit I have to take from Orion on a daily basis, sometimes I have to wonder if Star is worth it. Does that make me an ass? Yeah, I don't give a fuck.

"I'm gonna go," I say as I stand up.

"About damn time," Orion says.

Suddenly, I grow some balls. "Why don't you just lay off? Fuck, how many times do I have to apologize?" And then those balls shrink back inside me, and I have no idea what the hell I just did.

Orion stands up. "Excuse me?"

I walk towards the door, "Nothing, just forget it."

He's following me. "No. C'mon. You got something to say? Say it to my face, fucker."

"Just forget it," I mutter as I reach for the doorknob. His hand swats the back of my head.

Just like my dad always did to me.

Every gear in my head stops grinding. Turning around, I shove his shoulder. Then I realize what I did and whip the door open and dart onto the porch. I'm just stepping off the porch when I see a dark-haired woman walking toward me. For a second, I think it's Sky.

It's not.

Starla

Sometimes I wish Ray would just disappear.

But really, I don't know what I would do without him.

He's been a part of me for so long,

long before part of him grew inside me.

Now I can't seem to shake him,

or this part of him that's inside of me.

I have nine more long,

agonizing,

painful days until my due date.

And then life can get back to normal.

Me and Ray can go back to being the way we were before this debacle.

Orion can leave him the hell alone.

OR

We can go our separate ways because

I'm not sure I will ever get over

giving away part of my flesh.

And seeing Ray everyday will never let me forget that.

Orion

It was nice being a father.

That's what I'm thinking as I follow that fucker Ray out the front door. I'm sure I'm gonna kill him. And by kill him, I mean literally kill him. Like, bye-bye, I'm going to prison for life.

It all changes when I see Sky's doppelganger walking up the driveway. Except I know exactly who it is.

My mom.

I take a step back. "Sunny," I say evenly into the house. Then I realize she's already there, stepping onto the porch along with Austin, and a very pregnant Star.

"Hello," Amy Jo Hollis says.

I clear my throat. With Sky being gone, I have to take control. Seems I've been doing a lot of that lately. "Can I help you?"

She smiles gently, but I can tell she's as nervous as I am. "My name is Amy Jo Hollis. And I'm pretty sure you're Orion Hollis, my son."

Star speaks. "Our mom is dead. She died when I was born."

Amy Jo looks at Star. "Starla?"

Star steps off the porch and crosses the yard to where Ray stands watching. "I'm not dealing with this right now."

Amy Jo watches her climb into the passenger side of Ray's SUV and drive away without looking back. She looks at us and tries to smile. "Well, um," she looks at Sunny. "I'm pretty sure your name's not Haley, but I can't decide if you're Skylar or Sunshine."

So she *did* know it was us at the restaurant.

"Sunny," my sister says so quietly I barely hear her. Austin puts his arm around her shoulders.

"Do you want to come inside? It's really cold out here," I offer.

She nods and takes a step forward.

As I lead my mom into our house, I wonder what my dad would think. Should I call him? Should I call Sky?

I see our house like I'm seeing it for the first time. It's dirty. Our furniture is old and ripped. Our carpet is stained. The kitchen smells. And now Amy Jo is seeing it all. Seeing how her kids were raised. Seeing how horrible our dad did with us.

"Can I get you anything?" I ask.

"No, thank you." She smiles again. "Thanks for not making me leave."

"Honestly, it's tempting." I shrug. "I'm not sure our dad would want you here."

She nods. "Is he not here?"

"He's at work."

Her eyes wander the room. "And Skylar?"

"She moved out a few months ago. When she turned eighteen." I leave out the part about her moving in with her teacher, who doubles as our future uncle since Dad popped the question to Melissa at Christmas.

Amy Jo nods. "Well, after you guys came to see me, and I figured out who you were, I knew I needed to do this. Obviously, you guys were curious about me, and I think about you all the time. But in my mind, you're still little kids."

I manage a smile. "Definitely not."

"Starla, she's pregnant?"

"Due in, like, a week."

"Isn't she only fourteen?"

"Fifteen," I say, and add, "I have a daughter. She's seven months old."

"Wow."

"O," Sunny says. "I think we should call Dad."

She's probably right. I nod and pull my cell from my pocket while Austin introduces himself.

"Um, Dad?" I say when he answers. "Uh, there's a lady here, uh, she's our mom."

"What?"

"Our mom is here. She just showed up."

"Are you fucking kidding me?" He laughs. "Why? Why after fourteen years?"

"Um, I'm not sure, really. Do you want to talk to her?"

"I'm just getting into town. I'll be there in a minute."

He hangs up on me. I take a deep breath and try to smile. "He's almost home."

She nods. "Is it alright if I sit down?"

"Yeah, sure."

"I have to...," Sunny says before turning and darting up the stairs.

Austin's eyes meet mine. "Go with her." He nods and disappears up the stairs.

Sunshine

Who does she think she is, just showing up here like she has some kind of right to see us?

I mean, it's one thing if me and O want to sneak around and spy on her, but she can't just show up like she knows us and expect us to be okay with it.

My
      Life
            Can't
                  Handle
That. She has to go away.

Austin can't make this go away.

And, of course, I'm higher than the clouds on Austin's damn pills.

    I'm sure that doesn't help the situation.

.

Austin

Sunny tries shutting the door in my face but doesn't try too hard because I come in and shut the door behind me. Her room is the room that used to be Sky's. While she was in the hospital, Sky moved out and they moved all Sunny's stuff in here.

Pausing in the middle of her room, she faces me. "Austin, look, I love you, but you might not want to be in here right now."

Whoa. *What?*

My heart skips a beat and I lean back against the door. All I hear is those three words. Did she say them? Or did I imagine it? I haven't heard her say that since the first time she said it. "I love you, too," I choke out over the lump in my throat.

She doesn't hear me. I know she doesn't. Her hand is reaching above her window, fishing around for something on the ledge. Finding what she needs, she stands at the edge of her bed and unbuttons her pants, pulling them to her knees before sitting down.

Now I'm paying attention.

I watch as she stares at her legs, pulling at her skin.

"What are you doing?" I take a few steps and sit beside her.

She has a straight razor in her hand.

"Sunny, no," I say, resting my hand on her arm. "Don't. You'll regret it." She doesn't respond. I see the faint scars from all the times she's sliced herself before. It's like her own barcode.

I can't help watching as she runs the smooth razor across her skin. She doesn't flinch. She doesn't whimper. She doesn't wipe away the blood. She just does it, quickly and efficiently, four slices appear on her thigh.

"One two three four," she says under her breath. "One two three four." Her eyes are closed, her face placid. I don't think I'd ever seen her look so serene. I plant a kiss on her cheek. She faces me and smiles. "You won't tell, will you?"

I shake my head as she finds my lips with hers. "You love me?" I ask when she pulls back.

"I do."

I can't help smiling.

With a start, she jumps up, touches her fresh wounds, and pulls her pants up. "What sucks about this room, is I can't see out front." She faces me. "I don't want to go downstairs until she's gone."

"You're not even curious why she decided to show up all these years later?"

Falling on the bed next to me, she says, "Nope. Not at all. Actually, I better call Sky." She gropes her pants pockets. "Where's my phone?"

In my mind, I see it sitting in the cup holder in my truck. "I think you left it in the truck."

She sighs. "Give me yours."

I hesitate. I really don't want her calling Sky from my phone. But who am I to tell Sunny no? I find Sky in my contacts and hand the phone to Sunny before returning to the fact that she just sat here in front of me and sliced her legs like it was nothing. Like she hadn't just gone almost five months without severing her skin. No remorse. No regret. Like she'd done something routine.

She hangs up and looks up at me. "You must have her old number." She shifts her body and lays her head on my lap. "I can't believe I just did that."

"Did what?"

"You know." She shrugs. "It was the only thing I could think of."

I run my fingers through her corn silk hair. "Do you feel better?"

"I did, but now I regret it. And I'm worried you're gonna tell on me."

I should. It would be the right thing to do. "I won't."

She looks up at me. "I won't do it again."

Skylar

My mom?

Really?

After all these years?

This I have to see.

I have to referee.

I'm sure Dad will be on the offense.

I don't blame him.

He's been on his own for fourteen years,
doing the best he can.

But I want to hear her side of it.

I want to hear her say why she left.

Why she didn't want to be a mom.

What she thought was more important.

Why she didn't want us.

Ray

"Do you want to go back?" I ask.

Star shakes her head from her spot in the passenger seat. "She didn't want anything to do with me back then, well, then she doesn't deserve to know me now." Opening the glove box, she pulls out a napkin and blows her nose. "And, you know, why the hell would she have to show up now, when I'm fifteen and a million months pregnant. She must think I'm a total loser."

"You're not a loser."

"I know, but she saw me, she knows how old I am, and that's just what she's gonna think. She probably thinks I'm some kind of whore."

"Does it matter what she thinks?"

She shrugs and slumps back. "I don't know. I mean, she is my mom, technically. So in a way it does, but in a way it doesn't."

I get it. I used to care so much about living up to my dad's standards for me. But now that he's out of my life, there's a part of me that doesn't care anymore. But then again, he's still my dad, and some part of me wants him to be proud of me. It's part of the reason I stopped fighting the adoption. That and I felt like I was losing Star.

"I don't know." She looks over at me. "Think I should go back?"

"It's up to you."

"What if I never see her again?"

"That's possible."

"Will you stay there with me?"

I hesitate, maybe too long, because she sighs loudly. "I'm pretty sure Orion was about to kick my ass." I want to add that she didn't seem interested in stopping him, but I restrain myself.

"Just don't say anything to him." She looks at me, her blue eyes red and tired, pleading. "Please, Ray, I need you."

I let out a heavy sigh and head back toward her house. When we pull up, her dad's car is parked in the driveway. "Oh, good. Your dad's here."

She smiles weakly. "I guess you're safe then."

Safe. Yes. Orion won't touch me if Mike's there. At least I don't think he will. And if he does, Mike will probably step in.

I follow Star into the house. Mike is sitting next to Orion on the couch, while their mom sits on the chair where I was earlier. Orion stands and points at his seat for Star to sit down. She does, and he comes to stand next to me, which makes my heart pump and my palms sweat.

"So, your brother tells me you're due soon, Star," their mom says.

She nods. "Yeah."

"Do you know what you're having?"

Star looks at me. Her eyes tell me she wishes she wouldn't have come back.

Mike speaks. "They're giving it up for adoption. So, no, we don't know what she's having."

"Oh, well, that's probably a good plan then." She smiles softly at Star. "You're pretty young still."

"That's Ray," Star says, her finger pointing at me. "He's my boyfriend and I love him more than anything. He's the only guy I've ever been with. I'm not some whore that got knocked up on a one-night stand or something. We've been together for almost four years."

"I didn't think you were a whore. I know accidents happen."

"Were we accidents?" Sunny's voice came from the stairs. She appears behind me and Orion, Austin by her side. "Do you regret us?"

Their parents exchange a look. Mike speaks. "None of you were planned. You know that."

"But don't you think you would've figured out after a time or two how *not* to get pregnant?" she asked. "I mean, I really doubt Star and Ray are gonna have another baby anytime soon. And I'll bet that Orion has plenty of condoms on hand these days. You're supposed to learn from your mistakes, not repeat them."

"If we'd learned, Sunny, you wouldn't be here," Mike says.

"Exactly."

"Um," their mom says, "as I'm sure you know, we were young. Not as young as you guys, but still too young to have kids. And there were other things that were priority in our lives then." She shakes her head. "I don't regret having you guys. I regret staying gone for as long as I did."

"So why'd you decide to come back now?" Star asks.

Sunny answers. "Me and O found her on Facebook, figured out where she worked and went there. She figured out who we were, except she thought I was Sky. Then she tracked us down."

Mike glares at O and Sunny.

"It was her idea," O says.

"It was not! You're the one who found her on Facebook!"

The door opens and Sky steps inside tentatively. Their mom stands. "Skylar."

Sky covers her mouth and starts bawling. "Mom."

It's a touching moment for the five seconds it lasts. Then Sky faces me and Austin and says, "You two, get out of here. This is a family thing."

"No," Sunny says firmly, lacing her fingers with Austin's. "They're more a part of this family than she is." Her head tips toward their mom.

Mike stands up. "No, I think Sky is right. Austin and Ray, you'd better go."

I exchange a glance with Austin and shrug. I don't mind leaving but I can tell he's not ready to. Crossing the room, I give Star a kiss on the cheek and make my way to the door.

"Ray," Orion calls out. Pausing, I turn around. "We'll finish that up later, alright?"

I scoff and shake my head. "Sure, whatever." Life was easier in the hospital anyway. "Apparently you like being locked up."

"Goodbye, Ray," Sky says loudly.

I open the door and walk outside, leaving the door open assuming Austin is behind me. When I get to my vehicle, I see the door is still open and that he is just coming out. Right as I'm about to pull away, he appears at my passenger window; I roll it down. "What's up?"

"That's crazy, huh?"

He's talking about their mom showing up, but I say, "How? O's always wanting to kick my ass."

He shakes his head. "No, about their mom."

"Sure." I shrug and look through the windshield. "Honestly, I don't even care. I got more important things to worry about."

"Yeah," he says. "I guess you do. But I never thought of you to be one to say you didn't care."

I shake my head. "Things change." I look at him. "Think you can talk to Orion about laying off me? It stresses Star out." It doesn't. In fact, I'm not sure she even cares.

He raises an eyebrow. "I hardly talk to him anymore." He looks away. "Things change."

Starla

Things
> Change.

People
> Change.

I have
> Changed.

Ray has
> Changed.

Can my mom
> Change?

Has she
> Changed?

Are any of us ready for this
> Change?

Orion

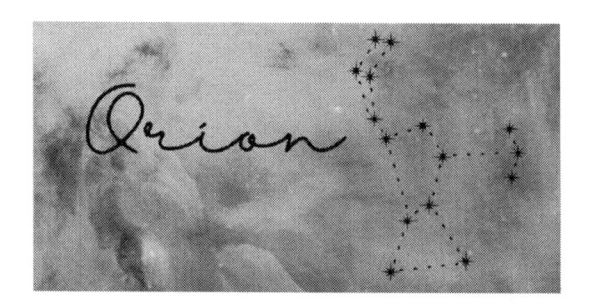

I breeze down the hall to the office. It's Friday; the weekend so close I can smell it. Off work tonight, get to see my daughter tomorrow afternoon. Oh, and it's payday. *Cha-ching*. I'll have to pick her up a little something. A new outfit, maybe a toy.

People can change, especially as time passes and circumstances change. Since I received confirmation that London is actually my daughter, she's been the only girl on my radar. I hadn't really doubted the paternity results; Rachel and I had been pretty intense. Like, on the daily.

I push the heavy glass door to the school office open and lean against the counter, waiting for the secretary to get off the phone.

"Why don't you ease up on my brother?" a voice says behind me. I turn to see who else is in there.

All I see is a tall blonde with legs that draw my eyes downward. They're bare and hanging out below her skirt. I lick my lower lip and turn myself all the way around, my back leaning on the counter now. "You talking to me?" My eyes wander back up. She's more than legs, and it all looks worthy of my attention.

"You see anyone else in here?" she snarls.

Oooh. Attitude too. I smile confidently. "I don't even know who you are, so you'll have to be more specific, sweetie."

Her eyebrows dart up. "Seriously?" She shakes her head. "I'm Tessa."

Realization hits me hard. "Whoa. Ray's sister?" I can see it now. But, *damn*! Last time I remember seeing her, she didn't look like *this*. Boobs, ass, legs. It's all here now.

People *can* change.

She smiles, probably amused by my confusion. "Yeah. How many people's brothers do you have a problem with?"

"Depends on the day, I guess." I shake my head. Don't need to think about Ray. Not with his smoking hot sister sitting here in front of me. "I didn't recognize you at all. You've changed." I shake my head again. "A lot."

"What do you need, Orion?" the secretary asks.

I face her. "She was here first," I say, jutting my thumb toward the new and improved Tessa.

"She's waiting for her mom. What do you need?"

I slide my court papers across the counter. "Here's the paper from when I had court the other day. And my dad thought maybe you could make a copy of this one that says when I go back. That way in case I forget."

She snaps the papers up and walks to the copier. I face Tessa. "Are you sick?"

"Do I look sick?"

"Not at all. Why are you waiting for your mom?" I don't even care. I just want to talk with her more.

"My skirt's too short." Her voice is thick with sarcasm.

The secretary gives me back my papers. "You need a pass?"

I shake my head and barely glace at her. "No. Jake knows I'm down here."

"Who?"

"Oh, Mr. Morris." I look at the secretary. "Sorry. My dad and his sister are engaged. I forget to call him Mr. Morris." Is there a formal name for an uncle/math teacher/brother-in-law? She nods and answers the ringing phone.

I walk toward Tessa. "I think your skirt is the perfect length." I shrug, then whisper, "Off would be even better, though."

A smile plays on her lips. She's not supposed to like me, but I can tell she's considering it. Her cheeks flush as I back up to the door, smiling at her as I do.

"I'll see you soon," I say. "Deal?"

She shakes her head, still smiling. "Whatever."

I open the office door as her mom walks up, a pair of jeans in her arms. "Hi," I say to Mrs. Douglas.

She shoots me a dirty look and mutters something under her breath. To Tessa she says, "Why would you even wear that? You know it's too short."

Tessa glances at me lingering in the doorway. I wink at her and let the door shut behind me.

Tessa

No, you don't know me.
                      And I don't know you.
You judge me by appearances, and mine
                            has proven to turn lots of heads lately.
Long and lean,
                    blonde and blue.
                                    Just call me Barbie.
                  Fuck that bitch.
                                        I'm not her.
She doesn't have demons inside of her.
                  Not like me.
                                  She doesn't have scars.
                  Not like me.
Go ahead, Orion.
                  Smile and flirt.
                                  It's all fun and games
                          until someone gets hurt.

Austin

"Austin?" Ms. Hoffman calls out. She beckons me to the front of the classroom.

A few heads look up as I make my way to the front. When I reach the teacher's desk, I see the paper I recently turned in on *MacBeth*. There's so much red ink on it I wonder if her pen exploded.

"I'm going to give you a chance to redo this." She looks up at me. "I know you can do better. You seemed to be engaged in the discussions we had in class. Is there anything you have questions about now?"

Embarrassed, I shake my head. I usually do pretty well in English, but the night before this was due, there'd been a basketball game, and then Sunny had come over and preoccupied me until she finally dozed off after midnight. This paper had been scribbled out sometime after that.

Back at my desk, I shove it into my folder just as the bell rings. Sunny is waiting for me in the hall. I slide my arm around her waist as we walk down the hall. "You okay?" she asks.

I force a smile. "I should be asking you that."

"Why?" Confusion is etched on her face.

I lean into her. "You took four of those pills, Sunny."

She pulls away. "And now I feel great. Isn't that what you want? For me to be happy?"

I try to lean close again but she backs up. "Yeah, but," I sigh and reach my hand out for her. She doesn't take it. "Are you? Are you happy?"

She smiles, but it's barely a smile, and steps to me. "I have you. That's all I need to be happy."

"Then why the pills? And," I lean close to her ear, "the cutting?"

She backs up with a shrug. "I like it. Whatever." Her gaze settles down the hall. I follow her eyes. "Is that a new kid?"

I see the guy she's looking at. His back is to us, but I recognize his orange hoodie. He was in PE and biology with me. "Yeah," I say. "His name is--"

"Carson," she says softly. She walks toward him, and I follow, like a little puppy who knows no better.

He turns around and smirks when he sees Sunny. "I was wondering if I'd see you." He holds out an arm and they hug. "How've you been?"

Okay, so the random new kid can get that close, but not me. Got it.

"I'm fine," Sunny says as she pulls back from the hug. "Why are you here?"

"For an education," he says, then chuckles. "My parents thought I needed a change."

I shift my weight, feeling like I'm eavesdropping on some confidential conversation. Sunny looks at me and frowns. "Austin, this is Carson. We met when I was in *that place*." She says 'that place' like it was going to poison her by speaking of it. She looks at Carson. "He won't say anything."

Carson nods at Sunny and looks at me, his too long hair falling in his face. "What's up?"

I shake my head. "Not much." I look at Sunny. "I gotta get to practice. I'll text you when I'm done."

She nods at me, her eyes on him, and I walk away.

Great.

Just freakin' great. Some loony from her mental hospital shows up when we're in the middle of a serious discussion and I get left feeling like the third wheel.

I change into my practice clothes while avoiding conversation. Seems I don't really talk to anyone besides Sunny anymore. Yesterday, when I tried to talk to Ray, he seemed like he would rather not. I finally understand what they mean when the say 'all alone in a crowded room.'

Practice is a blur of going through the motions. As soon as we are done, I grab my phone and am about to text Sunny but change my mind. Maybe we need a night apart. Maybe she needs to think I'm really upset about her stealing my pills (she took them all- and there were at least twelve full bottles) and slicing her legs up again. And why does she think she can do this stuff in front of me?

I remember where the cuts were before, when I first discovered them, traced them, realized how fragile, how *breakable* she was. Now she isn't so careful with them. She's done it every day this week right in front of me. They decorate her thighs like stripes on a zebra. Telling someone would betray everything I am to her.

When I step back into the gym from the locker room, I glance up to see my name on the player board- A Spencer 12- and know I need to get my head in the game for my own sake.

"Good practice, Austin," Mr. Morris says as he walks by.

I watch him go, knowing he's going home to Sky, and blame him for everything for the eight trillionth time.

Sunshine

Carson.
    He beat up his mom.
        Then tried to take his own life.
            That makes you crazy.
      Kinda like slicing your skin.
    And purging calories.
Locked up.
    That'll fix us right up.
        Pills, therapy, and group. Yep.
            That makes you crazy.
        Don't mingle on the outside. Nope.
      Not good for your health.
If we cared for our health,

    would we have ever been there in the first place?

.

Ray

I help Star gather all her books from her locker. Today was her last day of school until after the baby is born. Then she'll probably stay home for about a month. After that, life is supposed to return to normal. Whatever the hell that is.

She doesn't actually carry anything except her beach ball stomach through the school doors. Luckily, I don't have anything of my own to carry. I'm pretty sure her books and stuff weigh more than that baby, but I would never say that.

"You gonna miss school?" I ask.

She shrugs as Austin cuts in front of us, nearly running into us. "Asshole," she mutters.

I watch him disappear into the gym, longing to follow him. Basketball didn't seem like the thing to do this year. Not that I didn't want to, because I did. I actually went to the first few practices, and then Orion made some remark about he didn't think dudes who had babies should be spending their time shooting hoops when they had more important things to do. Not that I really had anything more important to do- other than follow Star around and feel worthless. It's not like I would actually have a kid to care for anytime soon.

"You know what I heard?" Star asks me as I start the car. I glance at her, expecting some tidbit of gossip. "Well, it's a way that could make my labor start."

I raise an eyebrow and pull into traffic.

"S-e-x."

I about give myself whiplash turning to see if she is serious. Her head is against the window, her eyes vacant.

"I want this thing out of me," she whispers.

"It's not a thing." I look away from her.

She sighs and shifts in her seat. "I know. I'm just so ready for this to be over." Her eyes settle on me. "I honestly wish this would've never happened."

Taking her hand, I tell her, "Me too."

"Oh, well. It'll all be over soon."

Over. Will it all be over? Will we end with the pregnancy? I shake my head to lose the thought. It doesn't matter how hard I shake my head, the thought is always there in the back of my mind, nagging me, eating me alive. How will we move on with the rest of our lives knowing a piece of her and a piece of me is out there calling someone else Mommy and Daddy?

The end is near.

"So what do you say?" she asks.

"About what?"

"You know." A glance her way shows a playful smirk on her lips.

I squeeze her hand. Sex. It's been, like, four months. As soon as she started to show, she wouldn't let me touch her. "You have to ask?"

She giggles and it takes me back to an easier time. Thinking back, it seems like we were so much younger then. Kids, carefree with our whole lives in front of us. Now we'll always have this dark cloud hanging over us. This blemish in our history.

Starla

                                                                                  I am done.

                  I have baked this bun long enough.

I'm ready to pop; stick a needle in me.

                                                                      This thing

                        (baby, child, tiny human, whatever)

is being served its eviction notice immediately.

                                No matter what I have to do to get it out.

           I refuse to be pregnant another Friday.

That may sound harsh,

                                  but I'm too young for this.

              IDK how it was ever normal for

girls my age

                                to carry little lives in them.

                 And actually,

I'm not sure why any woman

                           would willingly do this to herself.

Orion

At lunch, I find little Miss Tessa Douglas on Instagram and request to follow her highness. When I find her page, I glance across the room at her and send the request. I watch her face and wait. She glances up at me, smiles, and then I get the notification that she's accepted. Next, I go through all her selfies and heart every single one. And the truth is: I do like them. She is freakin' hot.

She sends me a private message. *Stalker.*

I chuckle to myself. *Just admiring what I see.* I watch her smirk from across the room.

She turns and talks to one of her friends, then looks back at her phone. *You haven't seen anything yet.*

This girl is good. She has game equivalent to mine, especially for a freshman. *I want to see everything you have to offer.*

I'll bet you do.

Can you hang out later?

She reads the message, meets and holds my eyes from across the cafeteria. Then she makes exaggerated movements, making it obvious she is locking her phone and tucking it in her backpack. Her eyes held mine the whole time, but she didn't give any indication either way.

Is it possible to be enchanted in half a day?

I messaged her several more times and the app indicated she saw every one of them, but she never answered. I get it. I'm the enemy. I put her brother in the hospital. But if I can look past the fact that she's the sister of the douchebag that knocked up my sister, then she should be able to look past what I did.

After school I picked up my check and cashed it before I started looking for plans for the night. By eight, Tessa Douglas was gone from my memory. I picked up my buddy Rory, Austin being MIA with Sunny every damn moment of his life, though he did say they were coming out to the same party tonight. I'd believe it when I saw it.

Around ten o'clock, I catch sight of her. *Tessa*. A freshman at an upperclassman party? She must've come here with someone. It's strange, but my stomach feels hollow when I realize Tessa could easily have a boyfriend already. She probably does. Why didn't I think of that before I went all stalkerish on her profile.

Fuck.

Someone passes me a blunt and I take a long drag, holding it in as long as I can. Austin and Sunny did show up. I spot them in the next room over and get up to go see what's up.

I give Austin a one-armed hug. "What's up?"

He shakes his head and gives a sideways glance at Sunny. My sister has her back to him and is engrossed in conversation with some kid who just started at our school that day.

"Who's he?" I ask.

"Apparently he was in the hospital with her."

"Seriously?" I look him up and down. He's short with shaggy hair- not the stylish shaggy, the need a trim shaggy- his jeans are loose and his sweatshirt too big. Gives the aura that he's bigger than he is. My guess is he's a toothpick.

"Yeah. Seriously."

I look at Austin. "So they're, like, best friends?"

He shrugs. "Whatever." He looks past me. "All I know is I had to pick him up. Oh, and she's said nothing to me since. Is there beer? Smoke? Anything?"

"All of the above." We get beer and find some smoke that's open for sharing. I spot Tessa again, looking right at me. I look away, face Austin. "Everything okay?"

"Bro, I should be asking you. You're the one whose mom returned from the dead yesterday."

I shake my head. "Not dealing with that now. Tell me what's up with you."

His eyes search the room, looking for Sunny. He shrugs. "Nothing."

"Hey," Tessa says as she walks up. "Thought you wanted to hang out."

I stare at her now that she's close. *Damn*. I could look at her all night and not want to look anywhere else. She's wearing the skirt she'd had on at school that was too short, and a scoop necked white top. Her wavy blonde hair is down around her shoulders, her lips colored a delectable shade of pink, and her blue eyes lined with expert make-up (having three sisters has forced me to take note of the little things). "I did. You never answered me." I shrug. "So I figured it was a no-go. Besides, aren't you here with someone?"

She cocks her head to the side. "Nope."

"How'd you get here?"

"My brother."

"Ray's here?" I glance around.

She shakes her head, her blonde hair shifting on her shoulders. "He dropped me off on his way to your house." She smiles. "I told him I had a ride home."

I smile and nod. "I can handle that."

"Orion Hollis," Austin says, "No offense, Tessa, but, O, not her."

I scoff. "We're just talking. Besides, this has nothing to do with Ray." I look Tessa over. "Nothing at all."

Austin shakes his head and walks away. Whatever. He was probably out of oxygen being so far from Sunny. Tessa steps closer to me. "Beer?" she asks.

"You sure?"

She nods. "It's all good."

Tessa

He doesn't know

        what's coming.

He doesn't know

        what I'm capable of.

He doesn't know

        what he's getting into.

He doesn't know

        I'm not your average freshman.

He doesn't know

        how quickly I can destroy his life.

        He doesn't know.

Austin

Really, I'm not sure how much more of this I can handle. Watching Sunny dote on Carson the new kid is wearing my patience thin. She wanted to be nice, welcoming, so she invited him to ride with us to the party so he could meet people. Yet, he's spoken to no one except Sunny, looked at no one except her- sans an awkward glance at me a few times.

I'm sitting on the arm of the couch in this crowded living room. Sunny is right next to me, Carson next to her. They're facing each other, smiling, and sharing stories or jokes or something. Her lips have worn a smile all night, little laughs slipping between them.

"I'm gonna go..." I start to say, but realize she doesn't even care, so I just get up and walk away. I walk through the house, shoot the bullshit with people I've known my whole life, and smile, pretending my girlfriend (who, don't forget, is *so* far out of my league) isn't sitting in the other room engrossed in conversation with some other dude.

Orion, once my partner in crime, is sitting on the floor in the corner of the dining room, Tessa Douglas straddling his lap in her little skirt. Their lips are meshed together, his hands under her skirt, resting on her rear. O has always been the type to mess with whoever he wants, but this seems kinda like crossing the line. There's been more than one girl who's wanted more from him than he's capable of giving. If Tessa ends up being one of them, it'll just add fuel to the Hollis vs. Douglas fire.

Ever since he found out he's a father, he's been a little more tame, telling me he was going to think twice before sleeping with someone. "You never know. Even with a rubber, it can happen."

"Did you and Rachel use a condom?" I'd asked.

"Hell no," he chuckled. "That's why I'm where I'm at." Then he shoved my shoulder. "Do you use rubbers with my sisters?"

I'm sure my face turned red. As if I've even been given an opportunity to with Sunny since that first time. Right before she went to the hospital. But I wasn't going to tell him that. It's awkward.

When I get back to where I left Sunny and Carson, I see that they've been replaced by Rory Anderson. His eyes are closed, his head resting on the back of the couch. "Did you see where Sunny went?" I ask.

He opens his eyes. They're bloodshot, his pupils dilated. "Who?"

"Sunny? Orion's little sister?"

"Never saw her," he says.

I move through the house faster this time, every worst-case scenario running through my head, making my stomach tight and my head feel light. In the course of maybe three minutes, I decide I'm done with Sunny and our relationship. I'm not getting what I need, and I don't just mean sex. I mean: she makes me feel like a place keeper. Someone to be her friend. Her sidekick. I don't feel like her equal. There's no need to feel that way, not at the hands of some girl.

I find them walking down the hall toward the bedrooms. Part of me just wants to let her go and turn away, but I can't. "Sunny!"

She turns around. "Austin! Where'd you go? We were looking all over for you."

"I was looking for you." I glance at Carson, standing awkwardly a few feet behind her. "What are you guys doing?"

"Looking for the bathroom."

"It's off the kitchen."

She shakes her head. "That one's too busy. We need somewhere more private."

My heart is thudding. I'm sure she can hear it. "For what?"

She takes my hand. "Just c'mon."

The hall bathroom is occupied, so she starts opening doors. "This looks like the master."

"What is going on?" I ask. Carson is following us, so I'm fairly certain she hasn't decided after five months of celibacy that tonight's the night.

She giggles. "I wanna try something Carson suggested."

"In the bathroom?"

"It's cool, man," the punk says. I glare at him. "It's nothing like you're thinking." He doesn't look at me when he talks.

I don't trust him.

Sunny flips on the bathroom light, and once the three of us are in there, she shuts and locks the door. She pulls my pill bottle from her pocket and opens it, pouring four orange capsules into her palm.

"Sunny, you've been drinking." I step closer to her.

She shrugs and takes a step back. "It's fine. I only took one after school."

"You're only supposed to take one each day." I shake my head. "Reality is you're not supposed to take any, ever. They're mine." I hold my hand out.

She looks up at me, her eyes soft and pleading, sucking me in like she has figured out how to do so well. "It's fine, really, Austin. I'm not even gonna take one." She sets the pills on the counter. "Carson said if you snort it, the high is better."

I can't believe what I'm hearing.

"And it's faster," he adds, like that makes it all better. Like I'm gonna be on board, pat him on the back. "You should try it."

"That's the stupidest shit I've ever heard. I'm not gonna try it." I meet Sunny's eyes. "I thought I was the stupid one in this relationship."

Her mouth opens like she's gonna say something, but she doesn't. She just stares at me, and I can't read her. Does she want me to give my permission for her to plunge even deeper into the hell she's bringing to her life? Does she want to take my hand and pull me down with her? What about Carson? Does he get to come too?

I shake my head and leave the bathroom. My heart wants her to follow me, say she's sorry, tell me again she loves me. I'd take her in my arms and forgive her. But she doesn't follow. She doesn't plead.

She doesn't love me.

I wait at the end of the hall for at least ten minutes.

Orion is still tangled up with Tessa when I find him. Their lips aren't together, and they're actually talking, smiles dancing on both their lips.

"Can you give Sunny a ride home?" I ask.

He nods. "You okay?"

"Sure." I walk away before he can read more into it.

Outside, flurries are dotting the night sky, and I watch my breath smoke out of my mouth. The air is frigid, and even shielded from the wind in my truck it's no better. I start the engine and flip on the parking lights. Why? Because any minute I know Sunny is gonna come looking for me. I need to be the beacon in the night waiting for her.

Twenty-four minutes and two cigarettes is all it takes for me to admit defeat. I lost her to a razor, a few bottles of my own pills, and some punk from a loony bin.

Sunshine

The high is faster.

And better.

But at what cost?

Where's Austin?

He needs to know.

Not about the high,

But that I need him.

More than I need to slice.

More than I need his meds.

More than I need anything.

I'm scared.

Ray

I drop my little sister off at her friend's house and head to see Star. She texted about an hour ago and said Orion had left for a party, her dad was working at the bar, and Sunny was somewhere with Austin. That meant she was home alone. When I told my mom this, and asked if I could go over there, she sighed. "I don't see why not. It's not like you can get her pregnant again." She shook her head. "I can't believe with a family that big, no one can stay home with her."

I pretended to agree, but I knew Star lied to Orion and said Sky was coming over so he would leave.

When I get to the Hollis house, I let myself in, finding Star lying across the sofa in her favorite position.

"You're just in time," she says with a smile. "I need some sherbet. STAT."

I chuckle and go to the kitchen to fulfill her request. As I dish the goods, she tells me the movie she's watching has about an hour left and proceeds to clue me in to what I missed.

She sits up when I come in and hand her the bowl. While she watches the rest of the movie, I contemplate how the hell we're going to have sex. She's huge. I can't think of any position that would be comfortable for her. I think about using my phone to Google it but decide not to. I wouldn't want her to see what I'm looking at. I guess we'll just have to wing it.

"Upstairs?" she says with a shy smile. That's the Star I love. The one who pretends to be shy about what she wants.

Our first time was planned. It was her idea and who was I to stop her. She told me she was ready, I was more than ready, so we decided on a day and a time and awkwardly implemented our plan. Nearly two years ago.

"No lights." She leads me up the stairs. "*I* don't even want to look at me. There's no way you're gonna see me like this."

"I want to see you," I say, shutting her bedroom door behind her.

She shakes her head. "It's gross. Bodies shouldn't stretch this way. It can't be healthy." I check out her ass as she climbs on her bed.

"I like how it's made your ass look."

She laughs. "Enjoy it while it lasts, Ray. Soon it'll be gone."

We sidle together in her twin size bed, my hands rubbing across her swollen belly. I've felt life move inside her, watched it move under her thin skin. I can't think about it. Can't think about how I will never hold the life we made. I won't see the first steps, first day of school, graduation, wedding day....

I feel a lump forming in my throat. Sex. That's what I'm here for. My lips find Star's and I try to block out that by this time next week, my baby will probably be in someone else's arms.

Starla

His arms feel so good around me.
                                                For real.

Things are like they used to be.
                                                For pretend.

We try to complete the deed.
                                                For real.

It's not awkward.
                                                For pretend.

We end with a half assed attempt.
                                                For real.

We say it was good enough.
                                                For pretend.

It's all pretend at this point.

.

Orion

It's nearly two in the morning when I decide to call it a night. I'm more than a little buzzed, and it's at least ten miles home. Tessa is wobbly as she walks behind me, refusing to let go of my hand or let me out of her sight. And I haven't let her out of my sight all night.

Sunny gets to the car before me, her loser friend leaning against the trunk. "I'll drive," she says. I try to eye her, assess her sobriety, but I can't. She's barely had her license for a month.

"Can you drive?"

"Better than you, I'm sure."

I fish the keys from my pocket and hand them to her. Her friend moves closer. "What's your name, dude?" I slur. "And why am I giving you a ride home?"

"Carson. I'm a friend of Sunny's."

I nod and let go of Tessa's hand. "Sunny's my sister. And Austin's my best friend. Austin being her boyfriend."

"I know that," he says as he turns away from me.

"It's fine, O," Sunny says.

Tessa is hanging from my waist now, her lips on my neck. Damn, I wish she would stop for just a second. I'm trying to handle this. "It's not fine, Sunny. Where's Austin?"

"Look, if you can mess around with Ray's little sister, then I think I can be friends with the new kid in school."

"What?" That's ridiculous. "Those two things have nothing to do with each other!"

"My name's Tessa," she says from my side.

"I know your name, Tessa," Sunny says as she gets in the car. I get in the back seat with Tessa. Sunny faces us. "He's messing with you to piss Ray off. Don't you realize that?"

I shake my head, bury my face in her hair. "Not true. Don't listen to her."

"I don't think so," Tessa says to Sunny. "He was checking me out before he realized who I was."

"And you think Ray would be cool with this?" Sunny asks.

Tessa scoffs. "He's not my dad."

"Ok, do you think your dad would be cool with this?"

"Fuck my dad, that piece of shit."

"Who's Ray?" Carson asks.

"Ray Douglas," I start, "is the worthless mother fucker who knocked up my fourteen-year-old sister. He's the one dude I haven't liked since the day I met him. Kinda like you, bro."

"What the fuck did I do?" He faces me, his eyes narrowed.

"Trying to come between Austin and my sister."

"No I'm not. Sunny's the only one I know here. She invited me to come out."

"Whatever," I say. Tessa has her hands in places that are making me forget why I want to argue with Carson.

"You almost killed my brother," Tessa says.

"I did not almost kill him."

Sunny says, "Ha. Yes, you did. He was in the ICU for weeks. You punctured his lung."

"Damn," Carson says.

"Facial fractures," Sunny added. "He doesn't even look the same."

I close my eyes, wanting to block out the conversation and just enjoy Tessa.

"Why didn't you just do it?" Tessa asks. "Kill him?"

I sit up, look at this girl laying on my chest with her hand down my pants. "Honestly, I saw Star crying, sitting on the floor all alone with that baby in her, and I didn't want her to go through all this alone."

Tessa looks up at me. "You have a heart."

"Somewhere in there. Especially when it comes to my sisters."

"Take me to your house," she whispers. I shake my head. "I told Ray I would get a ride there."

"He's at my house?"

She nods. "Can I get your number?"

I shift and pull my phone from my pocket and hand it to her. Her hand comes out of my pants, and I start to drift off. Next thing I know, the car comes to a stop. I open my eyes because I think we're home, but I see that Carson dude leaning toward Sunny.

I sit up, jarring Tessa from my chest, and smack him upside his head. "I fucking told you she has a boyfriend."

"I was giving her a hug, bro," he says. "Chill the fuck out."

"You chill the fuck out and get your pussy ass out of my car."

"Fuck you," he says as he opens the door.

Sunny is calling out some warning to me, but I don't hear it. I jump out of the backseat and go towards him, my arms outstretched. "You don't want to fuck with me, new guy. Trust me, you don't."

He just stands there. He doesn't come at me. He doesn't retreat. "You're right. I don't."

"Then stay the hell away from my sister."

"She can choose her own friends, can't she?"

I shake my head. "Go the fuck in the house and take this as your warning." If Sunny's boyfriend was anyone besides Austin, I wouldn't give two shits, but I can't stand by and let him get hurt by another of my sisters. I go to the driver's door when I get back to the car. "Move over. I can drive now."

Sunny moves awkwardly over the center console. "You don't have to be such an asshole."

"The fuck I don't," I say. "You think I'm gonna just stand by and let that fucker step in? I don't think so." I glance at my sister. There's a tear running down her cheek.

"Did he say anything when he left me there?" She looks at me. "Austin?"

I shake my head. "Just asked me to give you a ride home."

"It's cold back here," Tessa whines.

I turn the heat up to full blast and take Sunny's hand. When we get to our house, Ray's SUV is parked on the street. I feel the usual surge of anger I associate with seeing his vehicle in front of my house. My dad's Durango isn't there; he's probably staying at Melissa's.

After helping Tessa out of the backseat, I lead her into the house. The living room is empty. Sunny and I exchange a look, wondering where Star and Ray are.

"Where's your room?" Tessa asks me.

Sunny shakes her head and starts up the stairs. "I'll go see if they're in her room."

I nod at my sister and tell Tessa, "I'm not taking you to my room."

She flops onto our old couch, and flips one leg over the back, the other on the floor. I can see her lace trimmed panties. "Why not? Afraid my brother will catch us?"

"You're drunk...and sexy as hell." I lower myself onto her, our lips locking. It takes her no time to start tugging at the zipper on my jeans.

"Damn," I hear Sunny say from behind us. "No need to waste any time."

I sit up quickly. Tessa closes her legs and giggles. "Your brother's cute," she says. "I can't help it."

"Yeah, but he can." Sunny shakes her head and looks at me. "Star is sleeping. Ray woke up when we came in." She glances at Tessa. "I told him she was down here on the couch. I think he presumed she was alone." She bites her lip as she looks out the window. "I'm gonna go to Austin's."

We watch her leave. As soon as the door clicks behind her, Tessa uses one of her legs to pull me closer to her. Rubbing my hands along the length of her long legs, I lose myself and forget the fact her brother would come down the stairs any moment. I move my lips along those legs, shifting my weight so I can move upward. As I get closer to her lace trimmed panties, I push her skirt out of the way, kissing all around the edges of the lace. Her hands are in my hair and she is squirming with anticipation. Slipping one finger past the cloth, I look up to see her face.

She stops moving, her face frozen in anticipation. I slowly glide my finger around and watch her mouth open slowly. Her body tenses and she makes a little sound. Using my other fingers, I slide her panties over and move in to kiss more than just leg.

"Are you fucking serious?" Ray's voice makes my heart jump into my throat.

I jump up so fast, all while trying to conceal the serious boner I have. Tessa sits up, smoothing her little skirt over her legs.

"What's up?" I ask him.

He's glaring at me. "What are you doing with your head in my sister's skirt?"

I got nothing, so I stare at him.

He chuckles, glances at Tessa and then back to me. "You think this is gonna get to me, don't you? You're gonna make me mad, then maybe we'll fight. Then you can claim self-defense, so you don't get in trouble, right?"

My mouth opens but nothing comes out. I always have something to say to Ray's punk ass, but right now, I'm dumbstruck. Tessa moves closer to me. I step back.

"It's all good, Ray-Ray," she says. "It's not like we actually did anything, no thanks to you."

"He's using you, Tess. You have to know that."

"Is he?" She looks me over, brings her hand to her chest dramatically. "That would just break my poor little heart." Her hand falls as she stalks to the door. "It's all fun and games until someone gets knocked up, huh, Ray?"

Tessa goes outside, the door hitting the wall behind it. Ray looks back at me, shakes his head. "Suppose I should just let this go."

I open my mouth but can't say anything. Now I feel what he must've felt every time I walked in to find him with Star. "Ray, I--" I'm not sure what to say, but I have to say something. "I don't even--"

He shakes his head. "Let me know when you got something, bro." The door shuts behind him and I'm left to wonder WTF just happened. Did I really feel intimidated by Ray Douglas?

Tessa

I'm under his
          skin.
I'm in his
          brain.
The feel of his
          touch
left me   cold.
              hungry.
                  desperate
                            for more.

Austin

Zombies can only take my mind off Sunny for so long. I toss the Xbox controller aside and check my phone for the billionth time. Not even anything from Orion. I figured he'd at least text and let me know she went home. Alone.

Sunny and I don't go to sleep alone. Ever since she got out of the hospital, one of us has slept at the other's house every single night. Her dad never tried to stop it. My mom did, but Sunny'd just sneak back through my window, or I'd go over there, so she gave up. She gave me a jumbo box of condoms and said, "I don't need to see her looking like her sister."

As if that's even possible. Our bodies have no problem tangling together when our clothes are on, but the moment my hand brushes anywhere below the neck, she pulls away and freezes up. "I'm just not ready," she always says.

"But we already...," I try to reason.

She shakes her head. "I was in a different place then."

I don't understand her, or the cutting, or anorexia, so it doesn't make sense to me. What I do understand is that it's 2:30 a.m. and I have a *MacBeth* paper to rewrite tomorrow before I go to work. I flip off the small lamp next to my bed, pull the covers up, grab my phone and open Instagram.

Nearly fifteen minutes of scrolling pass when my bedroom door opens. I look up, half expecting my mom, but really hoping it's Sunny.

Hope wins. She's been crying. Even in the dim light I can see that. "You awake?" she whispers.

I pull the blanket back, welcoming her into my bed. She comes into my room, shuts the door behind her, and sheds her hoodie, shoes, socks, and pants. When she sidles next to me, her skin is like ice. "You're freezing," I say as I rub her legs, feeling the web of scabs that have found their way back to her body. As I start to trace them, she tucks her face into my neck.

"I walked," she says.

"From the party?"

"Do you even care?"

"What? Of course I care. I told Orion to give you a ride home."

"Why'd you leave me?"

I sit up and look down at her. "Sunny, what were you thinking? Snorting those pills? Why?"

She sits up. "I could run a marathon right now and not even be winded. That's how high I am." The way she says it, it's like she's proud. "I won't be falling asleep anytime soon."

"You like feeling like that?"

She shrugs, looks away from me. "I feel alive." Her hand finds mine and she wraps our fingers together. "The cuts, the pills, even talking to Carson, it makes me feel something. A week ago, I was just…I don't know. I feel better. Like I'm someone."

"You're my someone."

"Why?"

I shrug. "Why not? Or better yet, do you even still want to be with me? Now that you're someone?"

She gazes into my eyes. Even in the darkness in my room, I can see what she means. She's not herself. It's like something clicked inside of her, or just got snorted through her nose.

"You don't have to stay with me. I will keep your secrets even if we break up."

"Austin, I don't want to break up! Is that what you think? Do *you* want to break up?"

"No, but even you admit something's not right with you. Maybe it's me."

She cups my face in her hands. "You're the only thing that's right. You've always been what I've wanted. Don't you know that?"

I run my hands along hers. "You say that, and then spend your whole night talking to some other guy."

"I'm sorry. I wasn't trying to make you mad." She kisses me. "Can we just forget it?"

She kisses me again and doesn't let me answer. Her kisses don't end, her fingers running the length of my arm. I lean back, she falls on top of me. And when my hands cradle her perfect rear end, she doesn't stop me. Or when I pull her t-shirt over her head. Or her underwear off. No, in fact she whispers, "I love you."

Sunshine

Love Love Love

I really love Austin.

Mad Mad Mad

He really was mad.

Kiss Kiss Kiss

Let me kiss away the pain.

Better Better Better

I can do better.

Keep it moving, go all the way, use protection.

Happy Happy Happy

That smile means he's happy now.

What about me?

.

Ray

Saturday mornings around our house used to be for cleaning and chores. But now that Dad is gone, Mom doesn't make us get up as early. She still expects us to help, just not on a rigid, military type schedule. Even still, I wake at just after seven in the morning. My first thoughts are of Star and our baby, how the due date is drawing too close.

Last night was interesting. I can't say good, but it definitely wasn't bad. The labor inducing sex she'd hoped for didn't happen. Nothing felt comfortable for her or me. I wanted to cry. My heart is swollen with how much I love her. I hate seeing her hurt, and it seems that's all she's done the last few months.

"I don't think I'll ever want to have kids," she told me after we gave up on sex. "Just so you know." We were laying side by side on her bed.

"Why?"

Her eyes went wide, and she pointed at her belly with both hands. "Look at this! Do you see it?"

I smiled. "I see it, Star. Calm down." I turned my head to the side. "Think about it like this. What if this was ten years from now. I'm twenty-six, you're twenty-five. We're married, have our own house. And we're keeping the baby."

She doesn't say anything for several minutes, but then, "We'd have the nursery all decorated. We'd know what it was, have a name picked out."

"Boy or girl?"

"Boy." She sighed. "I might feel different in ten years. I don't know."

I squeezed her hand. "This changed so much for us."

"We'll never be the same. You realize that? We'll never be able to go back to the way things were before this." She faced me. "We can't let this break us, Ray. I don't want to break up, but I feel like that's where we're headed."

"I don't want that either."

I sigh and get up to shower and start my Saturday. Sometimes other factors besides what we want can determine a relationship. I guess one factor I won't have to worry about- for a while, anyway- is Orion.

Poor Tessa, but I can't tell her anything. She changed a lot over the last year. First, she hit puberty head on, which completely transformed her body, then our dad left. She was Daddy's Princess. Now she and my brothers get supervised visits with Dad. The social worker told Mom Tessa doesn't even talk to him, just sits there on her phone, ignoring him. At home, she basically does whatever she pleases, and Mom doesn't say or do anything about it, except say she needs counseling.

Regardless of Tess's reckless behavior, Orion is a dick. It's one thing to fuck with me, but something completely different to go through my vulnerable sister. I was actually surprised O wasn't more confrontational last night. Like I'd caught him completely off guard.

I turn off the shower, towel off, pull on some basketball shorts and head back into my bedroom. As I pull a shirt over my head, I grab my cell to text Star and see how she's feeling. She's probably not even awake, but it'll be there when she does wake up and she'll know I was thinking of her.

No, she's awake. Four missed calls from her and a few texts. Ringer was off. Damn. I had shut it off last night when we were attempting to bring on her labor.

She answers on the first ring. "Finally!"

"Are you okay?"

"Spectacular," she says. "What were you doing?"

"Showering."

"Oh. I want to go to the mall and walk around for a while. They say lots of walking can help bring on labor."

I nod. "I don't think the mall is open this early."

"I know. I haven't even gotten out of bed yet. Well, except to pee forty-seven times."

I glance at the clock. "We could go get breakfast."

"You have money?"

"I'll get some from my mom."

"That works. I don't think my dad ever came home."

"No, he wasn't there when I left." I snap my fingers and sit on my bed. "But I gotta tell you this. When I went downstairs, Orion was there. Him and Tessa were messing around."

"What?"

"Yeah, can you believe it?"

"What were they doing?"

It's not an image I want to see again. "His head was between her legs. You figure it out."

"Are you serious?"

"Serious as shit."

She's quiet for a minute. "You think he's just trying to piss you off?"

I shrug. "Probably."

"That's shitty. I'll talk to him."

Starla

When a rope gets frayed at the ends do you throw it away?

Or do you see all that it still has left to offer and keep it around?

When you face trials with someone you love,

your ends get frayed,

but you don't throw it away.

You hang on and hope for the best,

that it doesn't break when you're counting on it the most.

Orion

I was just drifting to sleep when Star threw my bedroom door open demanding to know: "What the hell were you doing with Tessa last night?"

I groan. "I need to sleep before I go get London. Can we talk about this later?"

"No." She waits for me to respond. When I don't, she says, "That's a really shitty thing to do, you know. There's no reason to involve her in your problems with Ray."

I roll over, facing her. "Why does everyone automatically think that? Why do I have to have an ulterior motive?"

"Your motive is obvious."

"Your fucking belly is obvious."

She slams the door as she leaves. Tessa and I had been texting ever since she left last night, which means I've been up for twenty-four hours now. My assumption is that Tessa fell asleep. She'd said she was tired, and she hasn't answered me in about thirty minutes. I roll back to my side, determined to fall asleep. I have to pick up London at noon. I only get to see her for six hours a week. After I drop her back off, I have to meet my sisters and our long-lost mother for dinner. Then I want to hang out with Tessa again.

I need to sleep now.

"Orion." The voice penetrates into my sleep bubble. "Orion! Aren't you supposed to be picking up London about now?"

I crack open my eyes to see Austin standing over me. Grabbing my phone, I see the time: 12:13 p.m. "Fuck!" I jump up, grab my shoes, phone, and keys, and dart downstairs. I need to call Rachel, but I have ten texts from Tessa. I debate reading them first, and decide calling Rachel is priority.

"Hello?" she answers.

"Hey, I'll be there in a few."

"I was starting to wonder."

"Yeah, sorry. I overslept."

"This late? Must be nice." Rachel has been pretty cool with me through this whole thing, so her sarcasm catches me off guard.

"No, Star is close to her due date and not sleeping well. I was up with her for a while last night."

"Hmm. Really? Because according to Snapchat, Ray was at your house last night."

Fuck. "He wasn't there all night."

"Whatever."

"I'm about five minutes away."

We end the call. I've never been late to pick up London. I don't know why she's got herself all worked up. I glance through the texts from Tessa. She had fallen asleep, and she's sorry, but now she's awake. I call her.

"Hey," I say when she answers. "I don't want you to think I'm blowing you off, but I'm on my way to pick up my daughter."

"Oh." She's disappointed. I can hear it in her tone. "I forgot you had a daughter."

I sigh. I don't suppose most girls think about that when they start talking to a guy. "Yeah, I have her on Saturdays from noon until six."

"Every Saturday?"

"Yeah. That's the only time I see her."

"Oh."

"Can you still hang out tonight?"

"I don't know. Probably." She sounds uncertain.

"Look, I'm here, but I do want to see you later. I'll text you. Or call."

Her heavy sigh can be heard through the phone. "Okay, whatever."

Tessa is still on my mind when I ring the bell at the Cotter house. I really don't want to disappoint her, not this soon into whatever is happening with us.

Rachel's mom answers the door. She never talks to me, never looks me in the eye. And I understand why. She walked into her kitchen one afternoon to find me and her daughter creating her first grandchild all those months ago. That was the first and last time I saw her until the court hearing a few months ago.

Inside, she disappears, and I head to the family room in the back of the house. Rachel is on the couch, textbooks and papers spread all around her. She glances up when I come in. "Hey," I say. "Where's London?"

"Have you even been home?"

"What?"

"Since last night. I know you were out at that party in Lynnwood."

"So? What does that matter to you?"

"You look like you slept in your clothes and stink like beer and BO."

I look down at my clothes-- that I slept in. They're wrinkled. "I overslept. I didn't have time to shower." I sigh and look down the hall. "Is she sleeping?"

"Emily's changing her diaper." She stands up, looks me over, her eyes judging me, then leaves me alone.

I fall into an overstuffed recliner and look out into their oversized backyard. It's several minutes before Rachel comes back, and I'm lost in thoughts of Tessa and the night before when she appears with London on her hip and her dad behind her.

"Orion," Drew Cotter greets me. "How're you doing?"

I rise and hold out my hand. "I'm good. How are you?"

He approaches me, his brow furrowed. "Have you been to sleep?"

My jaw clenches. I drop my hand and look back out the window. "I've had a few hours of sleep."

"What are you planning to do with London today?"

I straighten my posture. "I was going to go buy her a toy and maybe an outfit. Then probably go back to my house."

"Are you driving?"

My eyebrows draw together. "Yes."

He shakes his head. "No. Your eyes are bloodshot, and you smell like you've been drinking. I'm not letting you take her."

"I'm fine, I swear to God." My heart is pounding. Their judgmental eyes are attacking me. I will never be good enough for them or London, and they will make sure of it. "Completely sober. I just didn't have time to shower."

"Why don't you call your dad and see if he can help you out." He shrugs. "Otherwise you're welcome to stay here and visit with her."

I look past him at my daughter in Rachel's arms. Her hair is jet black like mine, and she has my dark eyes. She's chewing on a giraffe shaped teether, wearing a purple top and tiny little blue jeans with her Nike shoes that cost more than what

I pay in child support a month. The last thing I want to do is call my dad. "I'm fine."

"You can say that all you want, Orion. You're not leaving here with her."

I clench my jaw and turn away from him. Taking a deep breath, I pull out my phone and call my dad. He answers on the third ring.

"Dad, can you come pick up London?"

"Why?"

I explain the situation to him. After fifty million questions, he agrees to come out there. While I wait, I sit on the floor and try to play with London, but I feel Rachel's scrutinizing eyes on my every move. My phone has vibrated several times in my pocket.

"This is bullshit, and you know it," I tell her.

"I don't know it. You look high, you smell like a brewery, and are a mess. And why does your phone keep buzzing? Are you selling drugs? And don't swear in front of her."

"Selling drugs? Are you kidding me?"

She shrugs. "Never know with you."

"Wow, you're really...." I stop before I say something I'll regret.

"Really what, Orion? Protective of my daughter?"

I pull London onto my lap. "She's my daughter too."

"Yeah, those six hours a week and whopping hundred dollars a month makes you a *great* dad."

I grit my teeth and take a deep breath through my nose. I can't let her get to me. This is the best I can do. "I'd love to have her more, but my dad's not a lawyer, so I get screwed."

She chuckles. This evil side of her isn't the girl I used to actually want to hang out with. "It's sad, huh, that you can't pay for a lawyer with food stamps. Maybe use your drug money. Think you have a chance at custody? Oh, no, I doubt it. You're a junior in high school. Doubt you'll even graduate. Worthless loser."

I'm about to blow. She is being unfair, and she knows it. Standing, I keep London in my arms. "I didn't choose this. You never even asked what I wanted. Hell, you couldn't even tell me you were pregnant, or that you had my kid. You just decided what you wanted and now you and your family think you can control my life and my relationship with London." I take a deep breath and look out the window. "Where's her coat? My dad will be here soon."

"If you don't want anything to do with her, just say so. Walk out, just like your mom did to you."

I can't take it. "Where's her coat? And car seat."

"Use your own car seat." She doesn't move from the couch. "And diapers, and formula and baby food. That stuff's not cheap."

"Rachel, just stop," I say. "Is any of this helping anything?"

She shrugs, her chestnut eyes flashing. "Why don't you just fall off the earth? Disappear. She'll be better off without a loser for a father."

I chuckle. "Wow. Wasn't all that long ago you liked slumming it with this loser."

The doorbell rings and I feel a swell of relief. I can't remember the last time I was so happy to see my dad. Him and Drew come into the family room.

"Sorry, you had to come all the way out here, Mike," Drew is saying. "I just didn't feel comfortable with letting London go with him."

"I've asked her for London's coat, and she won't get it." I meet my dad's eyes. "This is ridiculous."

My dad looks me over, reaches out for London. "You look like crap, Son. Did you sleep in those clothes?"

"Yeah, and I overslept, so I just ran out the door." I threw up my arms and sighed. "Didn't know it was gonna cause all this drama. I just wanted to get here and pick her up."

Dad glances at Drew. "Can we get her stuff?"

Nothing else comes from Rachel's bitch mouth, thank goodness. She disappears for a minute and returns with London's coat, car seat, and diaper bag, setting them on the floor wordlessly. As I struggle while six eyes watch me try to dress my seven-month-old daughter and buckle her into her car seat, I think about how there was a time when Rachel and I couldn't get enough of each other. Now we can't stand to look at each other.

Star and Ray are making the right choice giving their baby up for adoption. If I'd had any say in London's life, I would've wanted the same thing. Not that the Cotter's won't make sure she'll have a wonderful life with all the opportunities Rachel and Emily have, but I don't want a kid. That might sound harsh, but no one asked me. A decision that will impact the rest of my life was made without me.

I glance at Rachel and wonder how much input she had in the decision to raise London. "I'll be back at six."

Tessa

I thought he was into me.
        I thought he wanted me.
                I thought I had him.
I thought too much.
        He's ignoring me.
                He's with someone else.
I've heard the stories.
        I've been warned.
                Not just by my bro.
Not just by everyone.

Wait   is that a text?   From him?

Sorry   he says   baby mama drama.

Austin

Sunny finishes my *MacBeth* paper in less than an hour. Then she does my algebra and makes flashcards to help me study for my biology test this week and convinces me to call off work so we can study.

"I think I'm starting to come down," she says. She collapses on Orion's bed next to me where I'm playing Xbox. We'd been here most of the day.

"It's about time." My tone shows my agitation, even though I hadn't meant for it to.

She sits up. "So, what? Now you hate me?"

"How did you get that from what I said?"

"You've been in a mood all day. If you're mad at me, just say so."

"I'm not mad at you."

She's quiet for a moment. "Can you look at me?"

I sigh loudly, pause the game, and face her.

"I'm gonna go in my room," she says quietly.

There's nothing to read in her expression. "I had to pause the game for you to tell me that?"

She opens her mouth but doesn't say anything. Then she jumps up and goes to her room, slamming her bedroom door.

Whatever. Maybe she'll fall asleep. I start my game again and feel a twinge of guilt. Not exactly sure why. I'm not the one snorting pills in the bathroom. I'm not the one who spent the whole night talking to some other guy. I'm not the one who decided sex was going to make it all better.

Sunny needs to sleep. In a few hours, they are having dinner with their mom. I should just leave her alone and let her come down alone, but I can't. I pause the game and go to her bedroom door. When I open it, she is sitting on the edge of her bed, a razor in her hand, thin lines of blood stripe her thighs.

"Sunny, why?"

Her eyes are glazed over when she looks at me. She's not focused, like she doesn't even see me. She looks back down at her legs, runs her finger through the blood. "One two three four." Then she lowers the razor to the other thigh and begins to cut. "One two three four."

"Stop, Sunny. You don't have to do that."

"But I don't know how not to," she says when she's finished. "I tried."

My heart tells me to go to her, comfort her, but my brain tells me not to, so I stay there in the doorway, our eyes locked.

"You won't tell on me, will you? They'll make me go back."

What do I say? I know I should tell. It's obvious she needs help, help I can't give her. Telling would end our relationship. She'd hate me. Especially after last night. Orion would be pissed. "No, I won't tell." I sit beside her. "But you have to stop."

"I wish you understood," she whispers.

"I wish I did too, but I don't."

She stands, pulls her pants up, and slides the razor under the edge of her mattress. Sounds of the front door opening downstairs are accompanied by Mike and Orion arguing. Sunny faces me, straddles my lap, and kisses me. "Please?"

"Please what?" I wrap my arms around her back.

"Please just be here for me. Try to understand that everything in here," she points to her head, "isn't the same as everyone else. But in here," she puts her hand over her heart, "feels so much for you." She kisses me softly. "I don't know what I'd do without you."

I shake my head. "I'm not going anywhere unless you are."

She smiles. "Never."

Later, after she leaves to go have dinner with her mom, I call Ray to see what he's up to. I can't just go home and be alone with my thoughts. Not tonight. Sunny will be back, but even just those few hours will make me dwell on everything that's wrong. Is it wrong that I want to peek at her phone to see if she's been texting with Carson? How is it that one moment I can be ready to walk away, and the next I'm freaking out that she will walk away from me?

Ray and I meet up at McDonald's. As we eat, he tells me about Star and how miserable she is with her pregnancy. "She's not sure she'll want to have kids later." He shakes his head. "This has taken its toll on her."

"That sucks. The whole situation," I say. "What's your thoughts on Orion messing with Tessa?"

He chuckles and leans back. "I don't know. Everyone knows he's just doing it to get to me, but she doesn't see that. She actually thinks he likes her."

"Maybe he does. But honestly, it was one night, so I guess time will tell."

"I kinda expected him to call me today but never heard from him." He shrugs. "That's why I think he's not really into her. I used to try and get on his good side all the time. I finally gave up."

"He might be a prick, but he's sure protective."

"No offense, but how come you can date two of his sisters and he's cool with that, but I've been with Star three years, and he still hates me?"

I nod, having wondered that plenty of times myself. "I don't really know, but my thoughts are that we've been friends longer than Sky or Sunny were even on my radar. He knows me, trusts me. He didn't know you. You were new and just suddenly appeared and were interested in Star. It's not that you're a bad dude, necessarily, but when Star ended up pregnant, that was it for him. I also have no doubt that if I did something that hurt his sister, that he would side with them. It'd probably be the end of our friendship."

"Good points," Ray says.

"Which brings me to something else." I glance around. "Sunny's been having some *issues* the last few days. Ever since their mom showed up. I'm not sure what to do."

"Issues like the issues she was having before?"

I nod. "Kinda. I guess I'm not totally sure what all issues she was having before, but I think it's similar."

"She was throwing up everything she ate and would only eat four bites at meal. And she was cutting, I guess."

"Yeah, definitely similar." I sigh. "Please don't say anything."

He shakes his head. "I won't." Leaning closer, he adds, "But you can't just stand by and watch her fall apart again."

I think of the scar on Sunny's cheek. Ray is right. If I really love her, or even just care about her, I shouldn't sit by and watch her destroy herself again. The pills made things worse. That look in her eyes, though, when she asked me not to tell. She trusts me. She needs me to be there for her, to care for her, keep her secrets.

I swear I've never felt more confused in my life. Even Sky didn't give me ups and downs like this.

"You guys are using protection, right?" Ray asks.

I can't help but chuckle. "The first time we didn't. The last time we did."

"What about all the times in between?"

"Yeah, there's only been two times."

Ray stares at me in disbelief. "All that PDA...and don't you stay over, like, every other night? I thought you guys were doing it daily."

I smirk and shake my head. "Nah."

"I've never stayed the night and get laid more than you. Well, *got* laid more than you. Not so much anymore. How'd you get those sleepover privileges anyway?"

"I just stayed."

"Yeah, I don't see that working out to well for me."

We both laugh. I glance at my phone. "What time you think they'll be back?"

He shrugs. "One of us should text and see how it's going."

"I will."

Sunshine

How's it going? he asks.

Ok, I guess.

That's good. Everyone being nice? he wants to know.

Not Sky. She's being a bitch and trying to make herself look better than us. Maybe I should mention that the guy she lives with was her teacher.

Go for it. he recommends.

I miss you.

I miss you too.

How much longer? he inquires.

Too long. I don't like my mom. She can never make up for what she did to us.

Sorry you have to be there.

Wish I was with you.

Me too. he agrees.

Orion

Unsure of the motivation behind the pizza and conversation, I just eat. Sky seems to have the talking portion down, telling Amy Jo how mediocre the rest of us are while Skylar herself is a stellar goddess who can do no wrong. We've covered the obvious (Star's engorged midsection), my arrest record and baby mama drama, and grazed over Sunny's not so sunny view on life. It really was all going fine until Sunny retreated and pulled out her phone.

"Put that away," Sky scolds like she's our mom even though Amy Jo sits right here, a slice of pepperoni pie hanging in front of her mouth.

Sunny barely entertains a side eye at Sky.

"Sunny." There's a warning in Sky's tone. Star and I exchange glances.

"Shut up," Sunny says without looking up. "How about we talk about the real you now?" She sets her phone on the table, face down, and looks Amy Jo in the eye. "Did you know the man Sky lives with is our math teacher? That's how they met. And Dad's engaged to his sister."

Amy Jo crinkles her forehead, her blue eyes on Sunny. "I see."

I sip my soda, watching for Sky's reaction. She's holding her head high.

Sunny continues. "Jake moved out of district so she could move in with him and go to school online when she turned eighteen." She shrugged. "Less chance of getting caught that way, I guess."

"As long as it's a consensual relationship, and your dad is okay with it, I don't see any issues," Amy Jo says slowly.

Sunny laughs. "You expected us to all be fucked up, didn't you? It's like you're not even surprised by any of this."

Amy Jo sets down her slice. "I didn't expect anything. I'm glad to have the chance to get to know all of you after so many years. But in the little time I've been around, I've observed a few things." She pauses, glances at each of us quickly before settling back on Sunny. "Sky is clearly the one in charge, probably the one who's been raising you, so good for her for moving on with her life and making your dad man up."

Wait, what?

"Orion is closely following in your dad's footsteps with the arrests and a baby already. Star is a child trapped in a body that's too old for her mind to comprehend, and you Sunny." Amy Jo looked down for a moment before meeting Sunny's eyes. "Sunny, your pupils are so dilated right now, I'm not sure if you're using meth or just stole someone's ADHD meds."

Wait, WHAT?

Sunny narrows her eyes at the birth giver across from her as my sisters and I try to see Sunny's black hole pupils.

"I am *not* on drugs," Sunny snarls.

"Sweetie, you can't fool a junkie. I know what I'm looking at."

Sunny stands up, gripping the edge of the table with both hands before flipping it to its side onto Amy Jo's lap. Sky and I jump up at either end of the table. Star stays seated beside Sunny, staring up at her deranged sister.

Restaurant staff come from the kitchen to see what the commotion is. The other diners stare in our direction. I'm too stunned to move, let alone say anything.

"We don't need you, you stupid bitch," Sunny yells. "Our dad did the best he could with what you left him. You left us for fourteen fucking years and want to just waltz back into our lives and act like you would've done a better job than he did. Why didn't you? Why didn't you come back? Why didn't you ever love us? We were babies! What did we ever do to you?"

Tears ran down Sunny's cheeks as her last words came out choked.

Amy Jo stares at Sunny, tears in her eyes and all of the pizza on her lap. "You would've been way worse off with me around," she says quietly. "I've only been sober for five years. And I've always loved you guys and wished I was a part of your lives, but I knew," her eyes dart to each of us, "I knew better than to come around. I was not a good person. I was not a good mom."

She swallows, her eyes settling on Sky. "You were three when Star was born. One of my most distinct memories from back then is of coming down from days of being high and you trying to wake me up because Star was crying." She looks at Star now. "I couldn't get up. I stared at your sister and told her to make you a bottle. I told a three-year-old to make a bottle. I have no idea where your dad was." She lowers her eyes and shakes her head. "Not coming home was one of the hardest things I ever did, but I wasn't a mom then and I am not trying to be your mom now." She starts to push the pizza and plates and parmesan cheese off her so she can stand.

We watch her struggle, seeing the sauce stains on her clothes and any pride she had when she entered this pizzeria dissipated. "I've loved each of you since the day you were born. I pray for you every single day. And whenever I see the moon, I know it's the same moon shining over you, wherever you are. The same moonbeams shine down on you that shine down on me. I send you my love in the moonbeams every time I see the moon. I always have." She's standing now, pulling her purse from the back of the chair. "I didn't even know if your dad still had you. I didn't know what happened to you. I just trusted that you were better off without me." She slings her purse strap over her shoulder. "I'm still sure I was right."

Amy Jo turns away, moving quickly toward the cashier. I look at my sisters, Sky and Sunny crying, Star apathetic, and I vow right then and there to always be there for London no matter how much of a bitch Rachel is. No way do I want my daughter to be anything like my sisters.

As Sky reaches down to stand the table back up, Amy Jo approaches again after paying the bill. "Every time you see the moon, remember that I'm sending my love in the moonbeams." Her eyes take in each of us one by one. "You know how to find me."

Wordlessly, me, Sky, and Sunny clean up the mess Sunny made. When we're done, I reach out to help Star stand up, and when she does, she makes a small sound and looks down. I follow her eyes to see wetness soaking her inner thighs.

Star looks at Sky, and so do me and Sunny, as Amy Jo walks out of the restaurant, leaving the mom duties to Sky once again.

But none of us look after Amy Jo, because we've made it this far in life without her, and we might all be completely fucked in the head, but we have each other through thick and thin.

And I realize, my sisters are the only ones I've ever really been able to count on.

Skylar

Count to ten.
Count backwards from ten.
Just because I moved out and on with my life, doesn't
mean I won't always be there for my completely jacked
up siblings.
They can count on me
 To be
  In their face
  In their business
   Pushing them to do the best they can with
    what they have.
Amy Jo and Mike brought us into the world and handed
 us approximately zero tools to navigate our existence.

Now
Star is in labor at age fifteen
 Sunny is on drugs at age sixteen.
  Orion has a rap sheet at age seventeen.
 Me?
   ??
At least I have Jake to keep me sane.

Ray

I'm following Austin to the trash can at McDonald's when my phone starts ringing. His dings at the same time. I spill my tray and excavate my cell from my pocket. It's Star. "Dinner must be over," I say as Austin eyes his screen.

He looks up at me. "Answer your phone."

And in that moment, I know. I know what time it is. *I know.* I just know it.

The baby is coming.

I stare back at Austin, my phone ringing in my hand, giving a little shake of my head. "No."

"No?"

"It's all gonna end after this. We will never be the same." I draw in a breath and look outside at the dirty piles of snow dotting the edges of the parking lot as my phone stops ringing. "I don't want this," I say through my swelling throat. Fuck. I cannot cry in front of Austin.

"Bro, it's too late for all that."

It is. It's way too late. My phone dings in my hand and I look down. *My water broke. On way to the hospital.* Nodding, I look up at Austin. What will be will be. Nothing is in my control; nothing is in Star's control.

As I drive the few miles to the hospital, I try to think about the wonderful life the baby will have. Star and I were able to choose the adoptive parents. Vince and Becca. Vince is a mortgage banker and Becca will be a stay-at-home mom. They're more than twice our age and ready and willing to raise the baby we never intended to make.

Star doesn't want me to see her in labor and said, "never in a million years will you watch a baby pop out of my coochie," so I'm not sure what to expect when I get to the hospital.

"She's hardly dilated at all," Sky says, like I know what that means. "But she has to stay here until the baby comes since her water broke, I guess."

I call my mom so she can call the adoption agency because I'm still a kid and that's a grown-up thing. "I'll call them and then take the boys to your grandma's. Text me if either of you need me to bring anything."

For over an hour I sit alone in the waiting room watching TikTok, refusing to think about the part of my life that's about to enter the world and vanish before crossing my line of sight. Mike shows up, looking overwhelmed, takes the seat across from me.

"They won't let you go back there?" he asks.

I shake my head, not looking away from the video of a cat drinking water from a bathroom faucet and hissing at the owner when they shut the water off. "She doesn't want me."

Mike's eyes penetrate my soul. "She doesn't want you?"

Sighing, I lock my phone and look at him. "Yeah, she doesn't want me. She doesn't want me back there. She doesn't want my baby. She doesn't want me."

Mike's eyebrows pinch together. "Ray," he starts, and I know he's trying to figure out how to placate me, convince me to hold on to hope that is long gone.

"Yeah, I know," I say harshly. "We're young, we have our whole lives ahead of us, blah blah blah, but you know what I see ahead of us? Nothing. Because there is no more us. This baby that we can't keep is fracturing us. And I don't just mean our relationship." I pause and look toward wherever Sky disappeared to when she returned to my one and only shining Star. "It's fracturing *us*, me and Star. We will never be the same again."

"How old were your parents when you were born?"

I look at Mike, more like glare. I've heard this argument a million times over the last few months.

"I'm thirty-six," he says. "Your parents are pushing fifty probably. I bet they already owned their first home when you were born. Went to college." He straightens his posture. "I was two years older than you when Sky was born and look at how their life turned out." He shakes his head. "You don't want that life for your child."

I know. I fucking know. "That doesn't mean it doesn't suck."

"I'm sure it sucks. But you are giving that child the only thing you have to offer right now."

He's right and I hate it. "I'm just not ready to let go. Not of the baby, not of Star." I unlock my phone and open Instagram, the first image I see being my trampy little sister trying to look like she's older than fourteen.

"Maybe you guys will make it," Mike says.

"Doubtful."

Starla

Fear. Terror. Trepidation. Panic.

These are feelings.

Feelings I've never had.

Because I don't feel.

Love? Four letter word.

But now.

Now I cannot imagine a whole ass child coming from the hole where

sometimes it hurts to put a

p-e-n-i-s.

So fucking what if I spelled it.

Austin

Sunny and Orion are walking into their front door when I pull up, and I feel a burn in my stomach at her sight. I'm still unsure why I was hung up on Sky for so long when she never made me feel the way Sunny does. If I had known what I feel now was something that could be felt, I would've endorsed Sunny's infatuation a little sooner.

I join them in the kitchen, anxious to hear about their dinner with their long-lost matriarch more than I want to hear about teeny-weeny Star having a baby. Instead, I hear O saying, "Just give me some, whatever it is."

Sunny laughs as I sit beside her at the table. "I don't have anything."

Orion looks at me, his mouth full of generic Doritos. "Look at her pupils. She's on something."

My heart skips more than a beat. "What?" I look at Sunny, pretend to investigate the status of her eyes, knowing her pupils all but drown out the pale amber of her irises. "She looks fine."

Sunny smiles triumphantly. "Amy Jo said I look like I'm doing meth."

I laugh. "Meth?"

Orion shrugs, shoving the chip bag aside as he pulls his phone out. "She's the expert on what a meth head looks like."

Sunny's hand slips over to my thigh and squeezes it. A simple, wordless thank you. But I'm already wondering if I need to speak up. Not just about the Adderall, but the cutting too.

"Anything interesting happen at dinner?" I ask.

"Other than Star's water breaking and Sunny flipping the whole table on our mother, no, not really." Orion looks up from his phone, his eyes darting back and forth between me and Sunny.

I chuckle, because I think he's joking about Sunny, but when I see her eyes focused on shoving around a crumb on the table, I say, "Seriously?"

Orion stands. "Flipped the whole thing on her. Pizza and all. It was epic." He holds up his phone. "With Star about to pop out a kid, seems the Douglas home is empty besides Miss Tessa and I have just been invited for a play date." He grins as he looks at me. "I'm gonna grab a condom from my room." Shooting his eyes to Sunny still foraging new life for the crumb across the scarred wood of the table, he says, "Help yourself if you need one."

In my mind, I scoff, because using a condom is the furthest thing from my mind. Sunny takes my hand while we wait for Orion to go up the stairs and back down again before he shouts, "I'll text when I'm on my way back."

Sunny sniffles beside me and I turn my body toward her. "What happened?"

Her voice is quiet. "She has no right to show up out of the blue and judge us. None at all." Her eyes find mine. "We're not bad kids. Yeah, we're all a little messed up, but we're not bad." Her eyes look past me. "Okay, maybe Orion is. But she said I looked like I was on meth, and, like, I didn't think anyone could tell."

I sigh. "So you flipped a table?"

She nods, trying to hide a smile. "Probably the most gratifying thing I've ever done in my life."

Laughing, I shake my head. "Sunny, I want you to give me the pills back."

Her eyes dart around. "Austin...I'm alive now. Don't make me give them back." Focusing on me, she smiles. "You know where O keeps the condoms, right?"

I swallow. No. Not this time. I pull out my phone as I ask, "When was the last time you went to the heart doctor?"

She looks confused by how I glide right past what she insinuated. "Like, a month ago."

"Do you go back again?"

She nods.

"Because you have a heart condition, right?"

She looks away from me, sighing.

"Hey, Siri," I say into my phone. "Should people with heart conditions take Adderall?"

Siri answers immediately in her robotesque voice. "Adderall use is especially dangerous for people with heart defects or—"

Sunny grabs my phone from my hand and locks it, discarding it to the table. Her huge eyes stare at me, challenging me to say more. But I don't need to. I made my point. "I love you. I can't sit by and watch you hurt yourself."

In a blur, she jumps up and darts up the stairs. I grab my phone and follow at a non-amphetamine fueled pace, finding her in her room. The jeans she'd been wearing are laying in a heap at her feet and she has a straight edge razor in hand, sliding it across the top of her thigh. "One two three four," she whispers. She stares at her leg. "One two three four," she says again, watching the little spots of blood come to the surface.

She lets out a sigh of relief. "What's wrong with me, Austin?" Lifting her head, she sees me leaning in the doorway. "Why can't I just be normal?"

I straighten. "Normal is boring."

Her eyes fall to her thigh again; she rubs the blood with her index finger. "Sit by me."

I do, well aware of the fact she is without pants. She slides the razor under her mattress and turns toward me. "Okay, I will give the pills back."

Relief is what I want to feel, but Sunny is manipulative. She kisses me then, pulling my arms around her while she lay back on her perfectly made bed. Within minutes, I've forgotten about the pills and the razor and that she flipped a table on her bio mom an hour or so ago. I forget about her heart condition and the *one two three four* that accompanies her whole life because she is amazing and beautiful despite all that.

So when she says, "Go get a condom," I don't hesitate. Except that I go pee first. Then I go in O's room, looking where I *thought* he kept condoms, but apparently, I don't know because they're not there. I rummage a bit before finding them shoved behind his lamp underneath a slew of popsicle wrappers. I snap one off the perforated binding holding them together in a strip and return to Sunny's room.

Her room is empty. I glance back at the bathroom; the door is open, light off. I look in the bedroom. Her jeans are gone.

Then I hear my truck start. "Mother fucker." I speed down the steps now, like I'm capable of moving at an amphetamine filled pace. I pop open the front door just in time to watch her pull down the street. I run back upstairs for my phone and call her.

Her phone rings on the floor beside her bed.

I stare at her closet, noticing now that it's open. It was closed. Closet doors being open start a fire for her OCD. My Adderall was hidden in her closet. Taking four easy steps to the closet, I reach up to the top for the plastic grocery sack she'd hid the pills in. It's gone.

Several thoughts fire into my brain simultaneously:

Sunny's gonna have a heart attack.

Sunny's gonna die.

It's gonna be my fault.

Ray's lifeless body on the floor of the cafeteria.

My body in a casket after Orion does more to me than he did to Ray.

And then, last but not least by any means, the death scene from *Romeo and Juliet*.

Sunshine

A heart attack?

    I think not.

Ridiculous?

    I think so.

Just going for a quick drive.

    Be right back.

Gotta find a spot.

    To hide the contraband.

        Carson smiles at me when he

        opens the front door of his house.

Orion

I leave my car in an undisclosed location and walk two plus blocks in the frigid three-degree night air to the Douglas abode per Tessa's instructions. *You know, in case my dad drives by.*

Okay. Makes sense. I saw what he did to Ray, but I'm sure I can take him because I also saw what *I* did to Ray.

Speaking of Ray, my preoccupation with Tessa has nothing whatsoever to do with Ray. I'm honestly not sure how I never noticed her before.

She is a

magnificent manifestation of metamorphosis,

suddenly a spectacular specimen of shimmering sex appeal.

I think the cold is getting to my brain.

She opens the door with a smile when I knock. I step into the heavenly heated home (okay, Orion, enough with that) and rub my hands together. "Where's your coat?" she asks, wearing a pair of spandex shorts and a sports bra, leaving plenty of skin in view for me to admire.

"I don't have one." Haven't had one since they stopped giving them out for free in elementary school.

She shrugs and leads me down the hallway to her bedroom. Not gonna lie, I'm a little thrown by this. I figured we'd chill for a bit, pretend to watch TV, or something. But when we step into her immaculate bedroom with a queen-size bed donning a white comforter, she faces me and starts kissing without a word. It takes me a second, but I match her movements, letting her call the shots.

Her mouth is warm, sending jolts of desire through me, concentrating on my stomach and groin. She pulls away as she sits on her bed, scooting to the center.

I look around, taking in the pristine, elegant look of everything from the white dresser and matching nightstand, the four-post white bed with pale pink tulle adorning each corner. A white wicker chair is piled with stuffed animals.

My eyes meet her eyes. "Hi."

She smiles. "Hi."

"You're really fucking hot," I tell her.

She giggles, pulling one of her knees up like she's suddenly bashful. Like she didn't literally text me and say *No one is home since your sister's having the baby so why don't you come by and we can pick up where we left off last night.*

Where we left off was my mouth moving its way up her thigh.

I pull my hoodie off and drop it on the floor before sidling beside her body, our mouths latching onto one another again. My hand begins exploring her exposed skin, then moving to the parts covered by the little clothes she wears. Her hands rub my chest through my t-shirt, and I pull it off wanting to feel her skin on mine. Trailing kisses down her neck I push up her black sports bra, her hand resting on my shoulder. When I put my mouth on her nipple, she draws in a sharp breath and arches her back.

I wasn't sure how into this she was until then. It's the greenlight I need to move to the other area concealed by cloth. She's more than responsive to my touch and tension builds inside me as she pushes her body against mine. I've been at her house less than thirty minutes when her spandex fall to the floor beside her bed, replaced by my hungry mouth.

I'm trying my best, I really am, but she stops moving after a minute or so, and I look up to see her staring at the ceiling, an arm draped across her forehead. "Hey," I say. She doesn't look at me. "You good? Want me to stop?"

She shakes her head but doesn't speak.

I lift myself up, hovering over her half-naked body, noticing she'd pulled her bra back over her chest. "Doesn't seem like you're into this, Tess."

Her royal blue eyes meet mine. "I am," she says softly.

It's then, it's her tone of voice, that finally makes it occur to me that Tessa is fourteen, maybe fifteen, and it's very, very, almost certainly possible, that she is a virgin. "Have you done this before?"

Because if she hasn't, it's not gonna be me to do it.

She smiles then, the mischievous smile that pulled me in just yesterday in the main office at school. "Of course I have." Her hands run down the length of my chest, and she starts unbuttoning my pants, her eyes closed now.

I watch her face as she reaches in my pants tentatively. She seems like she knows what she's doing. With one hand she pushes my jeans down around my hips while the other hand gently strokes my growing desire to leave this house with no questions as to the status of her virginity.

But I won't do it. I stay exactly where I am, holding myself above her for several moments, watching frustration etch her face as she hikes her hips upward, trying to get me to fuck her.

And I want to. I want to *so* fucking bad. But I will not be the one to take her virginity.

Instead, I kneel between her legs, pushing her bra back up so I can play with her boobs while she keeps rubbing my dick along her throbbing center. I've never had this level of self-control. Like, never ever.

"C'mon," she says quietly, desperately. Her eyes open and meet mine. "What are you waiting for?"

I smirk at her, amused by her desperation. "What is it you want?"

"You, silly."

I chuckle under my breath. "What is it you want me to do?"

She grips my dick harder, pulling it closer to her. "C'mon."

I lean over her again. "Say it, Tessa."

"Say what?"

"Say what you want me to do."

She closes her eyes again, bucking her hips upward as she angles my dick, aligning it with her. I push closer to her, let her think she's about to get what she wants.

"Say it," I whisper next to her ear before taking her left boob in my mouth.

"Fuck me. Just fuck me, please."

I almost choke on her nipple. Never in a million years did I expect her to actually say it. *Maybe she's not a virgin.* Maybe she really is just another slut with daddy issues.

Either way: today is not the day.

I pull back so I am perched between her legs, take my dick from her hand and she straightens her body for what she thinks is about to happen. With my reliable right hand, I take over what she was doing, and just to keep her anticipation up, I slide my fingers around in her wetness not caring one iota if she gets off.

"Orion, please," she says. "This is torture."

I smile, feeling myself close in on my finish. "Good things come to those who wait."

"Ugh, you're killing me."

Like I almost killed your brother. But I don't say it.

So close. So fucking close. I let my head fall back as I spill out all over the sacred spot between her legs where my mouth had been minutes ago when it first occurred to me that she could be a virgin.

And even if she's not, it's not because of me.

"What the fuck?" she hisses as she props herself on her elbows.

I stand beside the bed picking up her spandex from the floor to wipe my leftover sperm off the end of my dick before tossing them at her.

"We're not done, are we?"

"For now we are." She's pissed. I barely know her, but I can tell when I girl is pissed. "Good things come to those who wait." I pull my jeans up, fasten them, before I lean into her like I'm gonna kiss her and run my thumb along her bottom lip. "Good things come to good girls who aren't little hoes just trying to fuck."

Her eyes narrow as she pushes her bottom lip out. "So, like, what? You want to date or something first?"

I grab my t-shirt from beside her and pull it on before answering. "I don't know. Text me." *Hell no* I don't want to date. But I could do this again for sure. Grabbing my hoodie from the floor, I pull out my cell and the unused condom. Six missed calls from Austin. "I gotta go. Talk to you later."

When I glance at her, she's lying on her back, sliding her fingers in and out of herself, and I am turned on and in awe all over again, temped to strip and fucking give her what she was begging for.

But I don't.

And I wonder if it's possible for her to be shoving my sperm inside her body and if she is, can she get pregnant that way?

Now *that* would be ironic.

Tessa

Orion thinks that would be ironic.
He's about to see what irony is all about.

Yeah. I might still be a virgin.
but remember when I said:

> He doesn't know what's coming.
> He doesn't know what I'm capable of.
> He doesn't know what he's getting into.
> He doesn't know I'm not your average freshman.
> He doesn't know how quickly I can destroy his life.

He doesn't know.

I meant what I said.

Austin

Sunny left me no choice. After calling Orion at least five times, knowing he's probably preoccupied, I call Ray.

He answers on the first ring. "Hello?"

"Hey, how's it going?"

"I don't think she had the baby yet, if that's what you're asking."

It wasn't, but sure, we can go with that. "Oh, okay. So who all is there?"

"Me, my mom, and Star's dad. Oh, and Sky."

I nod, suck my lips between my teeth. "Can I talk to Mike? Like, is he able to talk?"

There's a pause. "Is everything okay?"

I let out a sigh. "Not really."

"Mike," Ray says. "It's Austin. He needs to talk to you. I think it's about Sunny."

"Hello?" Mike says loudly.

"Hey, so," I pause, not sure how to say whatever it is I'm trying to say. "Sunny's not doing well."

"What do you mean?"

"Well, she's cutting again and…." I lose my words.

"And what?" Mike says, his voice a cross between anger and urgency.

"She stole a bunch of pills from my house and has been taking them. Adderall. Like a lot of it. And I know it's not good for her heart." I continue, telling him how she took my truck and the pills and left her phone here.

"Was she talking like she wanted to kill herself or something?"

What the...? That hadn't occurred to me. "No, nothing like that. She was upset because I wanted the pills back."

Mike sighed. "Where's Orion?"

"Uh, I'm not sure. He didn't answer."

"I'm on my way."

Thirty minutes later, Mike and I are canvasing the streets looking for my truck. He starts talking about calling the police. And I think about how I don't have insurance on my truck. He reminds me she's endangered. Not right. Mentally unbalanced.

We give up and go to the police station. As we're walking inside, Orion calls me back.

Sunshine

I'm fine.

    Absolutely perfect.

  F l o a t i n g   h i g h   a b o v e

    my body.

Carson pours out the orange granules of another five capsules on Austin's center console and I watch him suck them into his nose one strong sniff.

                            He exhales,

                    followed by a groan,

                and his head falls back

                      against the glass

              of the passenger window.

I giggle, the sound

  still foreign to my ears.

                  I giggle because I have

          no clue what just happened.

Ray

Shortly after Mike leaves to deal with whatever is going on with Sunny, Sky comes into the waiting room and tells me Star wants me to go back there with her.

I shake my head.

Sky frowns, as does my mother. "She's not even close. She's dilated to four at this point. She has to be at ten for the baby to come out. We have hours. Lots of them, probably."

I find Starla in the hospital bed wearing a gown too big for her body, fear shining in her eyes. Wires and tubes come off her pocket-sized body and I haven't a clue what they're for or where they go.

She reaches her hand out for me. I take it, sitting in the chair beside the bed. "Hey," I say softly.

"Hey," she says. "How are you?"

I make a face. "How are *you*?"

"Scared to death." She looks at the ceiling. "It's gonna hurt so bad."

Yeah, probably. But I don't say that. Instead, "I'm so sorry, Star."

"It's not your fault."

"I know but you're the one who has to do this part while I just sit in the waiting room watching TikTok."

She laughs. "At least you won't be bored."

"Just trying to keep my mind occupied."

She nods, looking back at me. "Come lay with me."

I study the small bed, the wires, her more than abundant midsection. "You think I can?"

Nodding, she gingerly scoots over, patting the side of the bed. I climb in beside her, resting on my side, my hand finding nowhere to go but atop her stomach. She turns her face to mine, and we kiss one time. I feel like I'm gonna cry and my instinct is to move, but she's seen me cry ten plus times at this point, so once more won't change her opinion of me.

"You know I don't ever want to be without you, right?" she whispers.

The chance of tears just increased by one hundred percent. I nod, knowing my voice won't come out if I try to speak.

"We will get through this. We just can't let go."

"I know," I whisper, feeling the first tear spill from my eye and fall into my hairline above my ear. "If we can make it through this, we can make it through anything."

"I love you, Ray. I really do. You're the only person I've ever loved."

I know she means that literally. Love isn't a feeling she understands. She doesn't understand most feelings. In three and a half years, I've had time to figure that out. "I love you too."

Starla

Ray used to get so embarrassed when he would cry in front of me.

Not that it happens a lot, but lately it's been more often.

I was raised to believe boys don't cry.

Boys are tough.

Girls cry.

Orion never cried.

Sky and Sunny always cried.

I never cried, and still I wonder what tears feel like.

I know I said love was just a four-letter word, and yeah, sure,

I just turned fifteen a week ago, but I think maybe

I am starting to figure out

love.

Orion

Austin calls me six damn times and then can't even answer when I finally call back. Guess he and Sunny will be surprised when I walk in. But when I get home, Austin's truck isn't even there.

Good.

I'm exhausted. Thank God tomorrow is Sunday. I am gonna sleep until noon at least since I don't have to work until four.

I debate taking a shower, deciding against it since I didn't actually have sex. Just got off on playing mind games. I glance at my phone, surprised she hasn't texted me, noting it's past eleven already. I strip down to my boxers and plop on my bed, flipping on the TV. While I'm waiting for the home screen to load, the doorbell rings. There is no way in hell I locked the door. We never lock the door.

I'm not getting up to answer it.

The bell rings again and I roll my eyes. "Who in the fuck...?" And it occurs to me it's probably Tessa. She's probably hurt by my rejection and here to beg for more.

I gallop down the stairs with a smirk on my face and I'm still wearing that smirk when I open the door to find Mr. Douglas standing on the porch, his hands in his coat pockets, a hard look on his face. "Ray's not here," I say, a trickle of a memory reminding me Mr. Douglas is not allowed around Ray. As it's flowing into my brain, I remember that this man is also Tessa's dad and I see now that he looks pissed.

I start to shut the door, but he pushes it open. "I said Ray isn't here."

"Who in the *fuck* do you think you are, you worthless fucking white trash piece of shit?"

I open my mouth to say *excuse me*, and take the stance to fight this man, but he pulls a gun from his coat pocket and points it at my face.

Taking a few steps back, my hands fly up, not that he could possibly think I'm armed standing here in my boxers, and a million things flash through my mind: London, Star's baby, all three of my sisters, my dad, Austin, Rachel, Tessa. All the endings I'll never know, all the beginnings I'll never see, all the firsts and lasts, laughs and tears.

"Do you not understand the word *no*? You think you can just force little girls to do whatever you want? Did you think it was okay to make my little girl a part of your sick game of revenge against my son for knocking up your whore of a sister?"

So, if dude didn't have a gun pointed to my head, I would love to see his face as I explained that his daughter literally begged me to stick my dick in her, and also that my sister is *definitely* not a whore, and then maybe suggest to him that his own kids seem to have out of control fucking hormones that he should be worrying about instead of what I *didn't* do with his daughter.

Instead I say: "I have a daughter, sir. Her name is London. She's seven months old."

"I have a daughter too," he snarls. "She's fourteen and before tonight, she was a virgin."

What? Again, if not for the gun, I would laugh. Instead: I shake my head. "Sir, I didn't have sex with Tessa. I swear that on my own daughter's life."

His eyebrows pinch together, like he's considering my plea. "She's at the hospital with my wife now. The police are taking her statement."

I hear the click of him cock the gun as a car pulls up across the street. It's a quiet car with no squeaking brakes. So not Austin and not my dad. The people who live there usually pull into their garage, so I know it's not them and I am praying it's the cops. *Please, please arrest me, just don't let this bastard kill me in my boxers.*

He continues. "Figured I needed to get here before the police did. Handle things myself."

"Sir," I start, seeing now that it's Jake of all people (what the hell is he doing here?) walking up to the house, hands in his blue jean pockets, his warm breath making a fog in front of his face. I've never been happier to see my math teacher/soon to be uncle/guy my sister is living with. "Mr. Douglas, I'm not sure what Tessa *said* I did, but I promise you, I did not have sex with her. Yes, I know I lost my temper with Ray last fall, but he and I have worked past that. Tessa has nothing to do with it."

From the corner of my eye I can see Jake pause about ten feet from the porch, his eyes locked on the gun. He pulls his cell from his pocket and pushes the side of it, activating a call for help. "Orion," Jake says tentatively as he puts his phone back into his coat pocket. "I just came by to pick up Star's bag. Your dad said it was in her room."

My eyes stay on Mr. Douglas, his eyes narrowed on my face.

"Mr. Douglas? Is that you?" Jake doesn't move. "What brings you to the Hollis house? Everything okay?"

In a flash so quick I can't even comprehend until it's done, Mr. Douglas discharges the gun, shooting my right shoulder. I don't feel anything at first, then I feel my head hit the dirty ceramic tile of the entryway. I look to the side, seeing blood spill from my skin like someone left the hose on after playing in the yard on a hot summer day.

Except it's not a hot summer day and I am not playing in the hose.

Skylar

This is too much to handle.
This is why I moved out.
I am eighteen damn years old.

I can't even comprehend what Jake says when he calls. After he tells me how Ray's dad has gone off the deep end and shot my brother, he asks where my dad is.
I dial Dad. No answer. I text. Call me
EMERGENCY

I know he left to go find Sunny, so I call her. No answer.

I pull in a deep breath and let it out slowly before I go downstairs to the emergency room to wait for the ambulance stuffed with Orion and a gunshot wound.

How is this my life?

Austin

When Mike and I walked into the police station, he started to explain to the officer at the desk that Sunny is missing and endangered due to her mental illness.

Mental Illness.

I hate when people say that about Sunny. Such a stigma with that. I mean, yeah, I know she has all these diagnoses and does really weird things, but mental illness? No. Mentally ill people do things like.... I guess I don't know. Maybe being mentally ill meant you liked to slice your own skin, count everything in fours, be overly observant of calories and time, and steal pills and snort them.

Mike had just started to provide Sunny's information when another officer poked his head into the room, nodded once at Mike, and said, "Weird call about a shooting. I don't know what this is, but no one will be available for a bit."

"A shooting?" Officer One asks.

Officer Two shrugs. "Probably nothing."

I look at Mike who doesn't seem to care about a potential shooting in this no-name town, so I decide I don't care either. It's not like Sunny has a gun or anything.

Officer One looks at his paper. "Okay, Sunshine, goes by Sunny. Driving a 1990 Ford F150, black. What was she wearing when she was last seen?"

Mike looks at me. "Jeans and a red school hoodie. The back says Spencer 12 on it." I swallow. "It's mine," I add for good measure and to make it clear I'm her boyfriend more than anything.

The door opens behind us, and I turn to see Sunny come through the door, relief flooding through me before I notice she is panting and distraught. "He's not breathing. He's not breathing." She looks past me to Mike. "Dad, he's not breathing!"

"Who?" Mike asks.

Sunny points outside and Mike and the officer run out the door. "I killed him," she says. "It was an accident."

"Who?" I ask.

"I should've given you the pills back."

I go outside in time to see Officer One pull a body from the passenger seat of my truck and for a second, I think it's Orion. I jog to my truck, Sunny on my heels. Then I recognize the orange hoodie, the scraggly hair. Carson, the new kid. The kid Sunny met when she was in the hospital who just started school with us yesterday. Carson, who Sunny ditched me for at the party last night. And now, apparently the kid who OD'd in my truck on my fucking Adderall.

"What did he take?" Officer One yells at the same time Mike asks, "Who even is this?"

Sunny sobs beside me, her hands covering her face, leaving me to spill the...pills, so to speak. "Adderall," I say. "And his name is Carson. He just moved here." I look at Sunny. "What's his last name?"

She looks at me with her huge pupils. "I don't know."

Great.

We watch Officer One and Mike do CPR on Carson atop the wet asphalt parking lot for several minutes before Mike tells me to take Sunny inside because her sobs have transformed into wails of despair. We sit in the row of chairs along the wall, waiting for what I'm not sure. Sunny is crying next to me, rocking back and forth.

"What happened?" I ask softly.

"I'm so sorry. I'm so sorry."

I pull her to me because I know she didn't make Carson use the Adderall any more than I made her use it, assuming that's what it was. I have so many questions, but they can wait.

Several minutes pass before we hear sirens approach, and I remember what the other officer said about a shooting. I debate mentioning it to Sunny when the glow of the cherry lights floods the little lobby where we sit. We both stand to look out the door. The ambulance is from the next town over, the one where Sky moved with Jake.

Maybe the shooting was real.

We watch as the paramedics cut open Carson's hoodie, and I realize they're about to shock him with those paddles like you see on TV and I pull Sunny away from the door. Her eyes meet mine, her tears evaporated. "I need help. I need to go away again." She nods. "Tell my dad for me. Please. Tell him I said it."

I nod, pull her close. "I love you."

"I love you too, Austin. I love you so much and I am so so sorry for everything."

I hold her tight, realizing that just maybe love isn't enough to fix any of this and that I am definitely not strong enough to stand up to her.

Sunshine

I'm so sorry I'm so sorry I'm so sorry

I'm so sorry I'm so sorry I'm so sorry

I'm so sorry I'm so sorry I'm so sorry

I'm so sorry I'm so sorry I'm so sorry

I'm so sorry I'm so sorry I'm so sorry

I'm so sorry I'm so sorry I'm so sorry

I'm so sorry I'm so sorry I'm so sorry

I'm so sorry I'm so sorry I'm so sorry

I'm so sorry

I'm so sorry

I'm so

                                        fucking sorry.

Ray

"I don't know how, but you're at a nine," I hear the doctor tell Star from my spot in the hallway. "About time to start pushing."

I close my eyes and draw in a breath. It's a fight not to start walking- no, running- down the hall. Ninety minutes ago, Tessa was brought into the emergency room by ambulance after *supposedly* being sexually assaulted, so my mom went down there to be with her, and I haven't heard a word from her since. I barely had time to think about that because thirty minutes ago Sky stepped out to take a call from Jake, then popped her head back into the room to say she would be right back.

After hearing the doctor say it's time, I call Sky. That's the plan. Sky is the one in the room with Star. I'm in the waiting room. "You need to get back in here," I say when she answers. "They say it's about time to push."

"Orion was shot, and I can't get ahold of my dad. I can't come up there right now."

I don't think I heard her right. "Shot?"

"Shot, Ray. Your fucking dad shot him."

I open my mouth, but nothing comes out. *My dad?* What in the...?

"You're gonna have to grow up real fast and deal with this, Ray. I can't be up there and down here too."

My head is spinning. "Why?"

"Why what?" Sky asks.

Scraps of the last few days litter my brain, swirling like a snowstorm. Tessa and her vampish ways of late, Orion's head under her miniscule skirt last night. Sexual assault. Dad. Orion shot.

"Look, I gotta go, Ray. You have to be there for Star. You can do this."

I can't do it. I can't. She can't. We're kids. Isn't that what they keep telling us? How can they keep telling us we're just kids and can't make decisions for ourselves and then abandon us when we're about to deal with the most adult thing in the world?

"Where's her sister?" the nurse asks me.

I look into the room. I can't see Star from where I stand, but I know she's waiting for me, for Sky, for someone, to hold her hand. "She's...." I pull in a quick breath. "Something came up. She's not coming back."

Nurse wrinkles her forehead. "Will you be sitting with her?"

"We're giving the baby up for adoption."

She nods. "I know."

"We don't want to see it."

"I know."

"I don't want to see it. I don't want to know if it's a boy or a girl."

She nods. "Star needs you."

Star needs me.

The nurse leads me back into the room and turns the chair beside the bed away from where the baby comes out, so I don't have to see. I sit and meet Star's tired blue eyes.

"Where's Sky?" she asks in a whisper.

Shaking my head just slightly, I tell her, "I'm here."

She blinks a few times but says nothing because the doctor tells her to push. I take her hand because that's what they do in the movies. I can't look at her face, so I look at her hand, seeing her chipped yellow nail polish, a ripped cuticle on her thumb, and how her hand is barely bigger than half of mine. I thank God for modern medicine and the tube they looped into her spine so she wouldn't feel the pain that she should be in.

The pain I put her in.

I push my mind to leave the room as I stare at her smooth, pale skin, the freckle between her thumb and index finger. I push my mind to think about Tessa and Orion and my dad and try to decide if they really do all tie together, and if they do.... Despite everything Orion did to me, I don't want anything to happen to him, even if he did do something to Tessa.

Star needs him. Star needs Orion more than she needs me. Orion is stronger than me, and not just physically. Star needs her big brother to be here. Not here watching her grunt and make these noises I don't even want to hear, but here in her life.

I look at Star when she collapses back on the bed, her hair sticking to the side of her red face. "Why are you crying?" she yells.

With my free hand, I wipe my cheeks, unaware I'd been crying. "I'm so sorry I did this to you," I strain to say.

She doesn't get to reply because the doctor tells her to push again. I don't look at her again. I stare at the jagged yellow on her fingernails, noting how the paint on her middle finger forms an image that represents a mountain range.

This continues forever. A never-ending cycle of Star pushing and me crying.

When I eventually hear a baby cry, I look up. I look at Star. I look at her red, sweaty face. But she's not looking at me. She's looking right at the baby.

"Star," I say.

She doesn't hear me. Her eyes are locked on it. The baby. The baby we made. The human we created. The one we agreed we didn't even want to see. She's seeing it.

And then I see something I've never seen before. I've never seen it before because it's the first time it's happened as long as either of us can remember. Star is crying. Streams of tears are running down both of her cheeks. What she sees has made her cry.

I turn my head to see the doctor holding a screaming, slimy, red, tiny human without a penis as a nurse takes her, sets her in a little cart and wheels the cart out of the room.

Starla

She was the most amazing thing I've ever
$$\text{seen}$$
Those first thirty seconds of her life
$$\text{before}$$
she vanished from our lives were worth
$$\text{all}$$
of the pain and discomfort and ridicule
$$\text{from}$$
everyone, the judgmental stares, the
$$\text{whispers}$$
behind my back. My body grew an entire human,
$$\text{with}$$
just a little help from Ray. That human is going
$$\text{to}$$
make Vince and Becca the happiest people
$$\text{on earth,}$$
and I know she will be their pride and joy as well.

Orion

Sky stares at me, her eyes narrowed. "You can't question him without our dad being here," she says to the cop.

I look over at the cop, the first one who arrived at our house thanks to Jake showing up right on time to pick up Star's bag that no one had thought to get before then. The cop who held a kitchen towel to my shoulder and told me I would be fine, that it was just a surface wound. The cop who put Mr. Douglas easily in handcuffs and into the back of his patrol vehicle now wanted to put me in handcuffs and in the back of his patrol vehicle.

"You're seventeen now, Orion," he says. "We can question you without a parent present."

"Then he wants a lawyer," Sky says.

"We don't have money for a damn lawyer, Sky," I say.

"Public defender then. Whatever."

The cops shakes his head. "I'll be here until your dad gets here," he says as he walks out.

When the door shuts, Sky whisper yells at me: "What the fuck did you do?"

"I didn't do anything!" I whisper yell back.

She glares. "Start talking."

With my left hand, I reach up to my bandaged shoulder, thankful for the little things, like Mr. Douglas' shitty aim. "Skylar, I just got shot."

"Now, Orion!"

I roll my eyes and stare at the door. "I didn't even have sex with her."

"Then why would she say you raped her?"

"How would I know?" I glance at my sister. "I don't want to talk to you about this. Where the hell is Dad anyway? And did Star have the baby?"

Sky's face relaxes some. "I don't know. I should...no cause if I go up there, the cops will come back in here." She pulls her phone from her pocket. "C'mon, Dad."

As if on cue, her phone rings. "Dad!"

I can't hear what Dad is saying, and close my eyes, listening as Sky explains what's going on here. Sky starts crying so I look over at her. "I can't do this anymore, Dad. I can't keep holding everything together."

She can't. My strong-willed, big mouthed, opinionated sister is coming undone. But I guess we're all a little undone, aren't we? The difference is that my sisters all have someone to help them tighten their laces back up. Skylar has Jake. Sunny has Austin. Starla has Ray. Even my dad has Melissa.

I have no one but them.

Sky walks to the bed, her watery eyes on me as she holds out her phone. "Here."

I repeat what Sky said. "I can't do this anymore, Dad."

"What?"

"I don't know what I'm doing. Like, at all with anything."

"I'm not in the mood for games right now. I just did CPR for thirty minutes on some kid who's probably brain dead now. What did you do to that girl, O?"

"What?"

"What did you do to that girl?" he says slowly, each word enunciated.

Sky said Dad left the hospital to help Austin find Sunny or something, didn't she? "Who did you give CPR to? And why?"

"I don't know. Some kid that just moved to town. Tell me what you did, Orion, before I fucking lose my shit. I'm almost there and need to get my thoughts together before I see any more fucking cops tonight."

My mind was reeling. "I jacked off on her."

"As in you pulled out?"

"Never even put it in."

"You didn't put it in?"

"Nope."

"Why her, Orion? Why?"

"She's fucking hot."

Dad scoffs. "Was this some fucking revenge bullshit?"

"Not at all."

"So there's no evidence?"

"Evidence of what?" I ask with a chuckle.

"Evidence of rape?" He says it like I'm stupid for asking.

"Considering I didn't rape her, no."

"No evidence of sex?"

"Considering I didn't have sex with her, no."

"But you jacked off on her, so your fucking DNA is on her."

"Plenty of it, too."

"Shut the fuck up. I'll be there soon." He ends the call before I can ask about the CPR thing again. I hold the phone out for Sky. "Did he tell you he gave CPR to someone?"

She nodded. "Some kid Sunny was with. Guess he just moved here."

A lightbulb went on in my head. "Carson." What the fuck. "Why did he need CPR? Where was he? Where's Sunny? And Austin?" I try to sit up, my head swirling. "Where are Sunny and Austin?"

"I don't know. I don't fucking know. Just shut up."

"Is Tessa here?" I ask. "In this hospital?"

Sky stares at me.

"She is, isn't she?" I try again to sit up, my barely shot shoulder throbbing under the thick bandages covering the wound. "I wanna talk to her."

The door opens then, a nurse comes in. "You need to stay laying down," she says. She looks at the IV bag dripping into my arm. "How's your pain?"

"Only hurts if I move."

She nods. "That's why you need to stay still."

Dad comes through the door then, his face red, his hair tousled.

The nurse looks over at him. "Are you Dad?" When Dad nods, she says, "I'll let the doctor know you're here."

As the nurse leaves, Sky stands. "I need to go check on Star. And call Jake."

"Sky," I say. She looks back at me. "Thank you for being here for me."

Her lips barely lift as she gives me a small nod and leaves the room. When she's gone, I look at my dad.

"I don't know how you're gonna get out of this one, Son."

But I didn't even do anything wrong this time.

Tessa

To be fair, I never thought my dad would react like that.
      Like
            I knew he had a
                      Temper.
            I knew he had a
                      Gun.
      But
            I never thought he'd
                Lose his f'n mind.
            I never thought he'd
Unload a bullet in the guy who refused to unload in me.

          I guess this is
              why
        they tell us not to
              lie.

Austin

Sunny and I are sitting in the waiting area of the emergency room waiting once again for we don't know what.

What we know:

- Orion was shot. By Ray's dad. Tessa's dad.

- Orion was on his way to Tessa's last time we saw him.

No news past that.

- Starla's water broke hours ago.

No news past that.

- Carson snorted at least ten of my Adderall and basically died.

- The paddles gave him a heartbeat.

No news past that.

Sunny jumps up when Sky enters the waiting room. She runs to her sister who backs away from her, her arms out in front of her to keep Sunny from getting too close. "I have to check on Star."

Sunny stands frozen in place as she watches Sky disappear down the hallway towards the elevators. I go to her, take her cold hand in mine. "C'mon." She doesn't move. "There's a lot going on right now, Sunny. Let's just sit down and wait for news."

Her eyes find mine and she nods. We don't have words for each other. Everything is so overwhelming right now. We sit back down, and she lets her head fall on my shoulder. I try to relax, but I keep seeing Carson laying in the parking lot while Mike and the cop take turns doing CPR. His body bouncing like it was a toy underneath the weight of the compressions. His head falling to the side with every thrust.

I don't know Carson. I don't want to know Carson. I hated him immediately because Sunny liked him. Because he and Sunny were friends.

My thoughts should be on Orion, my best friend, my girlfriend's brother, and the fact that he was shot. Sure, he'll be physically fine. He's not brain dead like they say Carson likely is. But had Mr. Douglas aimed just a little to his right, Orion might not even have a brain right now.

I sigh heavily, wondering how long this day would weigh on us. Me and Sunny.

She lifts her head. "I have to pee."

I watch her walk down the hall for a moment and then lean my head against the wall, closing my eyes.

At least thirty minutes pass before I wonder where Sunny is, but at this point, I'm not sure I have the energy to figure it out. She still doesn't have her phone. Orion doesn't have his phone. In all the chaos of Sunny disappearing and then Carson and the CPR, it never occurred to me to get Mike's phone number. I don't have Sky's new number. Starla is popping out a baby.

That leaves me. I'm the only one who knows Sunny is either hiding in the bathroom or took off again. At least if she flew the coop, it wouldn't be in my truck this time. The police are holding it. Evidence.

I lean forward, rubbing my face with my hands. It's almost two in the morning. Maybe my mom has Mike's number. I don't want to wake her, but I don't see what other choice I have at this point.

"Hi, uh, I'm here for Orion Hollis," I hear a female voice say. "I'm his stepmom."

I look up to see Mr. Morris' sister. I can't think of her name, but she's engaged to Mike. Standing, I call out to her, "Mr. Morris' sister." She looks in my direction. "Sorry, I can't think of your real name."

She frowns. "Melissa. And you're Austin, Sunny's boyfriend."

I nod. "Yeah. And Sunny's gone again. I don't know if she's hiding in the bathroom or, like, left."

Melissa looks confused and I wonder if she has any idea what all happened tonight. "I'll check in the bathroom."

I follow her down the hallway. She goes into the bathroom for about thirty seconds before she returns, shaking her head.

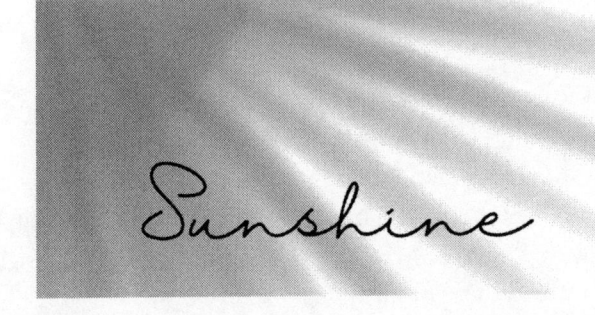

Sunshine

I'm so sorry I'm so sorry I'm so sorry
I'm so sorry I'm so sorry I'm so sorry
I'm so sorry I'm so sorry I'm so sorry
I'm so sorry I'm so sorry I'm so sorry
I'm so sorry I'm so sorry I'm so sorry
I'm so sorry I'm so sorry I'm so sorry
I'm so sorry I'm so sorry I'm so sorry
I'm so sorry I'm so sorry I'm so sorry
I'm so sorry
I'm so sorry
I'm so

                                          fucking sorry.

Arrest me.
Give me the electric chair.
Lethal injection.
Stone me in the town square.

Ray

We haven't spoken since the baby was whisked away just as we had asked them to do. We don't have words to say because what could be said? It was over. This looming project deadline had arrived, the project was completed early, and we turned it in for a grade.

The tears Star cried when she saw our daughter had dried and she was back to her stoic self. My tears which came so easily had also turned to desert conditions. It was all over now.

There's a light knock on the door before it slides open, Sky peering around it. "Hey," she says softly.

We look at her but don't say anything.

"How are you feeling?" she asks Star, who doesn't answer, her eyes glued to the wall. Sky moves to the bedside opposite me and takes Star's hand. "I'm sorry I wasn't here."

Star looks at her sister. "Why weren't you?"

Sky opens her mouth to speak, but pauses, her eyes settling on me. I shake my head. How was I going to tell Star her *brother* had been shot by *my dad* while she was pushing a human down her birth canal? Especially when I didn't have any answers to the million questions she would have undoubtedly asked.

"A lot of things have happened in the last few hours," Sky says.

"What could have possibly happened that would keep you away from *this*?"

Sky looks at me again, her steely eyes asking why I hadn't told Star what happened to Orion.

I clear my throat. "Orion got shot. By my dad. Has something to do with Tessa, I'm sure."

Star looks at me, her eyes wide as they fill with liquid for the second time today. "What?" She tried to sit tall in the hospital bed. "No, no, no, no." The tears form a waterfall on their way to her cheeks.

"He's okay, Star," Sky says. "He's absolutely fine."

"Why didn't you tell me?" she asks me.

For the next several minutes, I explain to Star why I didn't tell her about Orion and Tessa, and Sky updates us on his condition and Sunny's disappearance and subsequent return with some new kid who'd OD'd on Adderall.

I'm thinking about Orion. About how he and I have never really seen eye to eye, not to mention the whole incident where he literally rearranged my face and limited my ability to breathe last fall. But despite that, despite our differences and his asshole-ish personality, I know he's not a rapist. As soon as I can steal away from Star, I plan to find Tessa and talk to her.

Star squeezes my hand before looking at Sky. "Where's Sunny now?"

"Downstairs with Austin."

There's another knock at the door, but this time it doesn't just open. I glance at Star and Sky before I call out: "Come in!"

The door creeps open and a woman I vaguely recognize peeks inside. Her eyes settle on me first, then on Star. "Is it okay if me and Vince come in for a minute?"

Oh, yeah. Becca and Vince. The people we chose to raise our baby.

Our daughter.

"Sure," Star says.

They stand awkwardly by the door holding hands while me and Star and Sky stare at them.

Star looks at her sister. "Can you give us a minute? These are the adoptive parents."

Choosing the adoptive parents is the only thing I feel Star and I had complete control over. Our parents never met the families we considered. Just us.

When Sky leaves the room, Star says, "She's my sister."

Becca nods. "We just wanted to come in thank you again. From the bottom of our hearts. The gift you have given us...." She trails off, her eyes darting to her husband.

"What's her name?" Star asks.

Becca looks startled. "I thought you didn't want to know the sex."

"I couldn't look away. I knew it would be the only time I would ever see her...or him, so I just had to."

I stare at Star, tears threatening her eyes once again.

"Violet Moon," Becca says with a smile through her own tears.

"Violet Moon," Star repeats at the same time I'm letting the name roll around in my mind.

How fucking beautiful.

Star and I look at each other and she starts talking. She's looking at me, but I know her words are for them. "I just recently met my mother. She left when I was a baby and I have no memories of her. She told us that she always thought of us. That every time she saw the moon, she knew it was the same moon watching over us, me and my sisters and brother. She said she sent us her love in the moonbeams." Star looks at Becca and Vince. "When Violet Moon is old enough, if you choose to tell her she's adopted, can you let her know that every time I see the moon that I am sending her my love in the moonbeams?"

I don't see Becca's reaction because I cannot take my eyes from Star. My mind is swimming in the celestial seas where people are all named for all things above: The entire sky, a constellation, the burning ball of gas that makes our planet habitable, and the little twinkling lights people make wishes on as they shoot through the atmosphere. And I have no choice but to wonder if names are really by chance, or if they're predetermined by some cosmic influence we aren't privy to.

Because, really, what are the chances that our child's adoptive parents would name our daughter for one of all the things above?

Starla

Three generations.

    All connected.

        By the moon.

It's good to know Amy Jo thought of us.

It's good to know she sent her love even if it was in the moonbeams and not in the form of being present in our lives.

But I get it now.

Sometimes, love in the moonbeams is all you have to offer.

.

Orion

Dad comes back in the room after going in the hall to talk to Melissa. He'd been gone long enough for me to doze off.

"Tessa wants to talk to you," Dad says.

I scoff. "Tessa wants a lot of things."

Dad ignores me. "I spoke with Angela in the hall. They want to talk."

"This is fucking stupid, Dad. I didn't do anything. And if I did, then why would she want to talk to me. Like, that should be everyone's first clue that I'm innocent."

The door opens and Ray's mom, er...Tessa's mom walks in, Tessa behind her. I look away. Fuck. That. Bitch.

Angela stands by my dad near the foot of my bed; from the corner of my eye I can see Tessa still by the door.

I close my eyes, pushing the back of my head into the way too firm hospital issue pillow, content to doze right back off. Whatever they're dropping in my arm has me feeling nothing.

"Tessa," Angela urges, and I realize Tessa is here to apologize.

I open my eyes and look at her standing by the door in a hoodie and black leggings, her face splotchy and eyes red-rimmed. I clear my throat. "When I agreed to come by your house tonight, or last night, however you want to look at it, I thought we'd chill and pretend to watch TV. I thought maybe I'd get to know you a bit, and if you *let me*, maybe mess around some." I glance at my dad and Angela. "I'm sure you probably heard things about me. Most of them are probably true. But I know one thing you've never heard is that I made someone do something they didn't want to do." I pause. "Am I right?"

It's small, but she nods.

I glance at our parents to make sure they saw it too. "I have three sisters and a daughter. I might not have been raised by a mom, but I *was* raised to respect women."

Tessa lifts her eyes, glances quickly between me and her mom.

"It's why I did what I did to Ray. I felt he had done wrong to Star, and it is my job to protect Star. Did I go too far? Definitely. Do I have regrets? Definitely. Do I need to apologize still? I do." I crinkle my brow and look at my hands realizing I *do* need to apologize to Ray. "Apologies are hard."

Tessa looks up at me and I don't see the half-naked girl begging for sex that I saw earlier. I see a girl the same age as my sister who's upstairs giving birth as we speak. She's scared and afraid, just like Star.

She's not wearing any makeup now and she is still beautiful. Probably one of the most beautiful girls I've ever seen.

"You're a beautiful girl, Tess," I tell her. "I was honestly interested in you. Interested in *you*. Not just sex. I mean, don't get me wrong, I like sex, but just by you being who you are things were complicated immediately and I should've known better than to even find you on Instagram."

I close my eyes. *Was that really just two days ago?*

When I open my eyes, she's staring at me. "You're a virgin, aren't you?"

She doesn't look away when she nods.

I exhale. "I'm not sure if you said all this because I refused to fuck you," I pause realizing I shouldn't have said it that way in front of her mom but what's done is done. "Or if it was because of what I did to Ray. And I don't care what your reason was. I wanted to have sex with you. But I decided not to because something was off and even though you kept saying you weren't a virgin, I couldn't be sure. And I couldn't take the chance of being your first."

She's still staring at me so it's me who looks away now.

"You don't want me to be your first. No one should have a guy like me as their first." I close my eyes. "Something like that should be special."

My first time was anything but special. I'd only done it because Austin and Sky slept together, and then we all figured out Star and Ray were doing it too, and that was what got me. My best friend and my sister, and then my baby sister with someone my age. I was left behind. I needed to fit in. But there is nothing special about sex on the floor of the bathroom at the park with some girl whose press-on nails fell off when she pulled her pants down and whose name you barely remember and never saw again.

When I open my eyes, Tessa is standing beside the bed. I see tears littered on her cheeks. I push away the memories from the past and think of the one that brought us here right now. Her cocky little grin, the sparkle in her eye when she flirted, how she purposely ignored my texts and then acted like I blew her off. The taste of her skin, the sound of her breaths when I touched her, her fancy, white and pink bedroom. "You deserve someone who looks at you like Ray looks at Starla," I whisper, hoping I'm looking at Tessa the way Ray looks at Starla because I'm not even mad.

Tessa

Apologies are hard. Lies are easy.
        Someone should adjust the algorithm.
I deserve?
    Nothing.
        Definitely not the way he looked at me when it
        was all out in the open.
                (In front of my MOM)
He deserves?
    An apology.
        Definitely not a bullet to the shoulder and
        six weeks of physical therapy
                (Because of my DAD)

Austin

Melissa and I find Sunny at home. She's lying in bed staring at the ceiling with her pants off, slices covering her thighs from the top all the way to the knee on both legs. It's weird now to me how when I discovered the cuts on her thighs that very first time, I had thought it was beautiful. Seeing the cuts now in groups of four, each cut precisely the same length, I hear her voice echoing in my head *one two three four one two three four.*

There's not a lot of blood on the cuts but I see that her index finger is stained crimson from wiping it away.

Melissa stands frozen staring at Sunny.

"Those are all new," I say. "Like, since she's gotten home." I sit on the bed. "Sunny, hey."

"Should we call an ambulance?" Melissa asks.

"I think we can drive her." I'm relieved to see more of her wheat-colored irises than her pupil.

She smiles at me. "Hey."

"C'mon," I say. "Get your pants on."

She sits up, looks at Melissa standing behind me. "Where we going?"

I hold her jeans out to her. "Back to the hospital."

She takes them, and it's then I see the slices on the inside of her forearm. Groups of four from elbow to wrist. All even lengths. I grit my teeth together. *One two three four one two three four.*

"I need leggings," she whispers, setting the jeans to the side. She goes to her dresser and opens the bottom drawer, pulling out black leggings. "Is Carson okay? What about O?"

"That's why we need to go back to the hospital. So we can find out."

"Did Star have the baby yet?"

"I'm not sure." I glance at Melissa to see if she has an answer to that, but she's looking at her phone.

Sunny nods, grabs my red hoodie from the foot of her bed. "Okay."

I lead her down the stairs as she pulls the hoodie over her head.

"Do you need to grab your coat, Sunny?" Melissa asks. "It's below zero out there right now."

"I don't have a coat," she says as she steps over the smear of blood on the entryway tiles. She pauses, points at the floor. "Is this where…?"

I'm pretty sure it is where Orion was shot, but I don't answer; I touch her hip, guiding her into the bitter night air.

Melissa's car is still warm when we get in. I wish Sunny sat in back with me because I know I'm not going to see her again for a while. Sunny rocks in the passenger seat while we drive, muttering to herself. Most of what she says I can't make out except, "I didn't kill him, I didn't do it."

When we get to the hospital, Mike is waiting for us by the check-in desk. "Hey, Sunshine," he says softly.

She goes to him, his outstretched arms, and falls into them. "I'm not okay, Dad."

He squeezes her tight, his eyes on Melissa. "We're gonna get you some help, okay?"

Sunny nods and together, she and Mike are led behind the double doors to the treatment area.

Melissa and I look at each other for a moment and then find seats. I fall asleep almost immediately, my head propped against the wall behind me. There's sunlight flooding the waiting room when I'm startled awake by Sky, Jake standing behind her.

"Hey," she says. "Let us give you a ride home."

I nod and rub my face. "I need to say bye to Sunny first."

Sky stares at me, and I know what she's thinking. She's thinking I'm as crazy as Sunny. And maybe I am.

Sky nods. "C'mon."

No one questions her when she walks through the double doors, leading me through the emergency department. "How's O?" I ask as we walk.

"They moved him to another room for the night. He'll probably go home tomorrow or Tuesday."

I nod. "Can I see him?"

She looks at me. "Can we bring you later when we come back? We're both exhausted and I know you are too."

Sky and Jake are a *we*. A unit. A couple who makes decisions together. *We*.

Are me and Sunny a *we*?

Sky pushes open a heavy door to a dark room. Mike is asleep in the chair beside the bed. Sunny is asleep too, her face peaceful and I hope she's dreaming of anything except Carson.

Is that wrong of me?

I sit beside her on the bed, and she doesn't stir. I lean forward, laying my head on her chest. She draws in a quick breath and then her hand is on my head, her fingers running through my hair. "I love you, Sunny," I whisper over the lump in my throat.

"I love you too," she whispers back.

I tilt my head to see her face barely illuminated by the light seeping through the door. "Get better quick so you can come home."

"I'll try."

It hurts not knowing when I will see her again. I wish I had a miracle cure. I wish I could be her miracle cure, like I thought I was when she got home the last time and was doing so well.

I sit up and lean forward for a kiss. She gives me one, lacing her fingers with mine. "Austin," she says. "The moon. It's the same moon no matter where you are. When you see it, know that it's the same moon I see too."

I blink at her a few times trying to make sense of what she's saying. "I don't want to see the moon. I just want Sunshine."

She smiles softly. "Sometimes the sun needs to rest."

Sunshine

He doesn't want to say goodbye,
I can see it in his tired eyes.
    He's afraid I'll never come back.
    He's afraid I'll change and not need him,
want him anymore.
    And while I am little on the neurotic side,
        I still have a perfect GPA
and like to think I'm really, really smart.
    So that's why I know
    there is a 25% chance
        Austin and I will get married.
        And assuming we do,
    there is a 54% chance
    we will get divorced within
the first ten years.
I can't imagine there ever
    being a time I don't want Austin,
    but as it's already been established,
        I'm a little odd.
    Besides, if they hold me responsible
for Carson, it will be prison for me, not a future.

Seven Years Later

Mike

I watch my granddaughter London walk down the aisle in a beautiful frilly flower girl dress, hastily tossing flower petals as she moves too quickly to the front of the church. Her dress is blue, cornflower blue according to Melissa, as were the petals she dropped, her dark hair fixed up with a crown of flowers circling her head.

Earlier, when London got her own little photo shoot with the wedding photographer, she looked at me and said, "I always knew I was a real princess, Poppy."

I raised three daughters, but none of them melted my heart like London.

But then there's my other grandkids too: Noah and Scarlet, and Luna, just a few months old. They're all great, but there's something about that first grandbaby that just steals your heart.

We rise for the bride to make her way down the aisle. When she appears, my eyes fill with tears. She is stunning. Even without the makeup and elaborate hair, her rosy complexion and warm smile always made her stand out.

Melissa squeezes my hand. I look over at her and we exchange a smile. The couple getting married has had their ups and downs. But there was something I saw in the way they looked at each other that first time I saw them together. Did I think that look would bring us here? Never. But here we are.

When the bride reaches the front of the church, she hands her flowers to her maid of honor before facing her groom. They take each other's hands as the officiant says, "Friends and family, we are gathered here today to witness the joining of two lives. This is the marriage celebration of Tessa Catherine Douglas to Orion Michael Hollis. Who gives the bride away?"

Angela stands in the first row. "I do." Her fiancé smiles up at her from his seat beside her.

Orion

Tessa and I barely spoke until after she graduated high school. Sure, I saw her in the halls until I graduated, and we were cordial, but there was no conversation. Other girls came and went, but Tessa was always in the back of my mind. I left parties if she was at them. I unfollowed her socials at some point because I realized I had checked her page every day one week to stare at her selfies. Her profiles were all public so unfollowing didn't stop me from looking.

I wanted nothing to do with her, but I wanted everything to do with her at the exact same time.

Then the summer after Star and Tessa graduated high school, Star and Ray tied the knot at a backyard wedding at the Douglas house. Tessa came up to me that night, her cell phone camera on.

"Hey, O," she said, pointing her phone at me. "How have you been?"

"Are you live?" I asked. I knew from stalking her socials that she went live at least once a week.

"No, just wanted to be sure to record any interaction I have with you, so nothing gets twisted later."

I make a face at her and pull out my phone. "Then I'm the one who should be recording. It's my innocence that needs maintained."

"Record away."

And I do. When I play the video back (which I still do to this day), I am struck by the way she's looking at me at this part of the video. Like she knows she can break me but she's choosing not to because she can see me looking at her the way Ray looks at Starla.

"Do you remember where my bedroom is?" she asks, both cameras rolling.

I swallow. "Vaguely."

She cocks her head, looks into the camera on my phone. "Are you recording?"

I rotate the phone for a second and you see me, my eyes on her, and then it's back on her.

Her grin is mischievous, the same one she used on me way back before her dad shot me. "I'm consenting."

My heart jumps a little. "To what?"

She's on her feet, walking backward from me, but I didn't move the camera so you can't see this. "Come to my room and find out."

I remember the camera and turn it on her. "If I come, I'm recording everything."

She shrugs. "Maybe I'm into that."

Against my better judgement, I follow her, record her leading me down the hallway, kicking off her shoes, and sitting in the middle of her bed. Except this time, she's wearing a salmon-colored sundress and she makes sure it doesn't show too much.

"I feel like this has happened before," I say.

"Yeah, but this time, I just want to talk and get to know you. Like I should have done in the first place."

We talked for two hours on her bed. It had been three and a half years since I'd sat on that bed, yet it seemed no time had passed. She still enchanted me like the day I first laid eyes on her in the school office.

When I went back outside, my dad was getting ready to leave, and I told him, as I smiled at Tessa from across the yard, "I'm gonna marry that girl."

Starla

"I'm not sure what the problem is," I tell Ray. "But I'm really losing patience."

"Just let her look around," he says. "All the people and sounds are probably pretty interesting to her." He gets in her face. "Isn't that right, Luna?"

Her face lights up at Ray's silly voice and I smile.

Ray and I split up for about a month not long after Violet Moon arrived, but that was it. I'm not sure if we just don't know anything else, if we're scared of there being something else, or if the comfort has just made this okay.

After Ray graduated, a year before me, we both took college classes at night while I finished my senior year of high school, knocking out prerequisites for nursing school. We graduated with our associate degrees in nursing eighteen months ago, making me the first of my siblings to graduate college. Five months ago, we welcomed Luna into our lives.

We talk about Violet Moon sometimes, and trust that she's doing well. She should be in first grade now, which is so crazy to think about. Right after we got married, we thought about having a baby right away, but decided to wait.

"She hasn't eaten in, like, five hours," I say.

Ray shrugs. "She's not fussing. Just let her be."

I hand her to him and work to pull my dress back up to cover my milk engorged breasts. Stupid bridesmaid dress. I told Tessa she didn't have to make me a bridesmaid, but she did anyway. I almost wished Ray had been subjected to the same torture, but he wasn't. Orion was civil, but never went out of his way to have any type of relationship with Ray. Which was fine. Now that he married Ray's sister, we're all just one big happy family.

Sunshine

I want to ask Austin to dance so badly, but his baby mama is with him, so I don't. It's been so long since I touched him, felt his arms around me.

It's been years.

I suppose our relationship was doomed from the start. I was in the middle of losing my mind and he was barely over Sky. Once my medications were finally right, I thought things would get better, but we grew apart. I'm not sure exactly when we broke up because it just kinda fizzled with less and less talking and spending time together. Then there was all the drama with Haley Johnston and that was The End.

You'd expect I'd fall into the deep end of my bullshit again, but I didn't.

Austin has always been in my orbit. He and Orion shared an apartment for a while after they graduated. And then Tessa went to the same college as me, and sometimes Austin would come with Orion to visit Tessa. Tessa and I became friends in college and have stayed friends, which is why I'm wearing this godawful bridesmaid dress.

There was one drunken night of partying and getting high my second year of college when Austin and I hooked up and then we both cried and said I love you but then that was it. He already had two kids at that point, which was nuts because that was literally the third (and last) time I had sex in my entire life and every single time has been with him.

I think he has four kids now. I'm really not sure. I could ask him. That could be a reason to talk to him.

I look at Caleb, my date. It's our fourth date. I've never had a fifth date with anyone, and I'm not sure if that's because *one two three four* or just because I'm not interested in anyone. I say it's because I'm hyper-focused on my studies (I'm working on my master's thesis currently and really don't even have time for this stupid wedding), but I know I'm really just hyper-focused on my studies because then I don't have to think about all the things lacking in my life.

I think about going on to get my Ph.D. but am not sure a Ph.D. in English literature is really going to make a difference in my income or job opportunities without a little experience.

"Wanna dance?" Caleb asks me.

We go to the dance floor and dance a fast song and then a slow one. It's during the slow song I see that Austin has three kids. Well at least that's how many are at his table. His girlfriend of whatever she is- I think her name is Joslynn or something- is pretty. She's thin and wears her beach ball belly well.

I doubt I'll ever have kids, and that's okay. I have three nieces and a nephew, and there will probably be more to come. Noah is my favorite. I'm envious of him in a way. He doesn't have to talk, not that he can, and he is just always in his own little world inside his head while everyone caters to his needs.

Sky says he's trapped in his mind. I say he's free in his mind.

When I think about this, sometimes I'm pulled back to the long-ago memories of Carson and him overdosing right in front of me. Last I heard, he lived in a group home for people with brain injuries. I wonder if he's trapped in his mind or is he finally free inside his mind. I never got in any trouble for what happened, but the guilt I still feel to this day is a prison all on its own.

Skylar

"Can you watch her?" I ask my dad and Melissa. "Noah has to go to the bathroom."

I don't wait for a reply as I tug Noah across the reception hall to the bathroom. When we get in the bathroom, I pull his noise canceling headphones off his head. "It's quieter in here."

He tugs at his earlobe. I remind him of the motions of going poop in the toilet. I almost decided to put him in a pull-up for today, but it's just over a month until he starts kindergarten and I really want him to be potty trained.

Noah's developmental delays and autism already have the odds stacked against him. He doesn't need any other nuances to make him stand out from the other kids, but I have cleaned more poopy underwear than I'd like to acknowledge.

I help Noah onto the toilet for the third time tonight briefly wishing I'd just gotten a sitter, but that's not fair to Noah. Life would be a lot easier if Jake could be an active father to the kids.

Jake left Monroe High School where we met after that school year and started a job at a high school about forty-five minutes away from where we lived. I took classes at the community college, a social work degree on my mind. When I was twenty, he proposed, I accepted. We never really set a date because we were focused on me finishing college before anything else. But then I got strep throat; the antibiotics made my birth control ineffective and next thing I knew, Noah was on his way.

Noah was born exactly a month after my twenty-first birthday, so my baby shower served as an epic twenty-first birthday bash. By the time Noah was one, his issues were obvious, and he was involved in all kinds of therapies and had several appointments a week.

What started as a semester off school turned into never going back. Jake made the money, he had to work. We were making it just fine on his salary, so we thought when Noah got old enough to go to school, then I would go back to college.

But somewhere along the way, I guess I became too old, too mature for Jake. Or maybe it was that I now had a mom bod and not a teenager bod. Whatever it was, he was caught with his hand down the pants of a student in his classroom after school on a Wednesday.

The student was sixteen. The same age I was when he started checking me out.

It's weird how much age comes into play with things like this. Had she been eighteen, he would have lost his job, been shunned, and not much more. Seventeen, there probably would have been an investigation, he'd have been fired, maybe lost his teaching license. But sixteen, well, sixteen is very much underage. He was arrested, charged, made the local news, and served some time.

It was during all the melee that followed his arrest that I found out I was pregnant with Scarlet. Jake is out of jail now but must register as a sex offender for the rest of his life. His status means he is not supposed to be around children, so that limits his work opportunities, and his opportunities to see his own children until the judge says otherwise. He sees a therapist and is working to become rehabilitated, but for now, his visits with the kids are supervised.

I still love him, my engagement ring still on my left hand. But I see now that I was so desperate for attention from anywhere but in my own home that when he gave it to me, I latched on like a tick to a dog's underbelly. Jake loved me, he still loves me, and not just because I'm younger, because I'm not that much younger than him. He still tells me I'm beautiful and that he hopes we can move past all this and get married.

But I don't know. I really don't.

So now me and Noah and Scarlet, who is in the prime of her terrible twos, live with my dad and Melissa, back in the same dead-end town where I grew up. At least I'm not in public housing anymore though, even though I could have my own place that way. My dad and Melissa help me with the kids and their help is priceless.

After Noah poops in the toilet, I thank the sun and the stars and the moon and cheer like Noah just scored the winning touchdown in the Super Bowl. After I wipe him and we wash our hands, I put his noise canceling headphones back on him and we return to the reception.

I can't believe Orion married Tessa but until they became a couple, I had never seen my brother so happy. Tessa is a wild one. She barely finished college with passing grades because all she did was party while Orion worked forty plus hours a week at a manufacturing plant outside of town. Every weekend, he would drive to see her on Friday night, and they would party together. He never missed his visits with London though, and he now has her every week from Sunday through Wednesday and is very present and involved in her life. Orion is twenty-four and Tessa's twenty-two and they have zero plans of changing anything now that they're married. "Maybe when we're thirty," he told me. I'm super proud of him if I'm being honest.

When Noah and I get to the table, I see my dad and Scarlet gone. Melissa points out to the dance floor. My dad is hunched over, holding Scarlet's hands above her head while she bounces up and down, shaking her butt like she's twerking. I laugh aloud at the sight as Noah settles in his seat and lines up his Hot Wheels all over again.

Dear Friends,

This book, like all my books, would never come to see the light of day if it weren't for the support I receive from my friends and family. This book was released on August 15, 2023, almost four years to the day after I lost my own mother who had been my best friend most of my life. My mom, Catherine, would always tell my sister and I, and later her grandchildren, that she was sending her love in the moonbeams no matter where we were. I originally worked on the first draft of this novel over ten years ago. When I decided to dust it off all these years later, I found that it ended at the point the Hollis kids were about to meet their mother for dinner. It didn't make sense at first why I stopped there and I brainstormed for weeks on how to finish the story. And then it hit me. I knew I needed to share my mother's love in the moonbeams with the world. After checking with my family to make sure they were fine with me sharing this emotional heirloom with the world, the rest of the story flowed easily.

Thank you to Caileigh and Liberty for letting me blabber about things I make up all the time. Thank you to Caileigh (again), Ashley A., Nora G., and Debi O. for giving this a read and sharing your thoughts and feedback with me. Nora, you have been so supportive of my writing from the very start and it means so much to me!

Some of the feedback I received was the hope there would be a sequel but as you saw, I tied everything all up with a slightly tarnished bow at the end. That doesn't mean this is the last you'll see of the Hollis kids. *wink wink*

Thanks for reading! Love every single one of you!

Don't forget to leave a review!

sarah dawson powell
writer of real-life fiction

Sarah Dawson Powell was born and raised in the suburbs of Chicago, and currently lives in Central Illinois with her kidlings and too many cats. Her hobbies include doing laundry, washing dishes, petting cats, writing, reading, and talking to kids who have selective hearing. In her spare time, she enjoys working sixty hours a week, sleeping, and drinking lots of coffee. When she grows up, she wants to change the world.

Sarah has a bachelor's degree in sociology from the University of Illinois and has worked in social services since graduating. Her life hasn't always been peachy, but she's made the best of every situation. No one likes to talk about the dark side of life, so she decided to write books that would give people a glimpse inside that world. She hopes her readers take something away from her stories and loves to interact with them on social media.

visit my website & subscribe to my newsletter for sneak peeks at coming books and exclusive access to bonus material!
www.sarahdawsonpowell.com

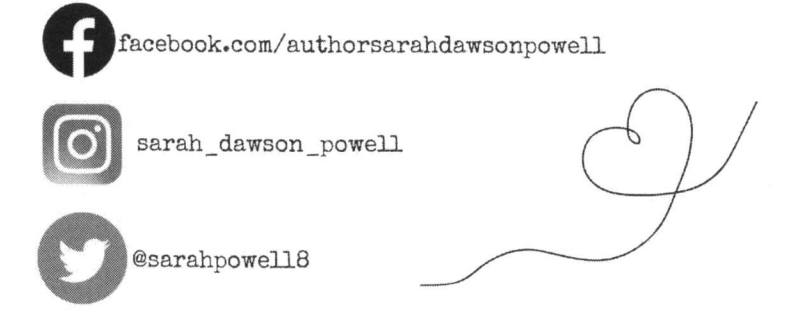

facebook.com/authorsarahdawsonpowell

sarah_dawson_powell

@sarahpowell8